HOPELESS, MAINE

NEW ENGLAND GOTHIC & ODDATSEA

Tom & Nimue Brown
&
Keith Errington

Published by Outland Entertainment LLC
3119 Gillham Road
Kansas City, MO 64109

Founder/Creative Director: Jeremy D. Mohler
Editor-in-Chief: Alana Joli Abbott

ISBN: 978-1-954255-12-8
EBOOK ISBN: 978-1-954255-11-1
Worldwide Rights
Created in the United States of America

New England Gothic Edited By: Meredith Debonnaire
Oddatsea Edited By: Nimue Brown
Cover Illustration: Tom Brown
Cover Design: Jeremy D. Mohler
Interior Layout: Mikael Brodu

Printed and bound in the United States of America.

Visit **outlandentertainment.com** to see more, or follow us on our Facebook Page **facebook.com/outlandentertainment/**

---c●)---

NEW ENGLAND GOTHIC

---c●)---

PART ONE
— ANNAMARIE —

The Hiring Fair

With the bunting up, and a few banners in place, the orphanage still didn't look cheerful. Reverend Josiah Witherspoon stalked amongst the tables, finding things to criticise. It started to rain, but they would continue anyway. They always did, even if no one from the town turned up. That had happened more than once, Annamarie recalled. At least this would be the last one for her. One way or another, she was leaving. The previous summer, she had run away twice, only to be brought back. It wasn't even like she was a proper orphan – she had a mother and grandmother on the far side of the island. They had thrown her out when she turned ten. *Bitches.* Not that she wanted to live with either of them. Going it alone would suit her just fine, but people kept interfering. *Bloody people. Do they have nothing better to do?*

"Hi Anna. Are you going to the hiring fair today?"

She smiled at the lad who had approached so quietly to ask her. Of all the people she'd been stuck with in the orphanage, he was the only one she liked or respected. He had integrity, and a good heart. Admittedly, he could be pedantic and stuffy at times, but she didn't mind that.

"I am. If anyone turns up to hire I'll be surprised. Though I can't think I'll get many offers even if there is a crowd."

"I hope you find something good."

She shook her head. "I'm not getting my hopes up. You on the other hand, are clever. Someone's bound to want you for something, Emanuel."

The young man looked down at his shoes. "I've had an offer already."

"Really? I'm so pleased for you." She meant it. He'd had a hard life in his sixteen short years. His parents and both sisters had died in a flu epidemic, leaving him to be raised by his grandfather, who then died as well. Emanuel was a solitary, miserable youth, and with good reason.

"I've been asked if I'll stay on here, as a teacher, an assistant."

Annamarie blinked in surprise. "I thought you hated the place?"

"I do, but perhaps if I stay, I can help to make it better, for the others."

"You're a good soul," she said.

"Reverend Witherspoon said he might even make a priest out of me one day. I'm not sure if he was joking."

"I don't think he ever jokes."

There were five of them at the hiring fair – three girls, and two boys – all of whom were deemed old enough to leave the orphanage's comfortless shelter. They had their meagre belongings packed. Missy Aubergine left almost at once, but she had the advantage of being wholesomely pretty, and able to show off all the things she had made. Annamarie had no talents that she knew of. None that anyone would employ her for at any rate. She smiled at Hilda Stubbs, a fat girl with bad skin. "If no one picks either of us, what say we set up a house of ill repute together?"

Hilda blushed, looking horrified and embarrassed in equal measure. They knew all about houses of ill repute. Reverend Witherspoon preached against them regularly, and Annamarie had done her own research on the subject. Anything the Reverend disliked held a certain appeal for her. The odds were that no one from the brothel would turn up recruiting, although she rather hoped they would. It would be worth it just to see the look on the Reverend's face when she left with them.

Two shop owners arrived together, fired off questions about weight and numbers, and left again. Annamarie could have answered accurately, but didn't want to. Being stuck in a shop would be about as bad as being stuck in the orphanage. If no one picked her, she would head off alone at the end of the day, and make her own fortune.

She shivered, feeling as though a winter breeze had blown into the summer's day. Looking up, she saw Vincent O'Stoat regarding her. Annamarie tilted her chin up and hoped he would move on. Every few years, the old man from the big house would show up and take a girl away with him. What happened to them after that, no one knew. There were rumours in the orphanage, stories spun on cold dark nights to frighten the youngest children – that O'Stoat ate the girls he hired, or that he sacrificed them to a demon that lived under his house. He was their bogeyman. Whatever happened, girls who went with him were said to vanish.

Annamarie wondered if anyone noticed. They were just poor orphans after all. Who would care if he did eat them? If he took her, no one would mourn. Her family would say good riddance, assuming they even heard. Tales about life on the island filtered through to the orphans in fragments. They had restricted contact with the rest of the world, and precious little insight. Annamarie knew just enough to suspect she was missing out on a great deal. *Today that changes. Everything changes.*

"Good afternoon Mr O'Stoat." Reverend Witherspoon advanced like an unsteady shadow.

"Good afternoon Reverend. I need a new girl."

"Of course, of course." He surveyed the two. "We only have these."

Hilda moved a little closer to Annamarie. They'd never been friends, but faced with O'Stoat, they were now allies and sisters.

"One rather fat, one too sharp looking," O'Stoat observed.

"Of the two, Hilda has the better temperament. She's not very clever, but she is diligent and biddable. Annamarie... has little to recommend her, I'm afraid."

She smouldered with resentment at his words. No amount of being talked about as though she were an object could ever make the experience bearable, and there had been a great deal of it.

O'Stoat steepled his fingers as though in prayer. "I'll take the fat one then."

At her side, Hilda whimpered.

Annamarie tried to think of something reassuring to whisper. "Don't worry. You can always run away."

Hilda shot her a look of sheer desperation. She was not the kind of girl to run, and they both knew it.

"Come along then," Reverend Witherspoon ordered. "Don't keep the gentleman waiting."

Annamarie wondered if she would ever see the girl again. *If no one picks me, I'll go there tonight and help her escape!* The scheme pleased her. She'd been waiting a while to lash out against her seniors, and liberating Hilda would be a nice way to start.

For what felt like an age, she stood around with the spotty boy who had spent the last few years pulling her hair and calling her 'Hannah-merely' and imagining he was being funny. She had found some solace in the past by adding beetles to his food whenever she had the chance. Today he looked edgy and did not bother to inflict his dull excuse for humour on her.

A couple of men in working gear arrived and eyed the lad. Whatever they did clearly involved labour. Annamarie kept her face straight. The useless boy couldn't even forage effectively for stew ingredients, much less work with his hands. Like everyone else, Spotty Jones wanted out of the orphanage, and would no doubt take whatever he could get. They took him, and she quietly ill-wished his departing back.

Being the last one left, she wished she could just walk out of the place. *No changes here then.* Whenever there was picking to do, she tended to find herself left at the end. *Could be worse. O'Stoat or a career with old Wither? With a bit of luck, I'm on my own.* They were clearing up the stalls. There would be all the excitement of seeing who had guessed the weight of the bucket of frogs, and then orphanage life would get back to normal. Only it would do so without her being there. It gave her a slightly hollow feeling.

The Reverend headed her way, with Emanuel in tow. This was a conversation she didn't know how to have. Bending down, Annamarie picked up her bag, and wondered where to spend the night. As she straightened her back, a short, black clad figure marched through the orphanage gates.

"How dare you come here?" She'd never heard the Reverend sound so angry before. His was a cold, seeping anger that she knew to fear.

"It's hiring day, isn't it?" the diminutive, aged woman said. Her voice rang with authority. Annamarie paid attention. Mostly people did not challenge Reverend Witherspoon like that. The woman had already won her respect.

"We're finished," he said, his tone pure ice.

"What about her?" the odd little woman pointed at Annamarie.

The Reverend turned, slowly, and eyed her. The expression on his face did not inspire confidence. "You want her?"

"She's what I'm here for."

He shrugged dismissively. "It's not like anyone else has a use for the little trollop. She's yours. Now get out of my sight."

Annamarie followed the small woman out through the gates. For a moment, she hesitated, glancing back over her shoulder.

Emanuel stood watching her, his expression pained. There had been no chance to say goodbye, but she waved. He responded in kind, turned, and walked away. "I'll see you around," she whispered to his retreating back. They'd been friends for years; adult life wouldn't change that, she felt certain.

"You're Annamarie, daughter of Clara, daughter of Evaline?"

"That's me, yes."

"We've not met before, but I believe I'm a distant cousin."

"Oh."

"I'll give you a year. If you're any good, you can stay and I'll teach you. If not, you're on your own, understood?"

"Fine by me."

They were heading for the woods, she realised. Orphans were not supposed to go into the woods, although she had sneaked there quite a few times during her night escapes. "What is it I'm going to be doing?" she asked, hoping it wouldn't be too dull.

"You my girl, if you have the talent for it, are going to be a witch."

In a Dark Garden

Lying in a comfortable, if makeshift, bed in the attic, Annamarie decided things had worked out fairly well for her. As apprentice places went, being taken on by a witch had a definite something. She hadn't even known there were any on the island. *And what else don't I know?* In the cloistered world of the orphanage, it was hard work finding out what real people did. Listening to Reverend Witherspoon's sermons, a person could figure out some of the juicier details. He disapproved of so much. There were dances, loose women, printers of godless trash, and other delights waiting for her to find out more about them. Her new mentor, Jemima Kettle, hadn't said much, but she hadn't laid down many rules either, and that boded well.

Annamarie wondered where Hilda Stubbs was that night. Whether she had a comfortable bed, or if something dire had happened to her already. With a witch on her side, she might be able to do something about Vincent O'Stoat and his vanishing girls. *I'm going to be a witch. I'm going to have real power, and be able to make a difference.* Drifting off to sleep, she thought about the people who were going to have boils on their bottoms just as soon as she learned how to do curses. It was quite a long list.

—⊂●⊃—

The reality of learning witchcraft wasn't very glamorous most of the time. There was wood to chop, water to fetch, herbs to grind up and all the usual labour of running a house.

"Why don't you use magic to do this stuff?" she asked her mentor.

"That's not what magic's for. It's not a toy, or a prop. It's for when there's nothing else to be done. And anyway, does a person good to keep her feet on the ground and some mud under her fingernails. Stops her getting silly ideas."

"What sort of silly ideas?"

"About meddling where she shouldn't," Jemima said, pointedly. "I've been a witch for forty years, and I wouldn't take on O'Stoat. Better not to be noticed by the likes of him."

Impressed by the insight, Annamarie didn't argue. "What is he?"

"Bloody dangerous is what he is. But, you're young and you think you know everything, and I know perfectly well you won't listen to me. I'm not so old I can't remember what I was like at your age."

"Will you help me?"

"Nope. You'll have to learn one or two things the hard way."

"But you aren't going to stop me?"

"It's your life, girl. I've told you what I think. If you live long enough to be a witch, you'll have to think for yourself. You may as well learn that now. But I get a feeling O'Stoat is part of your fate."

"Can you read the future then?"

Jemima looked past her. "Sometimes."

"Tell me mine?" Annamarie tried not to sound as enthusiastic as she felt.

"Often it's better not to know."

"I want to know."

Sighing, Jemima took her palm and considered it. "You'll die before your time, and the people you love and trust most in your life will either fail you or betray you, or both."

"Nothing else?"

"I did warn you."

She huffed, not pleased by her mentor's words. She supposed the woman might have got it wrong. "All right if I go for a bit of a walk tonight?"

"Wandering around at night's very much part of the job, girl. You learn things that way, when everything's quiet. You night walk all you want to."

"I think I'm going to like being a witch."

"Of course you are. That's why I picked you."

The moon hadn't risen, but starlight showed Annamarie the way. She saw well enough, and the island by night held no terrors for her. She had been running away to its wilder places for as long as she could remember, drawn to the woods and the sea. People might well be dangerous, but she had long since learned that most of them stayed in at night, or carried lanterns. It was easy enough to see them coming, and hide. Other girls believed there were monsters in the woods. If that were true, they paid Annamarie no attention. Sometimes she felt disappointed by this.

Years had passed since she'd last seen the O'Stoat residence. Memories of crumbling splendour returned to her. There were plenty of other dilapidated ruins on the island, but this one had a uniquely unwholesome air. *Or is that dormitory fear talking? Late night whispered tales created to scare the younger children.*

She remembered passing the house as a child. The feeling of being watched had troubled her, and the cold sweat that had broken out on her young skin. No one who left the orphanage for any job ever came back to visit, so why did they single out O'Stoat's girls for their grisly tales? Never did anyone suggest that the dress-maker ate girls, or that the fishermen deliberately threw orphans into the sea. She didn't know why that might be the case. *Hilda's probably fine. Still, won't do any harm to have a look.*

There were no lights in the windows. She could just make out the looming form of the huge building; a black space that hid the stars from view. Something skittered noisily on the roof tiles, making her jump. She entered the overgrown garden and wandered around the perimeter. There was a back entrance, which was locked, and nothing at all to indicate a cellar. Finding no signs of digging in the tangled garden, no bones, no smell of blood, she had to admit there was nothing that suggested violent death. *What were you expecting? Their heads on spikes?* She was about to give it up as a foolish idea when someone she could not see cleared their throat. The sound froze her.

"I know you're there." A male voice, impossible to age.

She remained silent, trying to work out how far away the gate was and what her chances might be if she ran for it.

"So, what are you doing here?" The voice had moved closer, approaching from behind.

Turning to face it, she decided to brazen things out. "I was just out for a walk."

"In my garden?"

My garden? He didn't sound like Vincent O'Stoat. "Sorry, I didn't realise this was a garden, not that I can see much."

He chuckled. "More like a wilderness."

"So you live here, do you?" she asked, playing for time.

"Not in the garden, but yes." He seemed amused.

"All by yourself?"

"My father, a few servants, others."

She hadn't known O'Stoat had a son. "I should be going."

"But you will come back."

It wasn't a question, so she didn't answer it. Instead, she took a few steps towards the gate. Something caught her arm, and fear shot through her at the cold touch.

"Be careful. Who knows what walks at night?"

"I walk at night." She shook his hand off and made her escape.

The Perils of Broad Daylight

Annamarie, isn't it?" The girl behind the counter beamed at her.

Nodding, the apprentice witch couldn't attach a name to the bland face. Another orphan, no doubt. Most of them hadn't made any impact on her at all. "How are you doing?" she asked, barely masking her disinterest.

"Good, good. I take it you've left Pallid Rock then. Coping with the real world?"

"I'm finding my way around." There had been more surprises than she cared to admit to. Simply learning to navigate the island was proving hard enough. It was bigger than she had thought. Despite her frequent escapes from the home, there was a lot to get to grips with.

She took up the bag of cakes, and set off. Jemima didn't pay much, but never having had her own money before, it was still a novelty to be able to walk into shops and just buy things because she felt like it. They didn't have cake at Pallid Rock, or ribbons to tie in your hair. Smiling, she walked through the streets, enjoying the feeling that for the time being, she could please herself. Afternoons off were also a delight.

Jemima proved easy enough to work for – demanding when she thought something mattered, but very much of the opinion that life was to be lived. Despite her advanced years, she had visitors – lovers, Annamarie suspected – and so frequently wanted her apprentice elsewhere. It worked well. She enjoyed the freedom to walk, to sit on the cliffs and look at the sea. Daydreaming and relishing having nothing to do occupied many a happy hour for her.

Without thinking about where her feet were going, she found herself back at the O'Stoat house. Daylight did nothing to make it seem pleasant. The overgrown garden looked uncared for rather than comfortably wild. There were some remarkably unpleasant statues as well, staring aggressively from amongst the rioting plants. Grimy windows with closed curtains made the place look deserted.

Hands caught her arms from behind, pinning her hard enough to hurt. She considered screaming, but decided to see if she was in any real danger before crying out. The daylight helped her feel bold.

"You didn't take long about coming back." The voice from the garden came from behind her back.

Although unsettled by his grip, she no longer felt afraid. She could talk her way out of this, undoubtedly. "I wanted to see where I'd been. It looks abandoned."

"It isn't though."

"And are you always this hospitable with guests?"

"I am being especially pleasant. You are fortunate, I find you interesting."

There were questions she itched to ask, but voicing them would reveal that she wanted to hear the answers. That wouldn't do, so she remained silent.

"Are you afraid of me?"

She grinned, feeling that she had scored a point if he had to enquire. "No."

"You should be."

She laughed. "I don't think so."

His words came like a chill breeze, barely above a whisper. "If you knew half of what I know, then you would be afraid."

"Maybe I know twice what you do, and that's why I'm not." She felt it could well be so.

"You ought to stay away from me, and this house, but I think you won't."

"It's not you I'm interested in, don't worry. I wanted to say hello to a friend from the orphanage."

"There are no orphan girls here."

"I was there when Vincent O'Stoat collected Hilda. He picks up orphan girls every few years, I hear."

"There are no orphan girls in my father's house." He spoke slowly, deliberately.

Hearing the menace in his voice, Annamarie shivered. "So where is she?"

"Who can say? Best not to trouble yourself. Best to stay away."

"Does he kill them?" She managed not to sound too melodramatic.

"My father is not a good person, that much I do not hesitate to say."

"But you won't go further. Are you afraid of him?"

Her question brought only silence, then he let go of her arms. "I'm saying nothing."

Annamarie spun round. From the strength of his grip and the depth of his voice, she expected an older, more physically imposing man. He was no taller than she, and looked to be about fourteen – awkward and with something of the rat in his face. Unable to stop herself, she burst out laughing.

An ugly sneer twisted his features. "You aren't a witch, not by any stretch of the imagination." When she didn't respond, he continued. "I have my sources, and I know who you are. If you have enough magical insight to call up a small breeze or a minor demon, I'd be impressed."

Flushing, she walked away from him. He was right. As yet, she couldn't do anything, and if it stayed like that, her prospects did not look good.

Out in the street, a round, red-faced woman hurried up to her. "Are you all right, my dear?"

"Yes. Why should I not be?"

"That O'Stoat boy is a nasty piece of work. I'd stay away from him, and that house if I were you."

Annamarie decided to play innocent. "I didn't realise."

In response, the woman tutted, took her arm, and led her towards the town. "No one lives near that house. You look. All the others are empty. I'm the nearest neighbour. I tell you, I don't always sleep well at night, and the things I hear sometimes... the screams..."

That caught her attention. "Really?"

"I swear it. It's a bad house, and they are monsters, father and son both."

"A friend of mine went to work for them. We were at the orphanage together." She had no qualms about claiming friendship if it would get her information.

"Oh you poor dear." The woman stopped. "If we had any kind of proper town council, he wouldn't be allowed to get away with it!"

"With what?" Her pulse accelerated.

"Whatever he does with them."

"What does he do?"

"I don't know, but they go in, and they never come out again."

"And no one stops him?"

"I've tried to tell people, but no one cares. All the people with influence seem to be on his side, and there's nothing I can do except bear witness."

Annamarie looked back at the house. Although she hadn't been close to Hilda, it was the principle of the thing. Men like the O'Stoats shouldn't be able to use young girls, kill them even, and have no one care to enquire about it. "It's wrong," she said.

"You stay away from there, Miss. You can't stop him any more than I can."

Turning on her best smile, Annamarie nodded. "There's more than one way to skin a cat."

If Jemima had any spellbooks, she kept them hidden. There were all kinds of items in the cottage, some seeming valuable, others little more than junk and driftwood. Annamarie had the feeling that looks were deceptive where magic was concerned. Some of the objects in the clutter were enchanted, but she couldn't tell what any of them might do. While her mentor dozed in the afternoon sun, the young woman pocketed a few things – a key made of wood, a string of holed stones, one of the many stoppered bottles with anonymous contents, and a small knife.

The Skinning of Cats

J ust as she'd hoped, the little wooden key opened locks. Annamarie tested it on a few doors as she made her way through town, and it worked reliably. She resisted the temptation to giggle like a maniac. This one small item gave her considerable power, and she had yet to try the others. The key wouldn't help in the slightest if a door had been barred from the inside, she soon learned. Everything had its limitations after all.

Picking the darkest shadow she could find, Annamarie waited outside the garden. The last thing she needed was another run-in with the creepy boy, and for all she knew, he might be lurking about somewhere. She could imagine he might have nothing better to do than stand around in his own garden late at night. Some people were not the types to make friends. *Oh, and you can talk, you're hardly a socialite.* For an uncomfortable moment she considered the possibility that she and the O'Stoat boy were in some ways alike. Repulsed by the thought, she brushed it aside.

After what seemed like a lot of waiting with no significant sounds from the garden, she ventured in. Dry things crunched and crackled beneath her feet. She hoped they were twigs, but in the darkness, her imagination conjured up bones and long dead flesh. The thought made her shiver, but did not slow her stride.

Having snooped around in daylight, she knew where to go, and made her way to the back of the house. There might have been a kitchen garden once – but now it lay in ruin, overgrown and unfriendly. She could smell herbs, their fragrance released when she brushed against them. It hadn't been a cared-for place in a long time, but once someone had bothered to plant things.

The modest porch, now almost lost under climbing plants, might once have led to the kitchen. Annamarie brandished the wooden key, and the door opened at her touch. She expected the door to creak, but it swung away with the barest whisper, opening into absolute darkness. A surge of triumph muted the remnants of her fear.

Annamarie stepped inside, closing the door behind her. She could feel a smooth, even floor beneath her feet, reassuringly free from debris. It hit her then, that she had broken into someone's house. Grinning, she retrieved a small lantern from her voluminous pockets, and lit it. The guttering flame showed her a surprisingly clean and tidy kitchen. The sight gave her hope, making her think Hilda and the other girls might be working unmolested after all. Having no idea where they might sleep at night, she crept from room to room.

It was a large, and strange house. Most of it felt unlived in, its contents there just for display. She couldn't imagine anyone sitting in the ornate chairs. There were displays of unfamiliar things – some pretty, some ugly, others unsettling for reasons she could not explain. Their nature and use were beyond her insight. Twisting tubes and bulbous vials. Things that looked like eyes. Objects that gave the impression that the inside of something once living had been inverted, to unpleasant effect. Things with blades and things that made ominous grinding noises when she explored them. Fascination and discomfort vied within her breast.

There were corridors between some rooms, others had connecting doors. There seemed to be no logic to it. One room had only bare floors, and a wooden kitchen table, strangely out of place compared with the luxuries housed nearby. The atmosphere made her skin crawl and she hurried away. After that, her nerves teetered on the brink of failure. In one long, narrow room she felt, or imagined, eyes upon her from the near-darkness. Panicking, she turned to leave, but in the maze of rooms she could not orientate herself or find the way. The lantern gave little light and she could not remember where she had been.

She pushed into another room, only to find it was little more than a cupboard, full of empty shelves and wire cages. Behind her, the door clicked shut. The sound sent a bolt of icy fear through her, but she tried to ignore it. *There must have been a draught.* When she tried the handle, the door refused to budge. Annamarie stood very still, holding her breath and listening. There might be someone else beyond the door: the creepy boy, or worse still, his horrible father. If she opened the lock with her key, that could turn out to be a mistake. She did not want to walk into something worse than her current situation.

Moving as quietly as she could, Annamarie backed up towards the window and considered breaking it to escape. It looked too small and high for an easy exit though, and the thought of getting cut discouraged her. She examined the room, looking for something to stand on. There were a lot of cages, many bearing tags. 'Cat.' 'Piglet.' 'Chicken.' 'Alice.' 'Deer Calf.' 'Crow.' 'Penny.' 'June.' She shivered. It all felt very wrong. Outside the door, a floor-board creaked faintly. She strained her ears, and heard something that might, perhaps, have been someone moving away. It took a lot of self control to wait rather than rushing to escape. Twenty breaths. Thirty. *Is that long enough?* Heart pounding, she took her wooden key and set to work. The door still refused to move. Whatever had been done to it, she could not make it open.

Annamarie swore under her breath. There was no other way out of the room. She couldn't get up to the window, much less through it, and she had nothing suitable for breaking the glass. The sound of it would surely attract attention.

With nothing else to do, the untrained witch sat down on the floor and considered her options. She played with the string of holed stones, but if they carried any enchantment at all, she had no idea how to access it. Opening the small vial of liquid, she sniffed at the contents. The smell was pleasant enough but that might not mean anything. She couldn't identify it, and Jemima had all kinds of things. It might be poison, or a cough medicine, or something to keep away mice for all she knew. The knife she had picked up could have its uses. She opened up the blade and kept it in her hand, knowing there would most likely be one chance to use it, at best. If she attacked whoever opened the door, she would have the element of surprise, and might be able to get out.

The light from her lantern grew dim as the hours of night advanced. She wondered if Jemima had noticed her absence. For a while, images of the canny old woman coming to her rescue kept her occupied. Then she remembered how nervous her mentor had been regarding Vincent O'Stoat. No. There would be no rescue. If she wanted to get out of this in one piece, she would have to find the means herself. She turned the holed stones over in her fingers, seeking inspiration.

"That will protect you from small curses and ill wishing but not much more."

Annamarie clutched the string of stones to her chest. She couldn't see anything, but the whispery voice had seemed very close. "Who are you?" she asked.

"Names are things of power. I do not give mine lightly."

"Fair enough. How did you get in here?"

"By magic, of course."

She supposed if this new arrival meant her any harm, she would be aware of it by now. It appeared to have all the advantages of being able to see when she could not. After so long spent in a state of nervous silence, talking to a mysterious magical person seemed infinitely preferable to carrying on alone. "Why are you here?"

"To see if you would like my help."

"Really?" She pondered this for a moment. Annamarie had learned enough magical theory to know that such things usually had some kind of price attached. "Why?"

"Because you are obviously in trouble."

"Well, that's true enough. What do you want in return for helping me?"

There was a slight pause before the voice replied. "Clever girl. I can only help you if I belong to you. You have to give me your blood to drink any time I want it."

"For how long?"

"As long as you live. In exchange, I will help you, now and always."

"What can you do?" Annamarie was desperate, but not so desperate as to jump from a frying pan to a fire.

"I can go places others cannot. I can fetch and carry. I know things and can find things out. I have my limitations, but you will find me useful. There is much I can teach you. I have belonged to many witches over the centuries."

"And what happened to them?"

Again the pause, the sense of something thinking carefully about how to answer. "They all died, in the end. I will not trap you with false promises. I cannot give immortality. But I can help. I can free you from this place before they take your mind and break your body."

A thousand questions exploded inside her mind, but she pushed them aside. Taking the knife, she cut the tip of her left thumb and offered her bleeding hand to the darkness. "Do it. Drink my blood. Belong to me, and get me out of here!"

"I will."

She felt the softness of it against her skin, the gentle lapping.

When it had taken enough blood, it spoke again. "I will fetch the key for you, and we will leave."

The Laws of Consequence

Y ou're a cat," Annamarie said out loud in surprise, once she was able to look around and notice. It looked cat shaped, at any rate. A cat that had been brought to life from a drawing. Elegant and sleek, but missing the details somehow.

"In a manner of speaking, yes. You may call me Lamashtu."

The sun had almost risen by the time Annamarie reached the cottage. To her relief, the door stood ajar and she could smell breakfast cooking.

"Some nice young man, was it?" her mentor enquired.

She hovered in the doorway. "Not exactly."

"You look like you haven't slept. Been visiting the O'Stoats, have you?"

"Yes."

"Well, you're still alive so you must have been paying attention to some of your lessons."

"Jemima, what does he do with the girls he takes?"

"I don't rightly know, but he's no good. Rotten to the core. Had some trouble with him, did you?"

"Less than I might have done." Annamarie glanced down at the talking cat.

Jemima followed her gaze. "Well bugger me!"

"Very pleased to make your acquaintance," Lamashtu said in haughty tones.

"You're a... one of them. I've heard of the likes of you, never thought I'd get to see one," Jemima said, apparently impressed.

"We are not common." Lamashtu swished into the cottage, taking a seat near to the stove.

Jemima went back to stirring the porridge. "You are full of tricks." She seemed pleased.

"I need to eat, and sleep," Annamarie announced.

"You do that, girl. We can work later. Did you pick up my constipation medicine by any chance?"

Annamarie removed the bottle of potion from her pocket. "This?"

"That's the one. Good. Thought I'd lost it. Need to drop that down to Marjory Aubergine today. Poor old soul."

Awake with the twilight, Annamarie sat outside, listening to the wind as it blew in from the ocean. She could taste the salt in it. Winds from the mainland had a very different character.

"Blood," Lamashtu demanded.

Thus far it had taken very little, and there was no menace in the request. It seemed they could work together and Jemima definitely approved. *I got something right then.* She reached for the knife, making a small wound on her arm. Her familiar dipped its head, licking up the crimson droplets.

"You are troubled," the cat-like being observed.

"Yep."

"Speak to me. Let us see what can be done."

"The house you got me out of. The man who lives there takes girls from the orphanage and no one ever sees them again."

"And this troubles you?"

"Well yes, don't you think that's wrong?"

"Right and wrong depend so much on where you are standing. How you look at things. They are such subjective, human notions. I do not appreciate them as you might."

"Oh."

"But it doesn't matter what I think. You are my mistress. I enact your will. That is my nature."

A plan began to grow in her mind. "You said yesterday that you can find and fetch things."

"I do that very well."

"Can you find and fetch people?"

"The living, always. The dead, seldom. The others – it varies."

She pushed aside the temptation to enquire what 'others' meant. "Right. So could you fetch me Hilda Stubbs?"

"It would be an honour." Lamashtu walked away, and gradually, where the shape of a cat had been, there was smoke, and then nothing at all.

Annamarie pulled her coat as close as she could get it. The old garment hadn't fitted for a long time, but there had been no scope for replacing it. The wind got in, and under, and around the edges, chilling her. Despite this discomfort, she didn't go in. She wondered how Hilda would take to being stolen away from the O'Stoat household. The girl had been resolutely dull and oblivious, able to miss all kinds of strangeness when it manifested around her. What on earth would she make of the cat?

The sun would soon sink beneath the sea, but she wanted to be outside with room and space to talk to the girl. The air before her churned. She stepped back, unsettled but not afraid. Hilda materialised.

"This girl?" Lamashtu enquired, sounding disarmingly innocent.

"This..." words failed her, and she retreated again. It looked like Hilda, certainly. She knew the face, the figure, the shabby dress even. "What's wrong with her?"

"Is she not meant to be like this?"

"No." Annamarie shook her head. Hilda had yet to move, her eyes blank, features slack and lifeless. "She looks dead."

"She isn't."

Annamarie poked her former acquaintance. The flesh she encountered felt real and pliable enough, but unpleasantly cold.

Lamashtu stretched and preened. "She isn't living either. Not fully."

The young witch growled. "Why didn't you say?"

"You did not ask."

"From now on, assume I want to know that kind of thing, ok?"

"Understood."

"What on earth am I going to do with her? Can we fix this?"

Her raised voice had drawn attention. "Fix what?" Jemima strode out into the darkening landscape. "By all that's sacred!"

"Can we do anything?" Annamarie tried to think pragmatically although her stomach churned with revulsion.

"O'Stoat's work, is it?"

Annamarie hissed. "Yes."

The diminutive witch raised her hands, exploring the air around Hilda's sluggish form. "This is obscene." Frown lines deepened in her forehead. "I don't know what kind of force it would take, or how..." She stepped away. "Her body lives, but there's no mind that I can feel. No spirit."

"How can he do that?"

"Girl, there are some questions best not asked."

Annamarie considered this, and found she agreed. Whatever it took to ruin a person in this way, she did not want to know. However, there were other possibilities to explore. "Lamashtu, can you bring her spirit back?"

"I can try." The cat slipped away into the ether.

"Don't get your hopes up, girly."

Annamarie stomped her feet in frustration. "What else can we do?"

"For now, send her back. There's no soul in that flesh, the body is irrelevant, but I'd much rather it was somewhere else."

"Agreed. I'll sort that out. Jemima, how do we stop him from doing this again?"

"Short of killing him? No idea."

Annamarie took a deep breath. "You think killing him would do it?"

"He's flesh and bone. But even so, I doubt it would be easy."

The two women fell silent for a while, both considering the direction their conversation had taken.

Jemima shook her head. "Enough words. We wait on your cat, and we sleep on it."

"Agreed."

The Wrath of Witches

Lamashtu returned silent, and alone. Where the cat had been and what it had seen, it declined to say, despite questions.

"Could her soul be properly gone?" Annamarie asked.

Nothing.

"Souls can be unmade, by all accounts. Taken, and used. I've not seen it done, only run into stories," Jemima said, her face furrowed and clouded.

Still the cat offered them nothing.

"If that had happened, if she'd been unmade in some way, could you find the pieces?" Annmarie asked.

"No."

It was such a firm, confident 'no' that it ended that line of thinking entirely.

Annamarie met Jemima's uneasy gaze and for a while, neither said anything, just considered each other's all too readable faces.

Eventually, Jemima said, "It isn't proper. It isn't respectful. A body shouldn't be wandering about without any spirit in it."

"What do we do?" Annamarie asked.

"We fetch what's left of her, and we put her in the ground. It won't be pretty work, not with a dead but moving body."

"Have you done this before?"

"Yes." Jemima sighed. "We'll have to cut her up, salt the cuts, put a rock in her mouth and lay the biggest stone we can find on top of her for good measure. It's hard work, this."

"I'll do it," Annamarie said.

"We'll do it together. Might as well get ourselves to a graveyard first, and bring her there." Jemima rolled up her sleeves, and started collecting knives. "Then, we think about our next move."

Jemima paced the floor. "Two of us might be able to do it where one would not."

"You really hate him, don't you?" Annamarie asked, intrigued by this display of emotion. Otherwise, Jemima had been entirely unruffled most of the brief time they had know each other.

"His whole family are a plague on this island. Rotten to the core, every last one. You know he's related to Witherspoon."

"I didn't know." Annamarie worked on pounding roots into powder.

"Back in my mother's day, there were a lot more of the O'Stoats. But a fair few moved on. Island not big enough for them. They've always been ambitious, see. One way or another. Quite a few have come to sticky ends as well."

Annamarie nodded, and waited to hear more, tipping her ground fibres into a jar and starting the next batch.

"They married into the Chevins. Queer family. Too long spent breeding with their cousins."

"I think I'm related to them, on my father's side."

"More than likely. You don't have to climb very far up anyone's family tree to find a connection to someone else."

Annamarie stopped her pounding and asked a question that had been on her mind for a while. "People don't come here very often, do they?"

"Only when they shipwreck, usually, although it wasn't always that way."

"Do many people leave?"

Jemima stopped pacing to consider this. "Not many."

"I'd go if I could."

"Who's to say things are very different anywhere else? What keeps people here is fear it'll be worse moving on, and apathy. We've a good deal of both. Something about this place I reckon. It's no good for your soul but I can't imagine leaving."

"I'll go," Annamarie said emphatically, setting to work on the next round of tough roots.

"No you won't. You'll die here." Jemima's tone had changed. She stopped her efforts, meeting her teacher's eyes, defiant. "We'll see. Now, what about O'Stoat?"

"I'm thinking."

"Could we curse him?"

"I usually do. It hasn't killed him yet. Sometimes things you do, they come back, in ways you don't foresee. It's not so easy."

"We could just push him off a cliff."

Jemima paused to stir the potion bubbling on her stove. "I doubt he'd give us opportunity. He's not without friends either. We do this and get caught, and they will burn us."

Annamarie nodded. "I understand."

"Worth risking I reckon, now there's two of us. We need to catch him when he's out of the house. That place has its own spirit, and a dark one at that. We'll need to be slick. Fast."

"Lamashtu can help."

"Very likely."

Inside the dressmaker's window, there were sleek fabrics that set Annamarie yearning to touch them. There were coins in her pocket, but not enough for one of those frocks. Her coat wouldn't quite fit around her shoulders or over her growing bust. Jemima's good food had put flesh on her bones, turning her from awkward girl into blossoming woman. But none of her clothes fitted very well as a consequence. There was a dark red dress in the window. She wanted it. She would have to buy a coat. New fabric did not come ashore very often. Very few new things did and usually as a consequence of a wreck. Annamarie daydreamed about finding a ship before anyone else did, and the wealth it would bring her. There would be beautiful dresses then.

"I thought it was you." The O'Stoat boy's voice made her jump. She sighed. "Yes, quite entirely me. Do you want something?"

"Just to say hello."

"Why?" She eyed him thoughtfully. "What do you want?"

"You interest me."

"I'm flattered, really." She couldn't keep the sarcasm out of her tone.

He smiled. It did not make him look more appealing. "No you aren't. But you don't seem afraid of me."

"Hell no."

"I find that strangely appealing."

Annamarie considered the boy, and made a decision. She smiled at him, trying her best to make it look genuine. "I'm guessing you don't have many friends then."

"Not a one. Most people do not appeal to me in the slightest."

"But I do?"

"A beautiful witch-in-training. You interest me. How did you get out of my house, incidentally?"

Annamarie raised her eyebrows. "I'm not going to tell you all my secrets. Not yet." She could see the hunger in his eyes. "So, were you going anywhere?"

"Not especially. Although... were you busy?"

"Not at all as it happens."

"I could take you to The Crow."

"I'd love that."

He offered his arm, and Annamarie took it, keeping the smile on her face. She felt deeply uneasy, but if they were going after O'Stoat, anything she could learn might help. Cultivating the boy seemed like a good way to proceed.

"I'm not fool enough to think you are drawn to my house by the possibility of seeing me. What do you want, Annamarie?"

It occurred to her that he might be trying to play her. "A friend of mine from the orphanage, went to work with your father."

"Ah. The fat girl with the squinty eyes."

"Her. Yes. Hilda."

He nodded. "Hard to imagine you two as friends."

Annamarie bit her tongue and planned her words. "It doesn't pay to judge too much by surfaces."

"Let me give you some advice, because I like you."

"Go on."

"There's no helping her. Give it up."

"I'm not sure I can."

They reached The Crow just as the rain started. There were plenty of empty tables, with little light and not much warmth from the barely glowing fire. The pair sat close to it, and ordered 'Surprise Soup', the conversation staying away from controversy.

"Did you know this is the oldest building on the island?" the lad asked.

"I didn't. What's your full name?"

"Durosimi Patrick Trismegistus O'Stoat."

She stared at him, wide-eyed. "That's a lot of name."

"And you are Annamarie what? Which family do you belong to?"

She considered this. No one had identified her father to her, although she had her suspicions. She had no desire to own any of her recent ancestors. Mind racing, she remembered her lessons from that morning. "Annamarie Nightshade." It felt right.

"The thing is, Annamarie, I hate my father. I'm as much his prisoner as your friend is. I might not be bound to serve him, but he gives me little freedom. My life is hell. I wish he was dead. I won't be free until he is."

The mirroring of her intentions startled her, but she did not trust him.

"Have I shocked you?" Durosimi asked.

"No. Surprised maybe, not shocked."

"I dream of poisoning him. It's the only thing I think would work." He spoke casually, as though jesting, but something dark flickered in his eyes.

Annamarie reached across the table and covered his pale, slender hand with hers.

The Choices We Make

Feeling herself watched, Annamarie straightened up and wiped the sweat from her brow. Her arms ached from wielding the axe, but she had broken up enough wood to last them a few days. Turning her head, she saw a familiar face amongst the trees, a faint smile on his lips. She knew he shouldn't be there, that he had taken some risk in order to see her.

"Old Witherspoon will have you doing penance for a month if he finds out about this!" she said cheerfully, lowering the axe and going to him.

"He will. But hopefully he won't know. How are you, Annamarie?" Emanuel stared intently at her as he spoke.

"I'm well. This life suits me. And you? I think you're as pale and thin as ever, my dear."

"He works me hard, but I feel useful. I have some purpose. I had heard..." he paused, more awkward than usual.

"Yes?"

"That you're walking out with Durosimi O'Stoat."

The query caught her off guard. "Oh."

"It's true then?"

She met his gaze, unable to see how she could explain any of it. Her long-time friend had a different moral sense to her own and would not understand the plot she was weaving.

With a nod, he looked away, talking to the space behind her. "It's all right. It wouldn't... I didn't... and of course now..." he frowned. "I wish you well, Anna. I miss you every day. I probably always will. But, you are to be a witch and I am to be a priest it seems, and you are stepping out with the O'Stoat boy."

"Emanuel I..."

"Don't say anything, please? We've made our choices, both of us. There is nothing to do but live with the consequences."

She stared, dumbstruck, hearing implications in the words that had never truly crossed her mind before.

Emanuel cleared his throat. "Better for both of us if I say goodbye. No doubt we will see each other, from afar now and then. But, we cannot be... friends."

Her hands shook. "Why do we have to go along with what everyone else thinks?"

"That's how the world works."

"Not for me!"

"Perhaps, but I have no choices. I have a path to follow. I cannot consort with witches."

Her temper snapped. "Well you don't have to consort with me if you don't want to!" She flung the words at him. "Go on then, turn your back on me if that's what you want. Pretend you don't know me. That's just fine. You were stupid coming up here. Like I'm going to care in the slightest what you do."

When she finished her tirade, Emanuel Davies turned silently from her and walked away. She watched him go, his spine ruthlessly straight, never once turning or glancing back. The rage burned out, leaving a trail of agonised expletives and tempestuous tears.

"Bloody stupid useless waste of a skin," she muttered at his rapidly vanishing back. "Pointless, crap arsehole... like I care. Like I care?" She sobbed. "How can you do this to me? How can you let everyone else be more important? I thought we were friends." Through her tears she wondered what would have happened if she'd said this in his presence instead of just lashing out.

He had reached the road, his narrow frame a dark line on the landscape. He stopped, but did not appear to be doing anything. Annamarie couldn't breathe, not knowing what was happening, or if he had somehow heard her later words. Emotions boiled and seethed within her, bubbling up as a mass of uncomfortable thoughts.

"I think I love you," she whispered, willing him to hear, to understand. The young witch knew as she uttered the words that she would never say them to him in person. Realisation set like ice around her heart. Whatever had been between them, was gone and could not be reclaimed. She had lost him. Only now did she realise how important the connection had been to her, but it was too late.

Why didn't I speak when I had the chance? Why didn't I realise sooner? Emanuel finally disappeared from her view. Slumping down at the foot of a tree, she succumbed to weeping, indulging the bitter rush of emotion.

"Now there's something I didn't expect to see." Durosimi sounded amused.

Resenting the intrusion, Annamarie sniffed back her tears and tried to reclaim some dignity.

"Don't worry, I've no intention of insulting you with false sympathy."

"Good." She stood up, her limbs trembling.

"Hard to imagine anything bothering you enough to make you cry," he observed.

"It's private." She folded her arms across her chest. "And it won't happen again."

"Tears are for the weak, but you are strong, Annamarie. You are proud and ambitious. Tears do not suit you." He sounded older, imposing.

"You are right. They don't suit me at all. What did you want, Durosimi?"

"Aside from the pleasure of your company? To talk about plants and potions."

"Ah." She had been expecting this, and had worked with Jemima on the issue. "Something that works quickly would be best. And that does not taste too strongly."

"You understand me perfectly."

"Stay here." Making a point of moving in a composed way, she walked down to the cottage to retrieve the poisonous brew she and Jemima had created. They had put it in an old bottle, unlabeled and anonymous. On returning, she presented it to Durosimi. "Use all of it."

"I will. I shall be back in a day or so, to tell you. If I am not, then most likely I will be dead. But you will not weep for me."

She smiled at this. "Of course not."

"That is better."

Jemima emerged from the cottage after he had gone. "It's an uneasy feeling, putting death into the hands of a boy like him."

"He can do what we cannot."

"Do you trust him, Annamarie?"

"Not in the slightest, but we are here, and they are a strange family. Perhaps we should take a stroll? It might not hurt to be seen." She couldn't stand still, agitation juddering all her limbs.

"Let's go down to the Red House. Lavender Bessom owes me a drink for getting her out of a spot of bother the other week."

"The Red House?" Annamarie grinned. It was one of Reverend Witherspoon's hated places. "I hear it's a den of vice and iniquity."

"That and more. We can drink something strong and not think about the O'Stoats."

"Fine by me." The face in her mind belonged to neither vile father nor murderous son. She needed to drink away the spectre of Emanuel Davies and forget the grief she felt at their parting.

The Colour of Her Heart

After a week, Annamarie could no longer bear the uncertainty. Nor could she stand being away from the town. Jemima was often too grumpy and dour a soul to be good company when there were no other distractions. If nothing else she could gaze through smeared shop windows and dream about being someone different. That no one had knocked their door down seemed to bode well, so she thought it no great risk to show her face.

She walked the long way round, passing the orphanage and the church. There were a few children picking leaves from the hedge, but otherwise no signs of life. It took some willpower not to loiter about. She wanted to catch a glimpse of Emanuel. Just to see his face, not to be seen, or to speak. The thought of him had haunted her. She did not want him to know any of this, and so she could not wait around and give him cause to suspect.

Walking along the main street, she saw plenty of familiar faces. A few acknowledged her with a brief nod, but no one spoke. That was normal. Everything seemed as usual in fact. A couple of crows were fighting over the corpse of a rat. A couple of women were arguing over the price of tentacles with the man from the fish shop. The weird guy whose decomposing hat appeared to be stuck to his head in pieces was having an argument with himself while walking round in circles, which he usually did. Annamarie managed not to make eye contact. A few weeks previously he had followed her for half an hour, making chicken noises.

At the end of the main street she stopped and considered her options as the roads branched in different directions. She could just go back to the cottage. There had been no signs of anything untoward and she had picked up no gossip. No one had stopped her or asked questions. There was no need to carry on down the road in the direction of Durosimi's house. No need at all. For a few minutes she tried to tell herself she didn't care what had happened.

She wanted to know what Durosimi had done, and whether he or his father had died as a consequence of it. Had he taken the poison and used it on his father? Had he been able to stand there and watch the man die? Possibly. Annamarie wasn't entirely sure if she could kill a person so directly. Being involved in this did not leave her carrying much guilt. Vincent O'Stoat had been a monster.

What if he lived? If Durosimi had tried and failed, he could be dead by now. She would not know unless she went to find out. Not fully decided, she took a hesitant step, then another. Somehow her feet made the decision and she trotted out along the stony track at a pace. It occurred to her she might ask Lamashtu to fetch the lad out. That would be safe enough and would give her some answers. Her familiar would come if she called it.

Approaching the house, she saw a figure sat in the garden, leather bound tome balanced on one hand, a glass of wine in the other. The empty chair beside him gave her an uneasy feeling.

Durosimi smiled at her, but the expression was cold. "I wondered how long it would take you."

She came to the gate. "You are well then?"

"Exceedingly. Care for some wine?"

"Of course." She tried to appear nonchalant.

"Take a seat then. There are plans to make. Things I will require of you." He poured her a glass of dark liquid and passed it to her. Annamarie sat down on the plush dining chair. "Require of me?"

"Oh yes. I think there is a great deal we can achieve together."

"You did it then?"

"Of course. I took great satisfaction in it. A shame you were not there to share the moment, but I have a feeling there will be others."

A great many thoughts buzzed in Annamarie's head. She chose not to voice any of them.

"My father was an accomplished occultist. Now I have his library, his tools. I have much to learn. He guarded his knowledge jealously. He thought I was too young." Durosimi smiled as though he had told a particularly good joke. "I will surpass him in every way." He turned a cold gaze upon the young witch. "You are going to help me."

"No I am not. I've done what I meant to do."

"Oh but you will," his words were frosted. "We are bound together, you and I. We have done things that unite us, and that can never be escaped from. We are partners in guilt, dear Annamarie."

She shrugged. "I don't feel much guilt. The world is a better place for your father being absent from it." She kept her voice low. "We both got what we wanted. That's the end of it."

Durosimi sipped at his wine, looking beyond her as though fascinated by the garden wall. "We shall see."

She put the untouched glass down, wary of its contents. "You sound like you mean to carry on much as he did. I won't support you in that."

"Oh no. I will not follow him. I shall be far better."

"No turning people into soulless slaves?"

His thin lips stretched in a smile. "Better in the sense of stronger, more powerful. The world at my fingertips."

"You'll find no friend in me then." She rose, heading for the gate. Durosimi's words followed her. "You will come back. Not because you are bound to me. Not because you like me, but because you want the same things as I do. Your own dark heart will draw you back here, again and again."

Although she did not want to hear his words, she stopped walking. "You will be unable to resist the lure of power. The intoxication of being able to entirely please yourself."

Turning back, she meant to argue with him, but the unsettling youth spoke again. "If I am a monster, then you are my equal in that regard, Annamarie Nightshade."

Finding she had no words with which to argue, she fled, skirts in her hands to make the running easier. Pelting up the muddy street, she kept her wild pace until she ran out of breath. She growled. "I'm nothing like you. Nothing at all." Maintaining a low and angry monologue, she kept walking. "I'm not..." What? Power hungry? Frustrated? Wanting more from life? Drawn by the idea of magic? As she worked her way through the list of similarities, there proved to be far too many for comfort. Only her recent flight from the house offered itself as evidence of difference.

"I'm not like him!" she announced to the open skies. "And I'm certainly not going to let him tell me what to do!"

His words circled in her mind. "Your own dark heart will draw you back here." Once the rage subsided, foreboding took its place. She had so little, and he had suggested so much.

"My dark heart," she whispered. "Maybe. But only if I want to and never on your terms, be sure of that."

PART TWO
— MADNESS IN THE BLOOD —

The Flesh is not Everything

He came out of the warm twilight of a late spring evening, eyes burning with their own peculiar light. Hearing the approach of heavy footsteps, Annamarie had already left off tending the herb bed and straightened her back. Lamashtu rubbed around her ankles, a presence that suggested catness, but lacked full solidity.

"I see it," the young witch whispered to her familiar, with no idea what exactly she saw.

Tail held high, Lamashtu approached the apparition. Golden eyes shifted erratically, weaving and wandering across the open ground at about the height of a human. Still Annamarie had learned caution. As the peculiar orbs grew nearer, she could make out a somewhat human shape, topped off by an explosion of insane hair. This appearance did nothing to reassure her. Two years in the study of witchcraft had encouraged her to look hard at everything, even if it seemed trustworthy at first glance. The peal of demented laughter didn't help.

"Hello, hello, is there anybody here?" The voice cracked with giggles. "Come out, come out, wherever you are!"

Annamarie stepped forwards. "I'm here. What do you want?"

"They told me there were witches here. They said you would help."

She decided he was very likely harmless. "That's right. Better come into the cottage and see Jemima."

Their guest looked no more sane once candlelight illuminated him. His clothes were a mismatched selection of tawdry rags patched with bright colours. The garments had been mended so many times that their original shape and purpose had long since been lost. Indoors, his bulbous eyes lost some of their luminescence. Annamarie tried not to stare at him.

Jemima looked up as they entered. "Balthazar Lemon! Well bugger me. I thought you were long dead."

"I've been lots of things, but dead isn't one of them, not yet, Mistress Kettle."

"Sit yourself down. Get him some tea to drink, girl."

Shaking her head, Annamarie brought out three cups and ladled hot liquid from the cauldron hanging over the fire.

Their guest smelled the brew suspiciously. "Don't go putting any spells on me, mind. They say you do that. You put spells on people." He laughed, his voice squeaking.

"That's right." Jemima seemed entirely untroubled.

"I went down to the sea and I talked to the crows of course."

Jemima sipped her tea, then blew on it before speaking. "Wise birds, crows. So, what's on your mind, Balthazar?"

"I mind. My mind is on my mind. Or in it. Was that it? What do I mind? All sorts of things, I can tell you. Mind what you say. Don't mind if I do." He turned to Annamarie and started as though he hadn't realised she was there. "What do I mind?"

Jemima fixed him with an intense gaze. "Slow down, Balthazar. Breathe. I need you to concentrate. Something bothered you to make you come here. See if you can remember and tell us about it, eh?"

His previously vacant expression sharpened, as though under his skin something had shifted into focus. "I need you to help with my girl."

Jemima's brow wrinkled. "She lived then? I remember delivering her, although that's going back a few years. Got her now. Ah yes. Thought I'd be called back to bury her in the week. Scrawny little thing she was, and silent."

"She lived. She lives. But she isn't right."

"By my reckoning, she must be sixteen, yes?" Jemima considered this. "And no mother. Ah. I think I understand."

"Her mother swam away like a fish. Right away. Never came back."

Annamarie listened with moderate interest. The people who sought them out were usually desperate, and working out what they meant from what it occurred to them to say was very much part of the job. However, even by the standards of their usual, troubled clientele, the startling Mister Lemon seemed as mad as a bucket full of rats.

"Don't you worry about a thing, Balthazar. Are you still living out on the coast?"

"I live with the light, and for the light. Do you think it will bring her back?"

"We'll pop round tomorrow and see how your little girl is. I'm sure we can sort her out. It'll be woman's things, and what with her mother being gone..."

"She's a fish. Did you know that?"

"Of course she is. Now don't you fret, let me deal with this." Jemima ushered their visitor out into the night.

"She isn't supposed to swell up like that."

"Girls do sometimes, but there's nothing to worry about. Perfectly natural. We'll put it all right," Jemima repeated, then pulled the door closed and sighed heavily. "God help us if she's pregnant."

Annamarie sighed. "He's not right in the head, is he?"

"Balthazar? A bit moon touched, and spends too much time by himself. It's like he looks at the world from a different direction to the rest of us, that's all. Not so bad once you get used to him."

"You know him then?"

"Not well, but enough. There were a few of them came ashore in a shipwreck, years ago. First new blood on the island in a long while. But they were an odd lot, funny ways."

Considering the ways in which residents of Hopeless chose to live, Annamarie wondered what anyone could consider 'funny' and was poised to ask when her mentor spoke again.

"It'll be interesting to see how the girl turned out. I'd not given her a thought in years! Her mother was a beauty. I saw her a few times. Cried a lot though, I remember."

"I'm not surprised, being shipwrecked here."

"There are worse places to be," Jemima said darkly.

"How would you know? You've never been anywhere else."

"The flesh is not everything, girl. There's more to knowing than what eyes can tell. Haven't you learned anything, girl?"

The remark stung. "Maybe there's things you ought to teach me then," she snapped back. They spent a lot of time sparring and point scoring.

Jemima shook her head. "It's not just about the learning, it's the understanding what you learn. That takes time. Life. You don't get to understand how people are until you've been through a few things yourself. I'm sure that to you, Balthazar is a mad old bird. Until you've walked on the other side of sanity a bit yourself, you won't know what to do with that. You think you understand how the world is, girly, but that's because you're young and you haven't lived enough to know that you don't know shit."

Unable to find a good come-back, Annamarie stoked the fire. It frustrated her that Jemima insisted on taking the teaching so slowly. She had the feeling it wouldn't take decades to learn to be a witch, if only she was given the scope to try.

"I can see what you're thinking, madam. You might well be a lot smarter than I am. I'll give you that. You've got Lamashtu and you know a thing or two. What you don't have is the least bit of common sense, and until you've gained a bit of wisdom, there are things I'm not going to teach you. Do you know why that is?"

"No, Jemima," Annamarie intoned, resigned being lectured on her shortcomings.

"Because I don't trust you not to do something stupid and get yourself killed. You'll learn, when I think you're ready for it."

"Oh good." Sarcasm dripped from her tongue.

"I don't much care what you think of me, but you're my apprentice and I mean to keep you alive long enough to inherit from me." Jemima paused, her expression intense. "And anyway, I happen to like you."

Speechless, Annamarie could do nothing but stare wide-eyed in response.

Living in the Light

Although Annamarie had been all the way to the base of the lighthouse once before, she had not realised anyone lived there. Now she came to think about it, obviously someone must tend the light. There were plenty of nights when she had seen its pale beams reaching out across the waves. It couldn't run itself. This was the kind of detail she frequently didn't bother to ponder, but today the question of how and why a person might live out here occupied her mind.

While most of the islanders made their homes in the town, there were plenty of farms, fisherman's cottages and places like Jemima's that were rather more isolated. Annamarie had mixed feelings about not being in the thick of things. Craving attention, but disliking most people, her current lifestyle was as viable as any, she supposed. The lighthouse appeared to have been stuck on the most lonely and desolate part of Hopeless. By the looks of it, high tides would separate it from the rest of the island. She imagined that in the depths of winter it would be a grim place to live.

As the two witches approached, a flock of crows took off from the nearby beach, wheeling overhead.

"Oh, you're worse than a bunch of old women!" Jemima exclaimed, waving her arms at the birds. They paid her little attention, filling the air with the sounds of wingbeats.

Running behind the flock, his arms flapping like a child imitating a bird, Balthazar Lemon made his way up the beach. The crows seemed untroubled by his presence, even when he added his voice to their harsh chorus. His clothes were dark with moisture and dripped conspicuously.

"More crows!" he shouted by way of a greeting. "Can you fly?"

"Of course!" Jemima shouted back. "Can you?"

Annamarie ground her teeth. Flying was one of the things her mentor steadfastly refused to teach her. It meant they had to walk everywhere, or she was left to follow as best she could. What was the point of being a witch if people couldn't see you doing anything out of the ordinary?

"I've been working on a machine!" Balthazar shouted. "It's amazing what you can do with machines, especially when they don't work in the way you thought they were going to." He reached them, his hair full of seaweed, and with something slimy trying to climb out of the collar of his makeshift garment.

"We came to see your daughter, do you remember?"

"My daughter? Why do you want to see her? Has she done something?"

Jemima put on the smile Annamarie associated with trouble. That kind of cheerful patience never boded well. "You came to see us yesterday, don't you remember?"

"I was going to see you. Yes. I meant to. I've been swimming. It's cold today. I think the fish prefer it that way, mind you."

"Your daughter," Jemima repeated, her smile becoming more rigid.

Annamarie drifted in the direction of the door. "You've left your door open, Mister Lemon. Shall I go and put the kettle on for you? I'm sure you must be cold after all that swimming."

"It won't fit you, but feel free to try!"

Taking this as permission, the trainee witch entered the light-house. From a quick glance around she had the impression that the ground floor room was meant to be a kitchen and scullery. There were no shortage of grimy dishes and pans whose contents she hesitated to consider. Littered amongst these items were other, less identifiable things. Some appeared to have been salvaged from the beach – there were shellfish still attached to them. Others were black with oil, or rusted with disuse. She could not name any of them. It took her a while to locate the stove, beneath a complex creation full of levers and pulleys. There was no heat in it, and from the looks of it, no one had used it in a while. Of the kettle, there was no immediate sign. With nothing better to do, she kept hunting. Eventually locating it, she could not work out how to part it from the impedimenta it had been wired to.

"What are you doing?"

Annamarie looked up, and found the owner of the rather sharp voice staring down at her. A pale face, with dark, haunted eyes, and no hint of any kind of expression. The dress this girl wore might have been expensive and fabulous, once, but looked as though it had been left out in the rain a few times too often, and then dried out in the oven. *Don't discount it.*

"I was just looking for the kettle. Your father sent me in to make everyone a nice cup of tea."

"I doubt that." The girl descended, moving with unsettling slowness. "Go away."

"Charming." Annamarie eyed the Lemon girl. She had a haughty look to her, but as she came closer, the shape of her body became more apparent beneath the complex folds and flounces of her dress. "You need a chat with Mistress Kettle."

The girl huffed dismissively and moved past her, stepping outside. Annamarie followed, keen to see how this all played out.

"Ah, this must be your little girl then," Jemima said.

"Melisandra," the creature replied, clearly not liking the description she had been given.

"Your father tells me you've had a few difficulties," Jemima said. Annamarie knew that the swollen belly would have been noticed. Very little escaped Jemima's attention. Little Miss Haughty clearly hadn't spent all of her time being so high and mighty. Hard to imagine anyone tumbling such a cold fish of a girl, but Annamarie knew enough about boys to appreciate that some didn't mind fish in the slightest. Or goats for that matter.

"Thank you, but I have no need for your interference," Melisandra announced.

Jemima chuckled. "You will have. You won't get that out without a bit of help. By the looks of you, it won't be many weeks away either."

"I have no idea what you mean."

Jemima stepped closer and pressed the palm of her hand to the girl's engorged middle. "That. Or are you telling me you don't know what that is or how it got there?"

The girl said nothing. Her face remained impassive, unreadable.

"You're going to have a baby," Jemima pressed. "You do understand that, yes? Staring at me won't make it go away, young lady. And by the looks of you, we need a bit of a chat about how it got in there in the first place, or no sooner will the first one be out but there will be a second on the way."

Annamarie watched for a reaction – a flush of shame, a twitch of remorse. *Nothing. Well, maybe she isn't right in the head either. Her father clearly isn't dancing to the same tune as the rest of us. Maybe she doesn't understand. Poor chicken. She's going to be in for a nasty surprise.*

"I am perfectly well aware of where babies come from. I have read books," Melisandra said, with disdain. "I have not undertaken that kind of action. I am not with child."

Jemima raised her eyebrows at this. "Can't think what else it could be. I've been delivering babies for longer than you've been alive my girl, and I know a pregnancy when I see one."

"You are mistaken."

Jemima glowered and it looked as though her attempt at jovial good humour would fail at any moment. Annamarie longed to see her mentor's temper break, and slash Melisandra. However, the older witch held firm, and managed to keep her smile in place.

"Tell you what dearie, when the pains start, you get your dad to come and fetch me. Then maybe afterwards we can have a proper talk about where babies come from and how yours came into the world."

"That will not be necessary." Melisandra turned on her heel and walked back into the lighthouse, moving with the same slow gait. She slammed the door behind her.

"I've seen babies," her father said. "They're slow. Slow as pumpkins and ripe apples. They don't turn up overnight like mushrooms."

"True enough," Jemima said.

"Hang on a minute, are you saying she wasn't like this a few days ago?" Annamarie asked.

"She was as slender as a reed and as pretty as a herring."

Jemima joined Annamarie in staring at Balthazar Lemon.

"She came up all of a sudden, on that day I came to you. So I knew it couldn't have been her sporting with some boy. They don't plant seeds that grow so fast. She won't tell me anything. She always was silent. Never cried as a baby. Never once."

"Listen to me, Balthazar. If she won't let us help, there's not much we can do. But, if anything changes, if she gets into difficulty, you come and give me a shout, got it?"

He nodded. "I wouldn't want anything to hurt her. She's all I have."

Jemima touched his arm gently. "We'll do whatever we can, but I can't make you any promises beyond that."

What the Crows Know

Having been sent out to see if the storms had washed up anything interesting, Annamarie started her search by the cluster of old fishing cottages. She knew there were people living in them, but never usually saw more than shadows of the occupants. The buildings were squat above the beach; brooding presences that gave her the impression they didn't trust the sea in the slightest. The high tide had brought in a lot of material – mostly driftwood, seaweed and dead things. She found a nice glass bottle with the stopper intact, and more decaying, stinking things than pleased her. Picking her way across the sand, she avoided the dense clumps of seaweed and debris, afraid of stepping on something that would crunch, or worse yet squelch under her shoe.

As the lighthouse came into view, she wondered if this had been deliberate on Jemima's part: giving her an excuse to wander by. Feeling quite nosy about the Lemon girl, Annamarie decided to walk out that way and have a look. The crows were out on the beach, feasting on the dead things. They paid her no attention. With the tide at its lowest, there was quite a lot of rock-strewn sand exposed, and she did not need to encroach upon their feeding ground.

Annamarie could make out a figure in the waves and supposed at first it must be Balthazar Lemon.

"Don't notice me," Annamarie whispered, concentrating on not being obvious. "Don't notice me, I'm just another crow, just a piece of fabric blown in the wind. Nothing to see. Nothing to notice." It wasn't a way of becoming invisible, but it made her easier to miss. A little will-working to bend the shape of reality slightly. Making her way up passed the lighthouse, she saw a plume of smoke. Balthazar was beating out the flames that surrounded a peculiar metal structure.

"Why have you done that? It isn't meant to go like that!" he swore repeatedly at the thing.

She slipped past him, unnoticed and proud of her growing skill. Then a thought struck her. If it wasn't him in the sea, it must be someone else. She doubled back, finding a suitable place in which to hide and watch. It was a warm enough day and she felt like taking a rest. The figure in the waves remained there, disappearing under the water from time to time. Warm sunlight made it easy to sit and daydream a little. The sea made its journey back up the beach, bringing the lone swimmer with it, until Annamarie was in no doubt. Even with her dark hair plastered against her scalp, and the dress gone, Melisandra Lemon remained identifiable.

The sun shone high overhead when the bather at last emerged, naked, from the water. The swell of her stomach was dramatic. Annamarie knew more theory than anything else where children were concerned, but it looked a lot like pregnancy to her. As the lone figure made her way up the beach, the bloated curve of her distended stomach drew the young witch's eyes. She couldn't imagine how any woman could want such a thing. *Not me. Not ever.*

Once Melisandra had vanished into the lighthouse, there wasn't much else to see. Quickly bored, Annamarie decided to head inland and walk back the less direct way, past the orphanage. Her routes frequently took her the long way round, but she seldom saw anyone. This time, she was crossing the road by the church when two black clad figures emerged. They were deep in conversation and did not recognise her, but she knew them all too well. Old Reverend Witherspoon had made her life miserable for a good many years. By his side, and dressed in ominously priest-like attire, walked Emanuel Davies. Her heart lurched at the sight of him. He looked so pale and serious, listening intently as Witherspoon spoke. The words did not carry across the street.

"Look up," she whispered. "See me. Please, just this once. Notice that I exist."

He didn't.

For more than two years, they had not been on speaking terms. Annamarie would have given anything for an opportunity to make amends, but the chance hadn't come. As soon as the young man's back turned towards her however, she cursed under her breath. "Damn you. I won't come crawling to you, Mister Davies. Perhaps if you beg me for my forgiveness, I'll think about it." Smothering the ache in her heart with anger, she continued on her way.

Turning down one of the more run-down side roads, onto Silver Street, Annamarie knocked on an anonymous looking door. It opened for her readily enough, revealing a girl with a pretty face and dishevelled clothes.

The fake smile melted into a real one. "Oh, it's you darling. Come on in."

There were four girls in the kitchen, in various states of undress. They plied Annamarie with what they claimed was coffee and what was unequivocally gossip. Having been raised by the orphanage with a clear idea of what a good girl should be, Annamarie found she preferred the company of the other sort. She felt easy around them. They were fun, rude, and not prone to judging.

"Did you know Melisandra Lemon's got a bun in the oven?" she said casually, wondering if this news might bring her some further information on the subject.

"I haven't seen her since school," Cassy, the youngest of the set replied. "Odd girl. Don't think I ever heard her say a thing. Who's been poking her then?"

"No idea," Annamarie replied.

"Old Lemon's got a girl the same age as you?" Desdemona asked, raising dark eyebrows.

"Yep." Cassy grinned.

"Old goat," Desdemona responded, with some warmth.

Sensing an undercurrent, Annamarie ventured, "Client of yours, is he?"

Cassy grinned impishly. "You know we don't talk about what we do, it's like being a priest. It's like hearing confession."

"Of course it is," Annamarie concurred, with a tone of faux respect. "Very serious profession yours, wouldn't think of asking you to break a confidence my dear."

"He's an odd one though," Desdemona continued. "Not that I'm telling you this mind, dearie. But some of the things he's asked for, I wouldn't have thought of in a million years."

"Sexual things I'm assuming?" Annamarie tried to sound casual.

"Well, for him maybe. This one time, he just wanted me to stand around in my underwear with some seaweed in one hand and a bit of driftwood in the other. Who knows what goes on in his head?" Desdemona chuckled. "He's always got something to give away though, and it's easily earned from him."

"We eat a lot of fish," Desdemona added with a chuckle.

Transparent Jones stopped brushing her long hair to speak. "You don't think?" She paused dramatically. "No."

They all turned their attention towards her.

"Silly idea," she said. "Don't mind me."

"Come on Tran, what were you thinking?" Cassy coaxed.

"Lonely place that lighthouse. And he's a funny old sod is Balthazar. What if it's his?"

"But she's his daughter," Annamarie protested.

"A bit of incest never slowed the Chevins down, or the Joneses for that matter," Transparent said. "I should know. Some of my family's very close indeed, if you know what I mean."

"Too close, I'd say. That's why you Joneses are all a bit mad, I reckon," Persephone, the quietest of the four interjected.

"Well, Old Mr Lemon is crazier than the lot of us put together," Transparent retorted. "It's not even like he's from around here."

"I should be getting back," Annamarie said. "Thanks for the coffee."

"Next time you're passing, I could do with some more of that cream Jemima did me last time," Desdemona said.

"Will do. See you soon my dears!" Around them, it was easy to fall into their speech patterns.

Walking home, Annamarie considered these latest insights. She had a feeling whatever had swollen Melisandra's belly, it wasn't her father. From what she'd seen of them together that didn't quite fit. Intuition suggested there would be a much stranger, and potentially less comfortable explanation. She considered asking Lamashtu, but when it came to understanding what happened between humans, her familiar was often at a loss. It could gather information, but it never knew which details were the ones that actually mattered. The more she asked of it, the more blood it needed so she tended to keep things minimal.

Thinking about the creature drew it to her, and together they meandered up the lane, stopping to pick occasional herbs, or to look at the view.

A Head Full of Storm Clouds

That boy's coming up the track," Jemima said, her tone making it clear she didn't approve much.

Annamarie's heart lurched, but the feeling soon passed. "Which one?" she asked, trying to sound careless.

"How many have you got?"

"Oh, a few, here and there. You know how it is."

"Then I wouldn't waste much time or breath on this one. It's the O'Stoat boy. If you want to hide in the attic, I can tell him you're out."

"He's nothing if not persistent. I'd better get it over with and see what he wants."

It wasn't as if she liked Durosimi. He had a slippery, unpleasant air to him that she recoiled from, and yet kept going back to. Unable to explain the fascination he held, Annamarie settled for pretending that it didn't exist.

Since his father's demise, Durosimi had adopted a more adult dress style. Where he got his money from, or the cloth even, Annamarie had managed not to ask. He dropped hints, but she hadn't taken the bait yet, thinking she could wait him out. He obviously wanted to tell her and she much preferred not to seem interested.

Sighing, she stepped out of the cottage to meet him. "What do you want this time?"

"You have such a charming way of greeting your friends, one could almost imagine you had studied the finer details of etiquette somewhere far from this social backwater."

"I say what I mean."

He smiled, unpleasantly. It occurred to Annamarie that she had never seen him smile with warmth or delight, only with malice, irony and cruel amusement. He was probably the kind of boy who had spent his early years pulling legs off spiders, and wings off butterflies. She did not imagine he would improve with age.

"I brought you a present, dear Annamarie."

She stiffened. It wouldn't be a gift, she felt certain. There would be a price attached, even if she couldn't tell what it was at first. Durosimi did not give without the expectation of receiving.

"That's very thoughtful of you," she said carefully, wondering what he was after.

"Don't you want to know what it is?"

"I'm sure you're going to tell me."

He held out his hand. On his palm sat a coil of fine chain, and a strange pendant, coiled and twisty. It radiated power.

"What does it do?" Annamarie asked, fingers hovering over the item but not quite touching.

"It is protection from evil. No supernatural forces will be able to harm you while you wear it."

"It's just the people I have to worry about, then," she said, lifting it. The amulet weighed heavily in her hand, but felt comfortable enough.

"It won't protect you from me, no."

"That comes as no surprise. But I have other ways of doing that, so don't trouble yourself about it."

"Do you now? I might have to test that some time." His eyes gleamed.

The amulet was like nothing she had seen before. It seemed to be stone, but not the sort you found on the island. "Where did you get it?" As soon as she spoke, triumph lit his eyes. *Well damn it, I am curious. Never hurts to know where a thing came from.* "My father had a very interesting book collection," Durosimi said. "I have learned a great deal of late. The trouble with a creature like Lamashtu is that in truth, they own you at least as much as you own them."

"It's a relationship," the young witch said defensively.

"Of course it is, and you know how I feel about that sort of thing. It struck me as being far better to be able to summon, posses and control, than being at any risk of compromising my own will."

"Is that what you've been doing? Summoning things?"

"I would appear to have no small amount of talent, where invoking and enslaving is concerned. My life has become far more pleasant of late. As you were so helpful to me, a little gift seemed in order. I had one of my minions fetch it for you."

"Very clever."

"I'm sure with all of your learning, and having a teacher, my small dabbling won't be of much interest to you."

Annamarie fought to keep her face straight. He was playing with her, luring her into revealing how much she did not know. "There is that, yes, but it was nice of you, Durosimi, to tell me what you've been up to."

"Perhaps one of these days you'll take the time to show me something."

That was it then, the payment he wanted for the amulet. Knowledge, or her humiliation.

"Or you could stop by at the house and I'll show you what I can do." She could hear the plaintive note in his voice. The boy needed an audience. What did it matter if you could summon up demons, spirits or the undead, if no one knew and was impressed by it? He would be suffering from not being able to share his discoveries.

Much as she hated to admit it, Annamarie longed to see what he had learned.

"I might, if I get an evening when I'm not too busy. You know how it is, people to see, mysteries to unravel." As this comment won her a look of disbelief, she continued. "You'd be amazed what happens here sometimes. You have to know how to look, and what to be looking for, of course."

"Of course."

She had the feeling he was mocking her. "Witchcraft isn't all about big impressive things, you know. It isn't showy. It's about getting the details right, noticing the small things that are going to turn into big things. It's not about being powerful, it's about being wise."

Durosimi laughed at this. "Oh, Annamarie, that must make it so very hard for you."

Before she could think of a suitably cutting answer, he turned his back and went on his way. Irritated, she stormed back inside, the amulet clutched in her hands.

"I heard what you said to him," Jemima said, causing Annamarie's spirits to decline even further. "Sounded like you have been figuring things out. I'd underestimated you, girl. You've more insight than I thought, and maybe you do understand."

"About the craft?"

"Yes. Perhaps it's about time I showed you a few more things. I think you're about ready."

Annamarie managed to remain composed, despite her enthusiasm. "That would be good." She opened her palm. "He gave me this. I think he's trying to impress me."

Jemima lifted it in her fingers. "It's old. Made with anger. There's some power in it, but not as much as there was meant to be."

"He said it would protect me from malevolent supernatural forces."

"I'd say he's right. It might keep off one or two. Never hurts to have a bit of something in that regard."

"Could I put more power in it?"

Jemima chuckled. "Wouldn't be hard. Depends a lot on how you feel about killing things. I get the impression it draws its power from sacrifices."

"Ick."

"The easiest power comes from hating, killing and taking. The people who go that way never see the costs, except when it's too late. More than one way a person can lose their soul."

"What about Lamashtu?" Annamarie asked, suddenly anxious.

"That one? If you used it all the time, it would take you over in the end. You're not doing so badly with it. I doubt you'll come to any harm, just so long as you don't get greedy."

"I don't mean to."

Annamarie could see how this would have implications for Durosimi, if he kept summoning unnatural things to do his bidding. She wondered what it would cost him.

Born of Darkness

L antern in one hand, Annamarie ran as best she could. She had long since lost sight of Balthazar Lemon, although he stopped frequently to shout encouragement at her. Rain trickled down the back of her neck, chilling and irritating in equal measure. *Typical melodramatic stuff, picking the middle of a stormy night to go into labour.* Jemima had flown on ahead, leaving her apprentice to make the journey across land, a state of affairs which had not improved the young woman's mood.

Out of breath and mud-spattered, she arrived at the lighthouse to find the front door ajar and a few candles burning. Balthazar bustled about in the kitchen, a frenetic and unruly ball of activity. He didn't appear to be actually doing anything, despite the appearance of busyness. Annamarie supposed he was afraid and trying to distract himself.

"Is there anything I can do to help, Mr Lemon?"

"Do you know the song about the girl who loses her slipper?"

"Can't say that I do."

"Probably not then." He started polishing one of his devices, then put it down again.

"I'll just pop up and see if Jemima needs any help then, yes?"

He turned sorrowful eyes in her direction. "It's Melisandra who needs the help. So much help, she needs. She isn't well."

Sick, I think, is the word we're looking for here. Annamarie smiled brightly and went in search of her mentor.

The bedroom looked as though it belonged to a very little and spoiled girl. It was decorated in pinks and purples, with lace and tassels dangling from every surface, and more dolls than Annamarie had seen in her entire life. Each of the dolls was immaculately dressed in a fabulous frock that someone had taken the time to sew. It could have been an enviable collection. They might have been beautiful, had someone not poked out their eyes and ruined their mouths. Many had lips broken off, leaving nasty holes in their china heads. Where the faces were made of fabric, a few mouths had been sewn shut with large stitches, while others had been painted black. Empty eye sockets stared blankly at the room and confirmed every suspicion Annamarie had about the state of Melisandra Lemon's mind.

A long, raw scream drew her attention to the bed. Dressed only in a white shift, her dark hair stuck to her face with sweat, Melisandra howled and writhed.

"Come on now girly," Jemima coaxed. "You've got to get up on your hands and knees. It'll be easier for you."

"I can't move," Melisandra hissed.

"Oh, I know it seems that way, but you can. It'll all be over soon. Quicker if you do as I tell you." She glanced round. "Give me a hand with her."

Annamarie had no desire to make any kind of contact with the labouring girl, but she was curious. Coming a little closer, she asked "What do you want me to do?"

"We're going to roll her over, as she can't move herself."

"Don't you touch me, you... hag!" Melisandra spat.

"Better if you do it yourself," Jemima said. She glanced at Annamarie. "It's always like this. Even the sweetest girls snap at you when their time comes. Never take it personally."

With obvious difficulty, Melisandra hauled herself onto her side. Scarlet flowers blossomed across her nightdress and as she rolled onto her knees, the blood dripped from her, staining the sheets. Jemima appeared untroubled by all of this.

"That's it girl, you just concentrate on breathing. It'll all be over soon. Let's see how you're doing." She pulled the nightdress up, ignoring her patient's furious complaints. "Oh come now, you don't have anything I haven't seen before. I birthed you myself girl, did all of this with your own mother and she wasn't too proud to have some help when the time came."

"Go away!" Melisandra said through gritted teeth.

"You were a hard birth mind, took her nearly seven hours," Jemima said conversationally. "I didn't think you were going to survive. I was concentrating on saving your mother. But, I did a good job there, and you lived."

"More's the pity," Melisandra replied.

"That's the pain talking. Once the baby comes, you won't feel like death is a good thing."

Melisandra laughed, the tone cold and grim. Movement drew Annamarie's gaze. Unable to make any sense of what she saw, she tapped Jemima's arm.

The older witch froze, and shot a warning look to her apprentice. Drawing the nightgown up a little higher, she reached between splayed legs. "Let's see if we can feel the head yet." Confusion played across her face, then alarm. "That's it dearie," she said, but the conviction had gone from her voice. Then, to Annamarie, "Get me a bucket, and something to cover it with."

Unnerved, the young woman was glad to escape the room for a few minutes. The smell of blood made her feel sick, and a feeling of wrongness had crept into her mind. Once outside, she gulped the fresh night air. The rain had stopped, and everything smelled clean.

"Is she there yet?" Balthazar asked, glowing eyes the only sign of his location.

"Nearly. Jemima wants a bucket." Realising this wasn't a diplomatic remark, she added, "For the afterbirth and the messed up sheets and all that."

"A nice big bucket then. I have one. It may smell a bit funny."

"Trust me, that won't be a problem."

Reluctance filled her limbs as she climbed back up the stairs. Melisandra's screams came regularly now. Gripping the bucket handle tightly, Annamarie re-entered the room. She took in her mentor's ashen face, the blood-drenched bed, and the fear in the atmosphere.

"Bucket," Jemima croaked.

"Here." She stepped closer, hungry to see the worst of it, wanting to be shocked. She had imagined a stillbirth, or something malformed. The previous year, one of the scarlet women from Murderer's Lane had produced a dead infant with two heads.

The thing slithering from Melisandra's body did not resemble a baby. There were spikes and tentacles. It had scratched Jemima repeatedly, and no doubt done the same to its mother, who howled all the time now. When it fully emerged, Jemima grabbed it and threw it into the bucket. Looking down at the thing she now held, Annamarie saw it was moving of its own volition.

"It's alive."

"Appears that way."

"What should I do with it?"

"Keep it where it is, if you can." Jemima shook her head. "I've seen some things in my time, but nothing like this. Let's try and get the girl comfortable."

Collapsed face down on the bed, Melisandra asked, "Is it over?"

"Yes it is. You can rest now," Jemima said, gently.

"Is it alive?"

"Yes."

"I want to see it."

Annamarie noted she hadn't asked if it was a boy or a girl. Perhaps Melisandra had known there was something unusual about her condition. Bringing the bucket nearer, she offered it for inspection.

The new mother peered down at her writhing offspring and nodded. "Put it in the sea."

"That's a good idea," Jemima said. "You do that, Anna. I'll clean up."

The sky had grown pale, although dawn was an hour away. Once she reached the sand, the thing in the bucket grew lively and she had trouble carrying it. The crows became restless, but flew towards her rather than away. She had to use an arm to keep them from flying into her face. Where the waves lapped softly against the shore, she tipped her charge over and let it flop out into the foam. It turned several baleful eyes upon her, and then splashed into the water.

In Pursuit of Knowledge

Getting the broomstick off the ground wasn't all that difficult, Annamarie soon found. A little focused attention and she could make it rise. Doing the same when she sat on it was a wholly different matter.

"How do you stay on?" she asked, brushing the dirt from her clothes and trying to ignore her growing collection of bruises.

"Practice," Jemima said. "And thinking about it the right way. You're trying to sit on it, like it's a horse. That's why you keep falling off."

Annamarie frowned at her airborne teacher. "You're sitting on yours."

"No. It may appear that way, but I'm not. I'm just holding onto a stick whilst flying."

"So you don't actually need the broom?"

Jemima dropped it, and stretched slightly, but remained aloft. "Not at all."

"So why bother with it?" Annamarie felt thoroughly confused and it started to show in her voice as irritation.

"People expect the broomstick. It's traditional, and it looks good. It's like the pointy hat, you don't have to wear them, but they change how people see you."

"I'm not doing the pointy hat, sorry. And I still don't see why the broom is necessary."

"Suit yourself." Jemima landed. "You can move the broom. You can move yourself. The main thing is, it doesn't feel so exposed, being in the sky when you have a nice solid bit of wood to hang onto."

"I'll take your word for it." She held the broom at an angle, climbed back on, and closed her eyes. Rather than trying to make the broom fly, she concentrated on the idea of both her and the broom happening to not be on the ground at the same time. Pushing off with her toes, she lifted slightly. This time, there was no awkward rotating around the broom and landing on her backside.

"That's more like it!" Jemima sounded pleased – a rare enough occurrence.

Opening her eyes, Annamarie nearly lost control. She had risen to the height of the cottage roof. A fall from this far up would cause serious injury, not just the bumps she usually suffered. She took a deep breath and managed not to panic. It was just a matter of thinking about where she wanted to be, and shaping that intent with enough precision. She dropped down, skimming a few feet above the earth.

"Find the speed that feels right for you," Jemima shouted. "You can go faster or slower than that of course, but you'll find there's a pace that seems natural and that one is the easiest to maintain."

Fast seemed preferable. She turned and twisted, steering the broom around trees and bushes, delighted by the rush of air against her face and the feeling of liberty. A startled bird flew out in front of her, snapping her concentration. Spinning wildly, she crashed into the ground, winding herself.

Jemima stood over her. "It's a lot like walking. You think how much trouble the little ones have learning that. Once you get the hang of it, you don't fall over just because you've been surprised."

"I'll keep working at it." Normally the prospect of work dismayed her, but Annamarie hungered for freedom, and the broom offered so many possibilities in that regard.

"There's a pot of salve to take out to the Lemon girl, and some herbs for her to make tea with. Why don't you take them out to her and see how she's doing?"

"On the broom?"

"I think so. Be careful, don't fly high, don't go over the cliffs or the sea. Make sure if you lose control of the thing it isn't going to kill you."

Annamarie grinned. "I can do this!"

Even staying low and avoiding the possible short cut over the cliffs, it took half the time to fly that it would have done to walk. Despite the prospect of seeing the Lemon girl, Annamarie landed in good spirits. She found Melisandra sat on the doorstep, her face uncomfortably thin, eyes glassy.

"I've brought some more things from Jemima. There's salve to help with the healing." She handed the jar over. Melisandra took it without even looking at her. "And this, you make up like a tea and drink it, to help build up your strength." That also was taken. "It's polite to say thank you when someone does something to help," Annamarie added.

The comment did not win her a response so after a little while she continued. "Jemima asked me to see how you're doing. Anything I should tell her? No? Suit yourself. It doesn't make any odds to me." She gave up and walked away.

"Before you go!" Balthazar called after her. "Something to say thank you." He pushed a bag into her hand. It was wet, smelled of the sea, and moved in ways that made Annamarie shiver. She had a horrible image of someone cooking and eating Melisandra's inhuman child.

Opening the gift, she was relieved to see a perfectly ordinary pair of fish, flapping their way towards death. "Thank you, Mister Lemon."

He met her gaze, expression sincere. "We all came from the sea, once."

Thinking of Jemima's instructions, she smiled. "I expect we did, yes."

"Some of us go back there."

Gripping the bag in one hand, she straddled her broom and set off before he could bother her with any other deranged observations. There were a few people working in the fields as she flew, but they didn't seem to notice her. Annamarie had the overwhelming desire to be noticed, and considered flying through the middle of the town. However, her skills in the air were not yet perfected, and she decided to wait until she could do so without fear of embarrassing herself.

"Good morning." Durosimi stepped out from behind a tree, as though he had been waiting there for her.

The broom turned. Annamarie rotated a full circle, but managed not to hit anything or fall off. She landed, irritated. "Are you following me, boy?"

"You're hard to miss, weaving about on that thing. So tell me, what takes you out to the lighthouse and the crazy man?"

"It's witch business, so I can't tell you."

"And he's paid you in... let me guess... fish? How lovely."

Annamarie scowled. "Is there a point to any of this? You might have nothing better to do with yourself, but I'm very busy today."

"Just being friendly," said Durosimi, in a voice that sounded anything but amicable. "You and Jemima do seem to be going to the lighthouse a lot these days. Perhaps she's sweet on the old lunatic. What do you think?"

"I think it's none of your business."

"My, my, you are in a nice mood today. Or is it you who likes him? Is that it?"

Annamarie ground her teeth. "If you're so interested in Mister Lemon and his useless daughter, why don't you just walk up and pay them a visit?"

"He has a daughter? Now that is interesting. I didn't know that. A very fine idea, my dear Annamarie. I shall take up your thoughtful suggestion." He smiled, the expression echoing the sarcasm in his voice.

As he walked away, whistling to himself, Annamarie had the feeling she had made a serious mistake. Part of her wanted to follow him and see what he got up to. The possibility of Durosimi O'Stoat and Melisandra Lemon communicating with each other seemed preposterous. What could two such people have to say to each other? She didn't like it at all. Both of them were monsters and the outcome... It wasn't that she cared what they did to each other. More a feeling that combined, they might be very bad news for her indeed. "They can be sullen and vile together and spare the rest of us from both of them," she muttered.

The fish in her bag had stopped moving. Dead, they were a lot easier to carry. She climbed back onto the broom and set off, but much of the sweetness had gone out of the day for her.

A Price to Pay

Durosimi came calling, with a smile on his face that suggested treachery. However, Annamarie had nothing better to do than go for a walk with him, so she agreed to his suggestion. At least he was something approximating her own age, and he had some ideas and energy. She missed Emanuel. Without him, there was no one to share her life with, no one to trust. Jemima was all right in her own way, but more as a teacher and adopted parent than someone to act as a friend. Trusting the O'Stoat boy would be deranged, but at least she could wander the edges of the woods with him and play at being companions.

"How long have you known Melisandra?" he enquired.

She thought he would ask about the girl, but wasn't happy to hear the question. "A few weeks. I wouldn't say we're close."

"An odd soul, but I feel a certain kinship with her."

Annamarie shot a glance in his direction. "I can see how that might work."

"Anyone would think you were envious, although whether of myself or of Miss Lemon, it would be hard to say."

"You talk some rubbish." He was right, but she could not have said which way round the envy ran either.

They paused in the conversation to use the stepping stones across a small stream. Annamarie tried to think of something that would divert his attention from this unwelcome topic, but no inspiration came.

Durosimi sighed theatrically. "She tells me about her nightmares. Things that press inside her head, and then claw their way out through her body. She says she cannot tell what is dream and what is real anymore."

"Some things run in families."

He snarled. "And some of us are more than the result of our parentage."

The young witch smiled to herself, feeling she had scored a point with that remark.

"But we digress," Durosimi said, taking on an unctuously pleasant tone again.

"Why don't you come out and ask whatever it is you want to know, rather than pretending you like me?" Annamarie asked. "It would make life so much simpler, wouldn't it?"

Durosimi stopped and turned to look directly at her. "Are her nightmares real, do you think?"

"I'd say she has some very real problems, yes." She considered turning back for home, ill at ease with his line of interrogation even though she had invited it.

"Is she imagining things, or did some horror tear its way out of her body?"

"What makes you think I'd know?"

"You and Jemima were tending to her for a while. I think you were there, dear Annamarie. I think you saw it all. Why not tell me? Aren't we friends? Isn't that what friends do?"

She recognised the attempted manipulation, but even so the words affected her. It was just the sort of thing she would have run to Emanuel with, back in the days before he rejected her. She missed that. Durosimi was no substitute, but was at her side and showing interest. That tempted her.

"You're right," she acknowledged, still cautious. "I was there. She gave birth to a monster."

"I knew it!" The glee in his voice was disturbing. "Was it alive? What happened to it?"

Annamarie wanted that enthusiasm to be focused on herself, but she couldn't resist the attention. "It lived. She told me to put it in the sea, and I did. It swam off."

He smiled in his usual, unlovely fashion. "Was it horrible?"

"Yes." She could tell he wanted more details and decided to give. "It was slimy and nothing at all like a proper baby. If I hadn't seen it born, I'd never have believed it had a human mother."

"I wonder how it happened."

He sounded genuinely perplexed. Annamarie eyed her companion. "You do know where babies come from, right?"

"Of course." Something about his tone suggested otherwise.

"Well you know how it is... takes two people to make new people and two cows to make new cows."

"Yes, I was aware of that," he said, the hard edges returning.

Annamarie ignored him and continued. "Well, for a girl to give birth to a monster, I reckon the father must have been something... not human."

"Is that possible?"

"Well it must have happened somehow, mustn't it?"

Durosimi nodded, but remained silent for a while. "Girls like flowers, don't they?"

"I hear some girls do. I wouldn't know. No one ever picked me any."

"Those are pretty," he said, pointing to some tall stems bearing purple blossoms.

"Those are poisonous." It amazed her how little he seemed to know about some things.

"They are? Perfect."

"You'd have to eat quite a few of them."

"That's fine, I wasn't planning on killing anyone just for now. But Melisandra would love them. Purple is her favourite colour, and she'll adore them for being poisoned. She's that sort of girl."

Annamarie stared at him in disbelief. "Have you totally lost you mind? Are you really going to pick flowers for her?"

The look on his face darkened to a more familiar expression of malice. "I have my reasons. Don't assume it's romantic. I want her to like me."

"What do you want with her?" Annamarie felt oddly protective. She didn't like it at all. Melisandra Lemon was not someone she had any desire to be looking out for.

"I'm not going to do her any harm. I just want to know where her monsters come from."

"And then?"

"We shall see."

Annamarie shook her head. "Look, I know you're too proud to admit you don't know about sex and babies and all that, but you're going to need to understand the technical details sooner or later."

"Are you offering to teach me?"

The look on his face made her shiver and step back. "That wasn't what I meant at all."

He laughed. "You wouldn't dare."

"No, I wouldn't want to, there's a whole world of difference. I like men, not boys. What I can do is loan you a book."

He hesitated, and for a moment looked his age, becoming young and strangely vulnerable. While the effect lasted, it inspired pity and protectiveness in Annamarie. Then Durosimi's face hardened and she could once more see the unfeeling adult he would become. She could not afford to care for him, and could sense that he would never do her any good. The passing years would make him darker, developing his innate cruelty into something truly obscene.

"I'll lend you the book," she reiterated. "It's Jemima's but she won't mind. You need to understand a few things. And don't argue with me."

"If that's what you want. I'll see you around." He took off on his own.

Watching him go, Annamarie sighed to herself. Unless she could get away from Hopeless somehow, Durosimi was about the most promising friend material she had. She liked the loose women, they were fun, but they weren't into magic and none of them struck her as being especially bright. There was so much she couldn't say to them. If she could improve her flying skills, escaping Hopeless might yet be an option.

Walking with the Dead

After Reverend Witherspoon's memorable shouting session, Annamarie made a point of flying past the church whenever she could. He called her "Child of Satan," "Jezebel" and "Evil seductress" in the initial, furiously shouted lecture that followed her down the road. Each time he came out to hurl abuse, she turned, smiled, and waved before heading off. Assorted citizens always stopped to watch her go by. She could count on gasps, pointed fingers, and other signs of recognition. Jemima might not approve of her making such a spectacle, but it seemed like a good way of advertising, and custom had been slack for a while. As anticipated, her display brought in a steady stream of girls looking for love spells and charms to make them pretty.

"I don't think it's ethical," Jemima objected.

"It doesn't do any harm, it gives them something to feel good about and let's face it, they get precious little of that."

Jemima hummed and hawed, but the prospect of a winter without money for food quelled her reservations.

There hadn't been any such dramas since, but she made an effort to stay visible, hoping Emanuel would notice her. With a bag full of provisions hanging awkwardly from one side of the broom, Annamarie cruised along the road by the church. The lights were on in the Town Hall, but otherwise the streets were unusually empty. For an early summer evening, this was odd in the extreme and she wondered if something had happened.

There were figures moving in the graveyard. Normally she wouldn't have paid this much attention, but an all too familiar laugh reached her ears. *Durosimi!* Landing the broom, she swung the bag over her shoulder and held the wooden shaft close to her body. It took a few moments to calm her breathing and clear her mind. Going unnoticed depended on placid emotions, she had found. Moving quietly, she advanced, making sure they would not notice her. Being caught spying was a humiliation she had no desire to endure.

"The O'Stoat vault is one of the oldest in the cemetery. If not the oldest. Some of the earliest dates are hard to read," he bragged.

The girl at his side said nothing. Her hand rested on his arm as they sauntered along one of the many paths between the graves.

"I have the key, if you wish to see inside?" He gestured towards the stone memorial.

"I want to see," came the whispered reply. "Are there dead people in there?"

"My father died a few years ago, his coffin has not yet crumbled as some of the older ones have."

"How did he die?"

Durosimi glanced around, and for a moment Annamarie feared herself caught in the act of following them. However, his gaze passed over her with no sign of awareness.

"He was poisoned," Durosimi said.

"Oh." Melisandra fell silent for a little while. "Did you kill him?"

"Yes."

"That's beautiful. I've never killed a person. I've killed other things. Fish of course, and birds. Small things. Did you watch him die?"

"I did."

"I wish I could have seen it."

Annamarie thought she had heard enough. Although she hadn't shed any tears over Victor O'Stoat's demise, this way of relating to murder left her cold and shaking. Hard to say which of the pair was the most monstrous, as they built a shared nightmare between them. She kept listening, held in place by morbid fascination.

"Durosimi, do you think I should kill my father?"

"I think you should do whatever fires your imagination."

Creeping a little closer, she watched the young man open the gate to his family tomb.

Melisandra tugged on his sleeve, the gesture urgent. "I want to kill someone. I want to know what it feels like."

"It is one of the most powerful feelings I have known. It certainly compares with the sensation of summoning a demon, or taming some other spirit to your will."

"I would like to see that also."

"Dearest Melisandra, it would give me great pleasure to share my arts with you."

He would have shared this with me, Annamarie realised. *He offered me as much. But I didn't want it. I don't want it. Power and recognition and nice dresses are plenty enough for me. Not dead people. Not demons.* She watched them enter the mausoleum, hand in hand, and envy cut into her. Their voices echoed from inside the grave, but the words did not carry well enough for her to hear their conversation. Rage boiled within her. There was no rational reason why Durosimi courting the Lemon girl in a graveyard should feel like betrayal. It did. That she had not wanted such attentions from him didn't seem to matter. Pain and frustration collided within her, the turmoil building its own momentum, demanding release.

"If you think it fun to play with the dead, then so will it be for you. May you never find any comfort or repose in the places living folk dwell. May you walk with the dead, live with the dead. May your lives be blighted, because you bloody well deserve it."

She felt a rush of power as the words left her body. The force of it dropped her to her knees, gasping for breath. Annamarie had never seriously tried to curse anyone before, but the intensity of her emotions had drawn a dark kind of magic from her. Shaking in the aftermath of her unconsidered spell, she did not regret the words. What they meant, exactly, and whether they would take any kind of effect remained to be seen.

Standing, she turned her back on the O'Stoat crypt, and walked amongst the graves. She did not yet feel steady enough for flying. The thought of going back and locking them in crossed her mind, but that seemed petty when she had laid such a curse on them. *Enough for one day.* Going back risked them noticing her, and she had no desire to speak to either of the pair.

There were a lot of graves. Many had stones, crusted with lichen and weather-worn beyond reading. Whoever lay there had long since been lost to memory. One corner of the cemetery was dedicated to the nameless ones who washed in on the tide from time to time. They had a single plaque between them. Poorer folk put up wooden markers that bleached and weathered away, leaving no trace behind. Her people mostly fell into that last category, as far as she knew. Very likely, the bones of her immediate ancestors were in here somewhere, but she did not know their names, much less where they lay.

For a moment she had the feeling that her life was nothing new, that she played a role in a story that had retold itself a dozen times down the years. The impression made her shiver. Looking at the nameless graves, and the sheer number of lives passed and forgotten, she was shocked by the apparent meaninglessness of it all.

"I have got to get out of here."

There was still time to buy cake, she realised. She could take it round to the girls on Silver Street, and sit by the fire in their kitchen. They would laugh and trade jokes, and not think about death. She nodded to herself. That would be for the best, and let Durosimi keep whatever morbid company he liked.

With the broom beneath her once more, and the graveyard behind, Annamarie felt more herself. A light sea mist had blown in from the sea, partially obscuring the town and giving everything a mysterious air. Lights appeared in windows, cheery and welcoming. "Best leave the dead to themselves," she muttered, banging on the plain wooden door of her favourite house of ill repute. A house didn't need to be a brothel to have an ill repute. Unruled women were Reverend Witherspoon's target of preference. No doubt she and Jemima were of ill repute too, with connotations of lechery, laziness, lesbianism, perhaps lycanthropy and other dangerous words beginning with the letter L.

Desdemona answered, her face freshly painted and a tired "Do come in," on her lips before she'd properly seen who was there.

"I bring cake," Annamarie announced. "I've got those funny seaweed ones Cassy likes, and some with honey in."

"You are an angel! Come in. I thought you were a punter!"

Following the scantily clad figure along the hallway, a weight lifted from her. For an hour or so, they could all pretend to be ordinary girls, and share laughter. Then they all had their dark and taboo arts to practice, she supposed.

The Sins of the Fathers

Knocks on the door at strange hours were nothing new. Still, Annamarie had a sense of foreboding as she went to answer the volley of urgent bangs.

"It's happened again," Balthazar Lemon announced before she'd even realised it was him.

"Come on in," Jemima shouted from the kitchen. "No point standing there on the doorstep. What's happened this time?"

Annamarie let him in and ducked into the corner, where she pretended to be working.

Wringing his hands, Balthazar stepped inside. "It's that girl of mine. Be the death of me, she will. I don't know what she does, but it came on yesterday all of a sudden and it looks just like before."

"Stomach swollen up, has it?" Jemima asked, in her usual unruffled way.

"Like a pumpkin, only probably not so orange. Or as good for making pies out of, and without a vine or any leaves."

"I get your drift, Balthazar."

He sat down at their table and buried his face in grubby, work worn hands. "I don't understand. It isn't right, and I don't know how it happened."

Jemima put a hand on his shoulder. "If she won't let us help her, there's not a lot we can do to stop it."

"I wouldn't mind if I thought it were a proper little one. A baby. Oh, she could have all the babies she wanted, bed every boy who caught her fancy and I wouldn't mind at all. But I'm afraid this will be like before, all sudden and wrong, and then you put it in the sea. It wasn't a proper baby, was it?"

"No. Nothing like a baby," Jemima reassured. "I'd raise a babe myself before I'd drown one, don't you worry on that score."

"What is doing this to her?" he wailed, and banged a fist against the table.

"I can't tell you that."

"But you're a witch, Mistress Kettle, you ought to know about these things, with strange powers and unnatural goings on."

"I might know some things," Annamarie ventured. When they both turned to look at her, she continued. "I saw her bathing naked in the sea, that seemed a bit odd. Maybe what happened to her... happened there. She wanted her offspring put in the water and it went off as happy as you please."

"It's a possibility," Jemima conceded.

After a moment's hesitation, the young witch decided to reveal everything she had heard. "She's been talking to... someone I know. Apparently Melisandra has nightmares about monsters in her head that are trying to tear their way out through her body."

"Has she talked to you about this?" Jemima asked.

"We aren't exactly close, so no."

"There's ways of looking into the past and the future alike," Jemima said. "I don't have much skill for it, but I can have a go, see what we can find out. It's the best I can offer."

"Thank you, Mistress Kettle," said Balthazar Lemon.

"And we'll be there for the laying in, and deal with whatever she gives birth to this time. At least we'll be ready for it."

Balthazar Lemon took both of her hands and held them tightly, then repeated the gesture with Annamarie. "You're good, good women," he said. "And my daughter is not. Breaks my heart. There's too much fish and cold slime water in her soul." With that, he let himself out.

Jemima turned to her student. "Well, now's as good a time as any to learn about scrying. I've no talent for it. I see things, but I can never work out what they mean until afterwards, which isn't much use."

"What do I have to do?"

"There's a covered mirror in my bedroom. Carry it through here and put it on the table."

Mirrors were expensive luxuries on the island. There was a glassmaker, who turned out window panes and slightly lopsided drinking vessels, but he didn't have the materials for mirrors. You could sometimes get polished metal ones, but they weren't very good. If a ship crashed, mirrors seldom survived, so most of the people lucky enough to have them owned pieces, not whole ones.

Not only was this mirror perfect, it was nearly two feet high and a foot wide. The glass was black. Annamarie had never seen anything like it, and gasped when her mentor removed the cloth that had been covering its strange surface.

"Sit yourself in front of it, but at an angle so as to make sure you can't see your own reflection. Then you gaze into the mirror and let your eyes go out of focus a bit. Think about what you need answering. Part of it is about finding the right question so you get the right answer. Things like 'where have I left my bottle of cold medicine?' are easy. I can do those. This is going to be a harder one."

"I think I understand," Annamarie replied. She bit her lip and looked into the mirror, trying to shape a question.

"Show me what happened to make Melisandra Lemon's stomach swell up this time." She was half afraid the mirror would show her an image of Durosimi, but it did not.

The glass misted, then a scene emerged, revealing Melisandra in her bed, tossing like one in the thrall of a nightmare. She sweated and strained, her back arching violently. Then the scene changed, to show the girl naked in the sea. Small creatures surrounded her, weirdly flat, consisting more of eyes than anything else. They swarmed over her body.

After that there was blackness, but it was deeper, darker than the mere surface of the mirror. The kind of blackness that burns, and scratches its way through your soul. A darkness so profound that it writhed with its own intent. Annamarie could hear her ears popping, and her mouth filled with the taste of blood. She covered her eyes, shaking and crying. "Make it go away. Don't let me look at it any more. Oh gods! Don't let it look at me. Cover it up, don't let it see me."

Jemima's hands on her helped to soothe the terror. "I've covered it. You're safe. I'm here. Let me get you a drink."

Plied with strong alcohol, a little of her courage returned. With the mirror covered, there were no immediate signs of the thing she had seen. Annamarie had the feeling it was still with them, lurking somewhere beyond the deepest shadows, just waiting for them to fall into its grasp.

"I saw it," she croaked. "The thing in Melisandra's head. I saw it."

"I'm truly sorry. I had no idea it would be like that for you."

"I am never using that mirror again," the young witch said, her hands still shaking.

"I wouldn't ask you to. I'm not sure I'm going to use it either. I don't know what that was."

"It's so hungry, and it's inside her head. It's not something she's doing. It's inside her all the time, trying to get out."

"I'll think of something to tell Balthazar." Jemima sighed. "I think this is beyond the both of us. Whatever has happened to Melisandra Lemon, she's on her own."

"We can't fight something like that." Annamarie shivered.

"We can't. Only one thing to do in this case, as old Granny Rosie used to tell me."

"Go on."

"In times like this, the only thing a self respecting witch can do is open a bottle of something good and drink until none of it seems quite so awful."

Managing a faint smile, Annamarie said, "Sounds like a very wise woman. So, what have we got to ward off the darkness with?"

"You sit tight dearie, and I'll have a look."

Alone in the room, Annamarie had the feeling the shadows were watching her, waiting for a mistake that would spin her into their grasp. She stayed very still, counting her breaths until Jemima returned. She had the feeling no amount of potent wine would keep this presence at bay for long, but she meant to do her best to blot it out, at least for now.

Twisted Ambition

The two women were prepared, and when Balthazar Lemon came knocking, it took very little time to collect what they needed. With Annamarie on a broom as well, both witches sped out through the night, the younger one staying close behind her mentor. They took the shortcut over the sea. The setting sun painted each breaking wave crimson, and gave the pale rocks a friendly glow. Annamarie concentrated on not becoming too intimately familiar with either. A grim sense of foreboding filled her, and even the beautiful evening did not lighten her mood.

In the previous days she had managed to shake the worst of the terror from her mind. It had taken a lot of effort. Now she shut out all traces of the mirror memory, aware that any stray thoughts in that line would destroy her concentration and send her into the sea. One of Melisandra's creations already lurked beneath the water. It might have grown by now, become something more akin to the parent that possessed her. The broom wobbled ominously, and Annamarie fought for a few panicked heartbeats before she regained mastery of it.

"Keep calm girl!" Jemima shouted. "We can do this."

Crows flew up from the sand, surrounding them in a confusing cloud of dark feathers. Jemima swore loudly at them as the pair landed. When the two witches approached the lighthouse, they found the door closed against them.

"Balthazar is a fool sometimes," Jemima spat.

Annamarie nodded. "I suppose we'll just have to wait for him to get here." Anything to stall the moment of going into that birthing room. "I'll get the bucket, while we wait."

"Do that." Jemima pointed her finger at the keyhole, and muttered under breath, then tried the door and uttered a few more choice expletives. "It's not locked, it's jammed shut."

"Why would Bal..." The name died on her lips as she realised that Balthazar could not have barred the door from within when he was still hurrying back from their cottage. "What is she playing at?"

"Melisandra, can you hear me?" Jemima shouted. "I know this must be very hard for you, but I need you to be a sensible girl and open the door so we can help you."

From the other side of the door came a scream. A high and violent sound, it tore through their ears and sawed into already frayed nerves.

"Her body will barely have recovered from the last one," Jemima muttered. "If she keeps on like this it's going to kill her."

"Maybe that would be for the best," Annamarie whispered back.

Jemima met her gaze, visibly torn. "If she won't let us help her, there's not much to be done."

"Should we even be helping her, if all she does is give birth to monsters? We might not be helping anyone else at all."

"I know." Jemima shook her head. "This is beyond me."

"Just go away," Melisandra shouted from her side of the closed door. "Go away. Leave me alone. I don't want you."

Annamarie nodded. "I think that's pretty clear."

So distracted were the pair by this predicament, that neither noticed the arrival of an additional player into the scene.

"Good evening ladies."

Annamarie jumped, then tried to hide her surprise. "Durosimi? What are you doing here?"

"I've come for Melisandra. Mind out of my way, if you would."

Stepping aside, Annamarie gave him room to approach the door.

"This isn't a good time, young man," Jemima said.

"That's why I'm here. She needs me." He knocked. "Are you there, Melisandra?"

"Yes."

"Ready?"

"Yes." The door opened.

If the Lemon girl had looked rough with her first birth, it was nothing compared to this. Her eyes were lost in dark shadows as though she had been physically beaten, and her hair hung lank around her face. She clung to the door frame for support. There were bloodstains on her dress, and sweat marks.

Jemima shook her head. "You should be in bed, girl! You'll make yourself sick."

"Go away, old woman. I do not want your help." The Lemon girl staggered forward.

Durosimi caught her before she fell. "Lean on me."

"Please, both of you, listen to me," Jemima implored. "Do not do this. Let us help you."

Durosimi smiled, showing his teeth. "I don't think so. I claim parentage of Melisandra's child. She's coming to live with me, so that I can take care of her and the baby. Now if you will excuse me, I do not want to make this any worse for my beloved than it already is."

Melisandra cried out, pain etching lines into her youthful face.

"You can't take her anywhere, she's in labour!" Jemima shouted.

"Watch me." Durosimi clicked his fingers, and something folded around them, like a giant fist of dark air closing over where they had stood. When it melted away, no sign of the unlikely couple remained.

For a long time, Annamarie stared at the space where they had been.

"Nothing but trouble, those O'Stoats," Jemima said.

"It's not our problem anymore." Annamarie straightened her back and tucked a stray lock of hair behind her ear.

"I wish I could agree with you. It's very much our problem. Where did that boy learn magic? He's picking it up from books by the looks of him. No guidance. No wisdom. It stinks of greed and corruption. No good will come of it, mark my words. And then it will be very much our problem. That kind of thing always is."

"Oh."

"There's always been witches in these parts. You know there's a story that we were here before any of their 'founding families', just living on the land and minding our own business. But when some fool of an O'Stoat starts messing with demons or raising the dead, who do you think has to sort it all out? Because you can be sure no one else will, my girly. When he goes too far, it'll be you and me who have to set things to rights."

"He told me he could summon demons. I didn't believe him."

"If he can't now, you can be sure he will. Not that it'll do him any good. They never learn. You don't get anything from demons; you get enslaved."

"We have some explaining to do." Annamarie gestured to the path, where Balthazar Lemon was fast approaching them.

The old man looked troubled. "Is she dead?"

Jemima stepped forward to meet him. "She lives, but I cannot say if she will survive this birth unaided."

"Where has she gone?"

"With a boy from the town. Durosimi."

Balthazar frowned, and nodded. "I couldn't keep her forever. The crows say she is evil, but do they know? I don't know what they know. It's all about beaches and territory with them, and the inbetween places and I don't know what they mean half the time."

He laughed raucously. "And everyone says I'm mad. It's as well they don't talk to the crows, isn't it?"

"Certainly," Jemima replied. "Will you be alright here by yourself?"

"But I'm not by myself, am I? I've got the sea and the crows, I'm never alone here. Never. She isn't coming back, is she?" Grief filled his eyes. "She swam out to sea and turned into a fish and even if I wait the rest of my life she won't come back to me. Perhaps when I am dead."

"That's how it goes sometimes," Jemima said. "If you get lonely, you can always come round to the cottage for a cup of tea."

"Melisandra is dead," Balthazar announced. "I have no one. I have no daughter."

A cold wind came in off the sea, gusting into the trio and whipping up the waves. There was nothing to do but go home, and wait.

Between Land and Sea

Autumn had come early. The mornings had a cold taste to them even though it was only the middle of August. Leaves yellowed and faded, not burning with their usual vibrant colours, but wasting away. Annamarie walked out over the headland, feeling as though all the colour was bleeding out of her life. The sky had been grey for days, with little sign of the sun. Traces of mist still lingered in the air. The day had started damp and uninspiring. At least the wind had picked up now, blowing the worst of it away.

From the cliff top she could see a boat coming in, drifting on the rising tide. It looked like one of the small fishing craft, but unmanned. A figure appeared from one of the squat cottages – a woman, with her hair flying wild behind her as she ran. Behind her came a boy, young and cautious. Sensing that something was amiss, Annamarie looked around. The nearest safe way down was some distance away. She did not have her broom. *It's not like the broom has any magic in it.*

Heart pounding, she willed herself to move, her feet lifting from the ground. She could see at once why Jemima had said the brooms were reassuring. However, she did not crash onto the rocks, but drifted down, her skirts billowing about her. Once on the beach, she ran towards the mother and son.

The woman was already in the sea, her long dress weighed down with water and hampering her as she tried to reach the boat. Reluctant to get wet, Annamarie eyed the boat. It was far too big for her to try and move. There was a rope trailing from the prow in the water however. Concentrating on that, she shifted it, making it reach for the land so that the bedraggled woman could catch the end. Only going into the waves far enough to wet her hem and ankles, Annamarie helped pull the boat to shore and tug it up the sand. Above them, the crows circled, their cries mournful.

A pale figure lay across the boards in the dory. His clothes were ripped, as was the flesh beneath it. There was a lot of blood in the boat. More than one person could have lost, and other things as well. At her side, the woman howled with grief.

Annamarie reached for the unmoving man, feeling for a pulse, beginning with the practical things that could be done. The skin beneath her hand felt far too cold, and she could find no trace of a heartbeat. "I'm sorry, I don't think there's anything we can do for him."

The woman gripped the wood until her knuckles went white. Shoulders shaking, she wept.

"He is dead then," the little boy said.

Annamarie turned to him. "I'm sorry. Was he your father?"

"Yes. I need to see." He stepped forward, his soft face filled with a desperate sadness.

For a long time, she did nothing but stand and wait, while the crows circled above them. One by one the birds came down, landing on every horizontal surface the boat offered. For a moment she thought they meant to feed on the corpse, and opened her mouth to shoo them away. Something else entirely was happening. With bowed heads, the crows kept silent vigil around the dead man.

"His spirit will become one of them," the woman said. "He will guard the shore as a shade, just as he did in life."

"How can I help?" Annamarie asked, deeply affected by the scene.

"Can you dig?"

"I expect so."

"Will you help me take him up on the headland then? We can cover him with stones. There are other cairns up there. Help me carry him."

"I will."

Between the three of them, they lifted the bloodied body and went the long way round onto the cliff tops. The woman returned for spades while the boy gathered rocks. He moved slowly.

"Are you alright, my lad?" Annamarie asked.

"I knew. I tried to tell him, but he wouldn't listen."

Hairs rose on the backs of her arms at this. "How did you know?"

"The sea tells me things. She whispers to me at night. She told me there new monsters growing inside her, and that they are hungry."

Annamarie shivered.

"I tried to tell him it wasn't safe, but it's what we do for food. I don't think he believed me, and although the sea tries to talk to him, he doesn't really hear her. Not like I do."

"I understand."

"You believe me, Miss?"

"Yes. I do. What can you tell me about these monsters?"

"They live in the sea. There are more of them. She said they are coming, and there is no stopping them."

"Where are they coming from?"

"Somewhere else. I don't know. It scares me, thinking about it."

"Best not to think about it then." She touched his brow, noticing how his eyes did not move. "You can't see."

"Not with my eyes, much, no."

The woman returned with spades, her eyes red rimmed and expression grim. "He wouldn't have wanted to go to the graveyard and have the minister muttering over him. His people never went for that sort of thing."

Annamarie nodded, accepted the proffered spade and set to work, cutting into the hard, thin soil as best she could. It took them several hours to clear a hole just deep enough to hold the dead man. The crows gathered around them, silent and watchful. Watching the child pile stones over the fallen man brought a lump to her throat. The small pale face, the troubled expression, the way the corners of his mouth tugged down as he worked. Her heart went out to him.

When at last they had covered the dead fisherman from view, the crows descended, taking perches on the rocks and turning the cairn into a jet black memorial. They cawed, voices raucous as they filled the air.

"Bless them," the woman whispered. "They do what they can, between the waves and the land. They stop things crossing over. I will see you when the crows fly, Silas. I will watch for you until my soul can fly with yours."

"I'll fish the shallows," the boy promised, his voice very small. "Mother won't starve. I'll see to that for you. And when I'm bigger, I'll find whatever took you, and I'll kill it. This I swear."

His words sent a shudder through her.

"Will you eat with us? I can only offer you bread and seaweed, but you've done a great deal for us. I don't even know your name."

"Annamarie Nightshade."

"Delores. This is my son, Seth."

"Thank you for the offer, Delores, but I should be getting home. Feels like it's going to rain."

"You've maybe an hour. Less if the wind picks up," Delores said.

"If there's anything you need, come and find me. I live with Jemima Kettle on the top of Fish Hill."

"The witch's cottage. I know that one. My aunt lived there, when I was a child. There were more of them, in those days."

Annamarie nodded, not wanting to admit she hadn't known this. Having nothing much else she could say, she nodded, ruffled the boy's hair, and headed for home. Her back and arms ached from the digging, and a sense of foreboding gnawed at her innards. She had seen the mess in the boat. The wash of blood, the things... like seashells, only harder, sharper and fiercer. The knots of dark green flesh. Those few snatched images replayed in her mind, as she tried to make sense of it. The dead man had fought something, and been killed by it. Whatever she had seen in the boat very likely came from the creature that attacked him. Had he managed to destroy it? The prescient child seemed to think not. It remained out there, hidden beneath the waves.

She turned, looking back at the sea, so vast in its mystery. Anything could hide beneath the waves. Memories of Melisandra's firstborn returned, and she wondered what had become of that particular monster, and what she had birthed since.

As she looked, a fine mist rose up from the waves, forming fine tendrils that twisted together. It thickened, until she could not make out the water at all, then began edging towards the land. After everything she had seen that day, this spectral fog was more than she could bear. Her fears blossomed into dark flowers. Turning her back on the scene, Annamarie took off at a run, afraid of being caught in that encroaching dampness. Just as the sea could obscure, so would that rolling blanket of fog, and she did not want to be trapped, unseeing, her mind free to populate the unknown with all kinds of improbable horrors.

PART THREE
— DREAMS OF LEAVING —

The Shape of the World

There were things Annamarie remembered with a shudder. Once a month or so, the school marched its students down to the library for special projects. It had done so for the fifty years that the town had enjoyed the presence of a school, and a library; these two gestures towards learning having arrived together. On the plus side, time spent walking between the two was not time wasted on the monotony of the classroom, and brought some joy to the local youths.

Like many of her fellows, both historical and contemporary, Annamarie hated the library as a child. It smelled of mouldering leather and old dust. The ancient librarian, one Theophrastus Frog, creaked his way around the place, joints popping audibly with every move. He had a habit of staring past your shoulder, as though he could see something there. Memories of time spent in that airless institution were not happy ones. There were a lot of things Annamarie preferred not to recall about her early years. Some of them she had locked away from herself entirely. However, as an adult she could see that a building full of books might have its uses after all.

Like the church, the school and the orphanage, the library was a place she had promised never to return to. Things had changed.

It had been a long, hard winter, with freezing fog and treacherous ice. Supplies had run out. Even foraging for fallen wood became too difficult. Jemima forbade her to use Lamashtu, having established that the spirit could not leave the island, and too proud to countenance it stealing from her neighbours. They went hungry, sleepless from the cold, and isolated from the town. Even at its worst, there had always been some warmth and food in the orphanage. There were a lot of arguments between the witches, tempers frayed and moods turned grim.

Over the bitter months, Annamarie made up her mind to try and get off the island in the spring. It gave her something to be hopeful about when everything else was grim. She devoted long hours to imagining how an escape might be achieved. Having no skill with boats that option lay beyond her, and she had no means to pay anyone else for assistance. Not that she had heard of anyone sailing away, in a long time. There had been no boats landing voluntarily on their shores for more than a year as well. Sometimes she dreamed of a fabulous ship that would cruise into the small natural harbour and whisk her away to a better place. It was just fantasy though, and she wanted more than that.

Having spent years gazing out of the window during geography lessons, the young woman had little idea what lay beyond her island home. She worked out that in order to escape, at the very least she needed to know where the nearest land might be. That meant the library.

On the first February day when the weather abated, she pulled a shawl over her jacket, knotted it in place and took the broom out. The cold air cut into her skin, so she went slowly. It felt good just to be out of the cottage and away from Jemima – confined together for so long their friendship had strained almost to breaking point. Ice still covered much of the ground, and drifts of snow remained in the many spots where the sun couldn't reach.

There were food smells in the town. Freshly baking bread. Frying onions. Her stomach rumbled, reminding her that there had been nothing to eat since Jemima had brought a bird down two days ago. It had tasted disgusting, but she would eat it again without hesitation, given the chance. The streets were quiet, but a few people went about their business, sliding around on the treacherous ground.

Turning a corner, she caught sight of the distinctive bowler hats of Jones and Son. The older Jones waved her over. Having not talked to anyone but Jemima in weeks, she decided to oblige and see what he wanted. They were an odd pair, this father and son team of news pedlars. She'd never heard anything about a Mistress Jones, and wondered sometimes if the younger one, Frampton, had been hatched out of an egg.

"And a very good morning to you, Miss Nightshade," Jones senior said, sweeping off his hat in an exaggerated bow.

"Good morning, Mister Jones, and Mister Jones."

Percival Jones gave her a thoughtful look. "Clearly a very handy thing to have in these dreadful conditions, Miss Nightshade. The broom, I mean."

"Oh, yes."

"Can hardly take the old bicycle out in this weather. Haven't been able to bear the news to half the farms and outlying cottages, much less pick up their payments or see how things are with them. I don't suppose you might fancy running an errand for me?"

"Mr Jones, I am not a delivery girl, I am -"

"I'll pay."

"I am however entirely open to suggestions," she said. Money meant food, and at that moment the dignity of witchcraft could, she thought, be compromised a good deal if it meant a decent breakfast.

They took her back to their house, and she had a brief glimpse of the infamous printing press before being loaded up. It was a complex machine, and she had no idea what most of it did. The many pulleys, levers and clunking parts reminded her of something Balthazar Lemon would make. As Percival Jones chatted away to her, his son remained silent, and watchful. The younger Jones seemed edgy, and she wondered how old he was. Given his gangly physique, thinning hair and doleful expression he might have been anywhere between twenty and forty.

With a borrowed scarf tied across her face, Annamarie set out across the island, delivering copies of The Hopeless Vendetta, and gathering coins. Cut off by the ice, many of the cottagers were glad to see her. They gave money, news, biscuits and other welcome nourishment. She soon took a liking to the job. There were old papers to take back for pulping, and coins aplenty. There were also stories; news of births and deaths, bodies that could not be buried, oversized rats on the prowl and taller, less probable things.

By the time she made it back to the printers, the young woman felt a good deal more cheerful. Percival was not excessively generous with his coins, but she could buy supplies for the next week or so, with a little care.

"You must be frozen after all that flying about," Percival said once she had recounted all the stories. "Do stay with us for a spot of lunch. I've made a bottom of the garden stew and there's more than enough to go round."

Annamarie knew better than to ask what was in it. Reverend Witherspoon's wife made bottom of the garden stew. It was a staple for the orphans. Most of them learned very quickly not to look at what they were eating, nor to object too much if any part of it moved. Much to her surprise, Percival Jones' stew consisted mostly of well cooked root vegetables, with a scattering of small, anonymous fragments of meat. It tasted good, was not at any point unpleasantly chewy, and did not move of its own volition. She emptied the bowl in no time.

"Help yourself to more," her host said enthusiastically. "There's plenty more in the pot on the stove." He chuckled. "Bottom of the Garden stew. It means don't ask. Don't think about it. Do you know where the name came from?"

"No."

"Back in my grandfather's day, there was a pie shop and a brewer on Watchman Street. They don't call it that now. You'd know it as Murderer's Lane. Well, it was a winter just like this one, only worse. People going hungry. Desperate times. Old Vortigern Frog kept that pie shop, and he never ran out of pies. Everyone guessed he was putting dog, or rat in them, but times were hard, you do what you must. He wasn't doing that though. It was people. Some of them were dead before he got to them of course. Some weren't. But they were the best pies you could get that winter, so no one asked questions. He'd do this hot broth with the pies. Bottom of the Garden Stew. It was him named it. Been a traditional local dish ever since."

"Only without the dead people," Annamarie said.

"Oh, most of the time," Percival replied with a wink. "The bones all went next door. Constance Jones, distant relative of mine but not a direct ancestor. She brewed cider. Strong stuff. Dissolved the bones nicely."

"What a horrible story!" Annamarie said, with no small amount of relish. "Thanks for lunch. I should be going."

"If the weather doesn't ease, come back next week, I'd be glad of your services."

"Will do."

With a hot meal warming her innards, the library seemed a far less intimidating prospect. None the less, she faltered at the foot of the steps, looking up at the gaping maw of the doorway. Whoever had built this place clearly wanted people to feel threatened by it. She'd seen children cry when forced to go in there.

It smelled exactly as she remembered it, with a lingering gloom and omnipresent layers of dust. A short figure creaked towards her, crunching with every step. Theophrastus Frog looked to be about a hundred years old. Wrinkled and sagging to the point of having barely discernible facial features, and with tufts of white hair jutting from the most unlikely locations on his head, he was even worse an apparition than she remembered.

"A girl," he said in a voice like rusted metal. "A pretty girl. You must be in the wrong place. This is a library."

"I want to look at some maps, please," she replied.

"We don't have any."

"So what are those on the walls?"

"We're closed."

"It said open on the door."

"Please go away," he said, staring at her.

"I want to see some maps please." She hadn't quite got the knack of forcing her will on people, but gave it her best shot none the less.

"I don't want you disturbing the dust," the peculiar librarian replied.

"I won't." Arms folded across her chest, and broom clutched tight, she lifted up a few inches.

"Like that is it, Miss? Alright. Maps."

Floating, she followed him. Something skittered in the gloom. Twirling forms in the corners of her eyes. Each time she turned her head, they moved out of view, but she felt certain they were there.

"No upsetting the dust," said Theophrastus.

She realized he wasn't walking on the ground either. She assumed the neat pile of bones in the second room were his. Whatever his companions were, she thought they weren't ghosts. Or at least, not the ghosts of anything she had previously encountered.

There were a great many charts salvaged from ships, on which Hopeless might have been a speck in the wide expanse of sea.

There were pictures of what claimed to be the world, and she couldn't see Hopeless on them either. "Isn't there anything that shows the island?"

Grunting, Theophrastus Frog removed a yellowed roll of cloth from a tube and unrolled it for her. It did not take her long to understand that she was seeing the island as though from a long way above. And there, not so very far away, lay the coastline of another place. "It's so near," she breathed, delighted. "Why on earth does no one leave if it's that close?"

The librarian chuckled. Or at least, she thought that might be what the scratching sound in his throat signified. "This isn't the kind of place you get to leave, girly. That's not how it works."

Committing the map to memory, she shrugged, and turned to leave. Half-way across the library floor she dropped to the ground, leaving a trail of footprints through the thick layers of dust.

Fond Adieu

The easiest way to go would be silently and without telling a soul. Annamarie considered this, liking the idea of leaving them all with a mystery. Perhaps those who had been less than kind to her down the years would feel remorse at her vanishing. Trying to imagine Reverend Witherspoon, Mister Haynes-Jones the schoolmaster, or for that matter her mother feeling anything other than relief rather ruined the scheme. There were others she owed the truth to – Jemima for a start. The girls of Silver Street.

She bought Jemima a large cake, and raised the subject over it. "I'm going to leave the island."

Her mentor did not even look up. "No you aren't."

"No, really. I've got it all planned and I'm serious. I'm going to do it, in a week or so when the weather improves."

"You can try, but something in my bones says you won't get very far."

"You aren't telling me not to?"

Jemima shook her head. "I've known you long enough, Annamarie. I'd be wasting my breath. You need to find out for yourself. You can always come back."

"Well, thanks. I don't mean to come back ever, but thanks, I appreciate it."

Her mentor nodded slowly, but made no further comment. Having psyched herself up ready for an argument, this placid acceptance felt like an anticlimax.

Cassy broke down and cried when she explained to the loose women of Silver Street. Flinging her arms around Annamarie she said, "We're going to miss you so much, honey!"

"I'll miss you all, but I have to try and do this."

Desdemona hugged her as well, then Persephone and Transparent followed suit.

"There's a whole world out there," dark eyed Persephone said. "I remember from school. All those names and places. You could see them, Anna. You could do anything."

"I mean to."

"I wish I was like you," the usually quiet girl continued. "But I'm not, and I won't ever amount to anything much."

Finding it impossible to answer that, Annamarie coughed, and dug about in her bag. "I bought you all some presents." They were small, pretty things she had salvaged from the beach and would no longer need for herself. The items won her a flurry of perfumed kisses and affectionate embraces, after which she fled as quickly as she could. Leaving was a far harder thing than she had imagined.

Stood in the middle of Silver Street, she had no idea what to do. There was a lump in her throat, and she hadn't even realised before how much she liked the girls. They were honest, playful, and utterly accepting. The young woman walked, because it drew less attention than standing still, her broom tucked under one arm. Without really thinking about it, her feet took her by the church, and up to the gates of the Pallid Rock Orphanage. The thought of walking down that path, and up to the door made her shiver. Another threshold she had not meant to cross again. To leave without saying farewell to Emanuel seemed unbearable, but would he even see her if asked?

A lot of time had passed since their previous meeting, and even longer since her final day in this unhappy place. Last time she had been here, the Reverend had been infuriated by Jemima Kettle's arrival. As a witch, she would not be welcome either, no doubt. It would be easier just to go home, but stubborn defiance won out over apprehension. Why should she let these people intimidate her?

Chin lifted defiantly, Annamarie strode down the path. For the first time in her apprenticeship, she wished for a pointed hat, just to reinforce the issue. Rather than use the side door as orphans were obliged to do, she knocked on the main one. After a few moments, it opened, revealing the all too familiar features of Cassandra Witherspoon.

"Oh, it's you!" the reverend's wife said in surprise. "What do you want?"

"I wish to speak with Emanuel Davies."

"Step into the kitchen and I'll see where he is." She stepped back, allowing Annamarie to enter. "Listen, my husband is in attendance at a deathbed and will be away for some time. Cause me no trouble, Miss, and I will cause you none either."

"Understood." She followed Mistress Witherspoon along the hall and took a seat on one of the kitchen stools. Her heart pounded as she waited. Time dragged.

"Annamarie. I understand you wished to speak with me?"

She stood, turning to look at him. Emanuel had grown taller and thinner since they had last properly spoken. Black attire emphasised the darkness of his eyes and the hollows in his cheeks.

She swallowed, her mind blank for several seconds, unable to think of anything beyond looking at him. "Would you step outside with me? There are things I need to say."

"I will." He sounded guarded, but followed her from the building and beyond the orphanage grounds.

Side by side, but with an arm's length separating them, they walked away from the gloomy orphanage buildings, following the lane they had walked every day to school for so many years. When she felt safely out of earshot and away from spying eyes, she stopped. "The thing is Emanuel, I'm leaving the island, and I wanted to say goodbye, before I go. I don't suppose I'll see you again."

He frowned. "How are you leaving?"

"With the broom. I know where the nearest land is and I'm going to fly out of here."

"Anna, that's madness. You could get lost... drowned... it might be further than you think." His voice shook with alarm.

It surprised her to find him so concerned. "I know, but I have to try this. I'll spend my whole life regretting it if I don't. I need more than this." She put the broom down, leaving her hands free.

He nodded, silent, and still visibly troubled. "Why are you telling me this? I thought you never wanted to speak to me again. Or did I miss something?"

Reaching out, she caught his hands in hers. They never touched particularly in the past; it had not been like that between them. She regretted it now. "You're the best friend I ever had, Emanuel. I was angry with you, and I thought you didn't want anything more to do with me. But leaving... I couldn't go without saying goodbye."

"You're the only friend I ever had," he said, squeezing her fingers. "I'm very sorry you are going, but I wish you well. I hope you find whatever it is that you need."

"Thank you." She stood on tiptoe, pressing a small, chaste kiss to his lips. All the things that might have been rushed through her. If she put her arms around him now, and let the turmoil of emotions pour out through her kisses, then everything would change. Visions of marriage, children, convention and security danced through her head, alluring and persuasive. All that and more would be possible, if she sought it. She could feel his heart beating hard against hers, as though it might break out of his chest at any moment. If she walked away, there would be no certainties and she might spend the rest of her life alone and regretting it.

He freed one hand from her fingers, and wrapped his arm around her waist. "Anna, I..."

Not letting him finish, she spoke instead. "I wish you well, my dear. Find a good girl, a nice girl. Marry her and be happy and have a good life. Don't ever look back, or wonder what if. Promise me that. I have to go."

He touched his forehead to hers. "I hear you. So be it then. I promise I won't spend my life waiting to see if you return. Go well Anna, and don't look back either."

"I won't."

She let go of him, picked up her broom and turned away. The not looking back was hard, and it hurt, but at the same time felt like the right choice. She was already a witch, and he seemed destined to take over from Reverend Witherspoon. Whatever emotions they might stir in each other, it was hardly happily-ever-after material. *All the more reason to get out of this place.*

Taking Flight

A gentle breeze blew off the land, making it easier to fly. Cliffs dropped away beneath her. A flash of beach and then there was only glittering sea beneath the broom. The water had never looked more lovely, with white crested waves rolling against the rocks. Annamarie whooped with delight and assorted seabirds answered her cry. She kept a good distance above the waves, not wanting to get wet from the spray. The first few minutes of her escape were glorious indeed, but soon the euphoria wore off. With no landmarks to judge things by, it soon felt as though she wasn't really moving at all. That, she realised, would make the whole travelling process a lot harder. *Until I can see land, then I just have to focus on that. Won't be too long now.* The library map made the nearest coast look very close. She had imagined it would take an hour or two at most to find it. Watching the sun creep higher in the sky, Annamarie started to wonder if the representation had been accurate.

There were a few fingers of rock reaching up out of the sea, with large, unfamiliar seabirds perched on their tips. She wondered if the land on the map could somehow have gone astray. Lost beneath the waves perhaps. Could it have sunk? How often did bits of land cease to be where you expected to find them? For all she knew, it might be a frequent occurrence. The irrational thought gripped her that the rest of the world might not actually exist, that beyond Hopeless there was only sea. Although that didn't explain where the occasional shipwrecks came from, so the idea soon lost credibility for her. *Why can't I see it yet?*

She gripped the broom tightly, feeling very small and exposed. Risking a glance over her shoulder, Annamarie found she could not see the island behind her either. Water stretched in all directions. Panic tightened its fingers around her. How would she find her way? She turned the broom in a circle, unable to see anything and losing track of where she was supposed to be going.

After what seemed like far too long, she remembered that the location of the sun ought to help her get her bearings. However, scanning the sky, she saw that a thin veil of clouds had rolled in and she could not work out the location of that potential guide. *Perfect. Bloody perfect. Now what? No idea which way to go, and I've only got as long as I can stay awake and focused for. Then I get to fall in the sea. Which will be worse? Drowning, or being eaten?* Neither prospect appealed. *Come on girl. Think! You are a witch. You have power. It's just a matter of working out how to use it. Like using the mirror... have to ask the right question.* That line of thought pulled her up. Asking the right question of her mentor's scrying mirror had taken her into some things she would gladly have missed. *Well, anything has to be better than death.*

Closing her eyes, she focused on the thought of land. Firm, solid land that she could stand on safely. Strong coastlines, people, life and shelter. She gripped the broom tightly, willing it towards solid ground, but not looking to see where it went. Unable to tell if she was even moving, Annamarie cast aside all doubt, not letting herself dwell on it. Every ounce of will went in to driving her broom towards land. She imagined how good it would feel to stand on the earth again, to be safe on some new shore. *Land. Bring me to land.*

When she heard the sound of breakers, her heart leapt and she risked opening her eyes. There was sand, pale rock, and some way in the distance, a squat cottage. The vision brought considerable relief. Exhausted, she made a poor landing, and fell into the sand, legs unable to bear her weight. For a while, lying still seemed like the best course of action. *It might be a different island,* she tried to tell herself. *Why shouldn't other islands look a bit like Hopeless?*

There were voices from the cliff top.

"The tide isn't in yet."

Recognising Melisandra, the young witch buried her face in the sand and resisted the urge to howl.

"It won't be long now. We can wait." Durosimi was the last person she wanted to hear.

"Yes. Or we could walk down and take it to the water now. I want to be rid of it. I do not want to wait."

"Of course my darling. As you desire, so shall it be."

Struggling to her feet, Annamarie tucked herself in under the cliff and set off as quickly as her tired legs would allow, willing herself to be unnoticed. The thought of running into those two was more than she could stomach. *At least I never said goodbye to him. He doesn't know. If he does see me, he won't be able to mock me for failing.*

Shoulders hunched, broomstick dragging behind her, Annamarie made her way along the sand. When she could no longer hear voices on the wind, her posture relaxed a little, but her mood remained grim. After all the farewells, how could she go back to everyone and admit failure?

So it went wrong. Doesn't mean I'm beaten, or that I have to give up. I can do it. I can try again tomorrow. She thought about her attic bedroom in Jemima's cottage. The familiar furniture, the smell of wood smoke and boiling potions called to her. Even though she had been absent less than a day, nostalgia and longing caught hold. It would be lovely to curl up in that bed and listen to the wind rattling round the eaves. But to admit to her mentor that she had not managed her great bid for freedom? That stung her pride, and Annamarie had never liked feeling foolish. *I can't go back. What will she think of me? What will she say?*

"I thought you'd be here."

Lost in thought, she hadn't seen the small figure approaching her.

"You are sad," the boy observed. "Come home with me. I told mother to set an extra place for supper."

"Hello Seth." She sighed. "That's very kind of you."

"Come on then." He offered a small, cool hand for her to hold, and walked silently with her down the beach.

Inside the cottage Delores greeted her with sorrowful eyes and a nod of recognition. "He said you would come."

"You should study the craft with Jemima," Annamarie suggested, trying to sound more cheerful than she felt. "You're a natural."

Seth smiled. "Thank you, but that is not for me. I belong here, between the sea and the land."

The three of them sat at a small wooden table, bleached to grey by countless years of scrubbing. Annamarie realised her chair must once have belonged to Seth's father, and wondered if her companions were thinking about that too. The food was simple – a broth made with things from the sea, and fresh bread. She ate ravenously, and only when the bowl was empty did she notice that her hostess had barely touched the food.

"How are you two coping? Did you have a hard winter?" Hearing about other people's problems seemed far preferable to contemplating her own, or worse yet, sitting in silence any longer.

"It was cold, no taking the boat out in that," Delores said. "We lived on seaweed and shellfish mostly. We survived."

"In the worst of the storms the sea came right up to the door," Seth said. "But never any further."

"We were lucky. With the ice, there was no way off the beach, but the sea took care of us." Delores sounded distant, as though most of her attention lay somewhere else. "She is good to us, the sea."

"Mother hasn't been well," Seth said. He turned sorrowful eyes in Annamarie's direction, enabling her to read the truth in his young face: he did not expect his mother to live, but he could not speak of it.

She covered his hand, feeling sorry for him. "If you need anything, you go to Jemima Kettle, promise me?"

"I will. But there's not much she could do." He glanced at his distracted mother then mouthed, "Heartbroken."

"I understand." Although she didn't. The idea that you could waste away and die because of losing someone perplexed her. No one had ever been that important to her, nor did she anticipate ever feeling that way. "But there's you to think about as well. If you need anything, don't go to the townsfolk, go to Jemima."

"I'll stay here. It's where I belong." He sounded so much older than he looked. "You are tired. I can share with mother and you can have my bed. Then tomorrow, you can try again."

She smiled at him. "You know about that as well, huh?"

"I know all sorts of things. But mostly what I know at the moment is that you really need to sleep."

There was a cat on his bed – a rangy thing with a tatty, striped coat and tufted ears. Its fur bristled as they approached.

Seth went to soothe the creature. "Don't worry Matilda, she's a friend."

The cat showed no signs of being reassured, its eyes luminous in the gloom.

"I wonder if she can see Lamashtu."

"What's Lamashtu?" the boy enquired, then followed with an "Oh!" as the familiar appeared.

Matilda cowered before the cat-like entity, then jumped down to hide beneath the bed. Lamashtu followed. There were mews, then he returned to the bed and the scrawny female retreated to the rug by the fire. Annamarie slipped beneath the blankets fully clothed, and was asleep almost at once.

Tides of Mist

During the night, the headland had vanished beneath a blanket of pale mist. Everything lay still, even the sounds of waves muted by the clogged air. Annamarie and Seth walked along the beach together.

"She doesn't want to live without him," the boy explained. "But she doesn't want to leave me either. It's hard for her."

"Just promise me, you won't go to the orphanage. I grew up there. It's a bad place."

"I won't go away from the sea. Not ever. I can look after myself, and there's hardly anyone knows I'm here."

"Good." She sighed heavily.

"Will you get away this time, do you think?" Seth asked.

"I don't know. I've got a plan though, and it should work. I can't give up, not yet." She patted his shoulder, lost in thought and not really sure what else to do with the boy.

"I don't much like this mist. It feels wrong."

"I don't need to see, it won't be much of a problem," she replied.

He touched her arm. "No Annamarie, not like that. I don't know how to explain. It's wrong somehow."

"I'll be fine." She clambered onto the broom, closed her eyes and thought of the map. "Take care of yourself, Seth."

"I will."

Lifting off, she rose high over the water, and closed her eyes. There wasn't much point trying to see through the mist anyway. Picturing the coastline she had only ever encountered in a drawing, Annamarie willed her broomstick onwards, directing it towards that land. Looking at things would only distract her, she felt. That had been the mistake last time – being too focused on what she could see rather than what she knew to be there. With her head filled by the thought of another shore, she raced forwards, chasing a new destiny.

Only when her hands started to ache from clinging so long to the broom handle, did she think about Seth's words. "It's wrong somehow." She could feel the chill, clammy mist on her skin. Her thoughts wandered towards the first time she had met the boy. Images of his dead father returned to her, and a recollection that Seth had issued a warning to him as well. *An unheeded warning to a man who was killed.* A cold, clammy feeling leached into her heart. *Was he trying to warn me? Am I in danger?* She shook off the thought, focusing again on an image of the coastline she meant to reach. Holding that picture of land became harder by the moment.

The temptation to open her eyes grew stronger. She fought it, trying to keep all attention directed towards her destination. *No faltering. No distractions. No letting fear get the better of me. Clear thoughts and intentions. I am leaving Hopeless behind me. I am going somewhere new.* From nearby, she heard the sound of waves lapping against something, and wondering if it signified arrival, she succumbed and opened her eyes.

All around her, there was nothing but fog. Thick, white and clinging tendrils covered everything, as though she had flown into the heart of a snowdrift. A faint sound of lapping waves reached her, but she could not tell what direction they came from, nor could her eyes discern any hint of the sea. It might lie inches beneath her feet, or a vast distance below. Either way she could find herself in trouble at any moment. *Maybe I've flown too high, maybe this is the inside of a cloud and I need to go down.* But going down risked encountering the water, and getting into other difficulties. *Oh shit!* She closed her eyes again, trying to re-find her focus and steer the broom. The necessary clarity had gone. With her head in such disarray, the risk of falling from the sky increased dramatically. Fear could so easily beget fear, so she fought the rising panic because her life depended on not being overwhelmed. Sounds of breaking waves came from close by. She focused on the steady noise, and dropped a little lower, risking impact with the sea. Out of the swirling mist appeared a cluster of jagged rocks, black and sinister against the whiteness. Some of the central ones were large enough to land on, so she brought the broom down, glad to take a rest and be able to think without risk of inadvertently drowning herself. The rocks were slightly damp from mingled droplets of spray and fog, but she managed to keep her footing. It wasn't a big space, and offered little comfort. Huddled in what little shelter she could find, Annamarie considered her options, and found none of them to her liking. *Stay. Attempt to go onwards. Give up and go back.* There had to be something else.

"Lamashtu, come to me, please," she murmured.

Her cat familiar materialised out of the mist, thinner and paler than usual as though he too was affected by the conditions.

His appearance bothered her. "What's wrong with you?"

"I belong to the island. The further I am from it, the less substantial I become." Even his voice sounded less real than usual.

"I didn't know it would affect you like that."

"You didn't ask."

Rather than re-start that familiar argument, she pressed on. "Can you take me anywhere from here?"

"I might be able to take you back to Hopeless. I am uncertain. I would have to bear you through the realms of spirit to do it though. I do not know what that would do to you."

"Could you find me a boat?"

"I could try. It may take a while."

"What about water, Lamashtu?"

"There is water all around you. How much water do you want? You are wet."

"Water to drink. I cannot drink this."

"Oh."

Both cat spirit and human fell silent for a time.

"How far is it to land? Not back to Hopeless but somewhere else. Anywhere else."

"Further than you can travel."

"Other people get to us on ships. People have left before now. Why can't I go?"

"It doesn't want you to. I cannot take you that far anyway. I cannot leave."

Annamarie hissed in frustration. "What doesn't want me to? I don't understand."

"The island does not wish you to leave. I thought after yesterday you would understand that."

"What?" She stared at the transparent creature, shaking her head. "That doesn't make any sense. Why wouldn't the island want me to go? The island? That's crazy."

"Should I remind you that you are talking to a cat, and that you are a witch? The island does not want you to leave, and so, you will not leave."

"So why did it let me get this far?"

"How far do you think you've come?"

"Miles, surely?" Her gut clenched in anticipation of the response.

"Half a mile, as far as its influence extends over the sea."

"So I'm almost free then?"

Lamashtu did something that looked far too much like a smirk. "The word is 'almost'."

Annamarie buried her face in her hands and swore under her breath, before speaking to her familiar again. "There's no way out?"

"There's death, and otherwise no, not for you."

"Well, that's cheering." She lifted her head and looked at the mist and sea as they swirled around her. "Why?"

"I do not know. I feel the intentions but do not understand the reasons. It is like Matilda cat with a mouse. It plays. It lets you run around. It will not let you escape."

"This is madness. You're starting to sound like Balthazar Lemon and I'm starting to think like him!"

"It may be because of me," Lamashtu added.

"How?"

"We are bound to each other. It is not just that I am bound to you. I cannot stray far from the island, perhaps that ties you also. I do not know what would happen to either of us if you did break away. I could not serve you beyond Hopeless."

"That almost makes sense. I wish I'd known before I agreed."

"If you hadn't agreed to bond with me, you would be dead now."

An unpleasant splatting sound reached her ears. Looking for the source of it, Annamarie saw a long slimy appendage emerging from the water and reaching over the rocks towards her. It slithered, finding its way over the distance between them. More of it emerged from the depths, and she shuddered to think what the whole creature would look like.

Grasping her broom, she stood, ready to defend herself. "What the...?"

Another appeared on the far side of her craggy refuge and moved towards her. A third came from a different angle. A fourth. There were more of them out to sea, reaching into the sky and drifting towards her. There were barbs on the sinister flesh, and they put her in mind of Melisandra's firstborn.

"Please let this be a nightmare. Please let me wake up now," she whispered.

"It isn't, and you won't," Lamashtu said.

The first tentacle slithered closer, merely yards away now.

"Get me ought of here!" she squealed. "I don't care what you have to do, but get me out of here."

"As you wish, Annamarie."

In the Realms of Spirit

In a matter of seconds, Lamashtu grew from the size of a domesticated cat, to a beast several times larger than his mistress. Jaws gaped, long fangs looking all too real. A few heartbeats of time ensued, during which Annamarie was able to wonder if she had made a fatal mistake. Hardly enough opportunity for feet to set down roots, much less scope to resist what was coming. Something slimy touched her skin as the tentacles reached her. She lashed out with the broom and had not quite gathered the breath to scream when the dire feline mouth came down, bringing darkness.

It did not feel like anything at all. She could not move, or find any sense of her body, but the lingering impression of existing still remained. Although she tried, her hands, if she still had them, could not be directed to make contact with the rest of her. *No breath! I'm not breathing. I have no heartbeat.* There was nothing at all beyond the fragile thread of her own thoughts. When she tried to voice a stream of irate expletives, there were no sounds. Attempts at employing sight, touch and smell remained equally futile, but she persisted, because trying seemed a lot better than letting the nothingness occupy her attention.

"You bastard Lamashtu! What are you playing at?" Hearing her own voice emerging from the void, Annamarie paused. "Oh!" The reply came from the darkness surrounding her. "You wished to leave. I used the quickest method."

At least now she had something to focus on. "You ate me! I'm inside you, right?"

"I did, and you are. As a consequence, nothing else managed to eat you. I thought you would be pleased."

"How do I get out of here?"

Lamashtu rumbled. "Well, we could wait until you pass all the way through me, or I could cough you up. The journey will be quicker and easier if I bear you inside me and release you when it is done."

"I want you to let me out. I can't stand the not seeing and not feeling!"

"As you will, but do not blame me if you do not like it."

There were tremors as feeling returned to her body, and the sound of cat-like retching filled her ears. It occurred to Annamarie that she might have added to her list of recent mistakes. There was no knowing where Lamashtu would cough her up or what hazards lingered out there. Bile filled her mouth. The world pulsed red and black.

Awareness returned. Annamarie found herself on something that looked a lot like the craggy island on which she had been swallowed. The angles were all different though, the shapes loaded with malice. Tentacles of black mist rose from the sea, exploring the air and creeping over the land. They looked worse in this less physical form – the ghosts of monstrous intentions reaching up from unnaturally placid water.

"Where are we?" the young woman asked, hungry for anything that would help her feel in control of this experience.

"One of the other layers," Lamashtu said. "Another kind of here."

"That doesn't help." The air tasted of wrong things, each breath adding to her profound unease.

"It is what I know. They are still looking for you, here," the familiar inclined his head towards the echoes of sea beasts. "It is not safe to stay. As you would not let me carry you, we must fly."

Feeling grim, she nodded and straddled the broom. "Which way?"

"Follow me." Lamashtu's form contracted and shifted, becoming less like the memory of a cat, then evolving into the semblance of a bird.

"I didn't know you could do that!"

"It is just a matter of will. I am a cat because I happen to like being a cat. It is not a form that goes well with waves, and it is easier to change myself than turn this into land."

"You could do that?"

"I expect so, eventually. I do not think you would like how long it takes."

Annamarie huffed. "Fine. We fly then. I just want to get out of here."

"If you let me, I can arrange that." Lamashtu growled. "But I must do as you bid me, Annamarie, and you have no idea where you are or what you are doing."

"Just shut up, and get moving."

It did not feel like flying. Nothing else moved. The sea below lay still as Jemima's black mirror, its surface an ominous glass that the young witch feared would reveal hideous secrets to her at any moment. The trouble with riding the broom was that looking down came too naturally. She tried to focus on her hands and the grain in the wood, or to look ahead at her familiar's bird form rather than down. The sea remained in her peripheral vision though, full of disturbing promises. Its stillness spoke of sinister mystery.

Shutting her eyes didn't help. The air did not move over her skin as it would in normal circumstances. With eyelids lowered, she had no sense of travelling, which was worse, and too much freedom to imagine what the water might be doing while she wasn't watching. She had visions of appendages snaking up to grasp her; things she could not feel taking hold and dragging her down into the depths.

The sky proved no better. It looked flat and unreal, as though someone had painted it there; a thin film of colour put up to hide the truth. Like whitewashing a wall to hide the flecks of blood. Memory stirred in her. Something from the distant past, a brush in her hand and the smell of fear in the air. Above her, the sky bleached white, echoing the recollection. Under the paint, there was blood and no amount of trying to hide it would make it go away. She could see it now, leaching through the pristine whiteness of the sky and dripping into the sea, stirring the waters in violent shades of crimson.

"Stop that!" Lamashtu commanded. She had never heard any suggestion of emotion from the creature before. Now it sounded afraid.

"I'm just flying."

"You are thinking... and drawing things to you with those thoughts. You are making the sky run with blood, and that is not safe, for either of us."

"I didn't mean to."

"It is the nature of this place. It draws forth the darkness. Makes real what you fear."

"Why do you travel here, then?" she asked, searching for something that would blot out the fearful, half formed recollections.

"It is not in my nature to regret, or to fear. I am myself, and there is nothing this place can draw forth. Alone, I am safe here. I could have carried you through without risk had you let me."

"Well, maybe I did make a mistake, but being inside you all of a sudden was bloody disconcerting. You didn't even warn me."

"I didn't have time. I had to eat you before anything else could."

A shoreline came into view. While it felt familiar, it looked more akin to the echo of a forgotten nightmare than anything she had actually seen. Shapes and forms writhed across the landscape, feeding upon each other relentlessly in an orgy of blood and violence.

"It is good to be home," Lamashtu said, sweeping low over the land.

"We can't land down there," Annamarie responded, panicking.

"How else do you propose to return?"

She scanned around frantically. "There must be somewhere that isn't... where they aren't..."

"Must there? Why must there?"

"Because..." she faltered. Maintaining control over the broom became harder. She feared losing control and plummeting into the feeding frenzy beneath her. There was no reason why any spot on this version of the island should be safe for her. "Well, I might as well have a look around, yes?"

"By all means."

The view from above did not tie in with her understanding of Hopeless. She couldn't always see the land shapes for the creatures covering it. Even so, she had the feeling this was not exactly the same place. Wracking her brains, she tried to imagine where might be safe. Jemima's cottage? The Church? Even assuming she could find their locations here. Which rather assumed that what happened on her layer of island related to what happened here... *And what if that's true the other way round? What if this is part of the island you know... the thing in the mirror... what if this could break through into our world at any moment?* Sickness clutched her stomach and the broom veered out of control. She skimmed low over slithering backs. A vast head full of teeth and eyes rose to greet her. Twisting the broom, she dodged its foul smelling maw and climbed into the sky.

"What is this place?" she asked.

"A layer, a way through."

"Do I have to land down there, to go back where I belong?"

"No. There are other ways."

"And how do they work?" She had a feeling they might turn out to be worse.

"I can eat you again, cough you up where you should be. It really would be easiest."

"Do it."

"I will try not to drop you."

"Thank you very much."

"Afterwards, I will need your blood."

"Understood." She watched the bird grow, until its beak opened to take her in. Compared to the other things that might feed upon her, it seemed like a haven.

Into the Woods

There had been bloodletting before. Drops here and there, requiring a little pain but no difficulty. Exhausted from the journeying, and disorientated, Annamarie was not ready for her familiar's hunger. Back in a catlike form, Lamashtu did not wait for an offering, but clamped down hard on her wrist, breaking the skin with sharp teeth. It hurt, and she fought the need to whimper. As her companion drank, it grew more substantial, but no more natural to look at.

"Please! Enough! You're really hurting me now."

Lamashtu continued, making her wonder how much blood a person could afford to lose. She remembered Jemima's words about what happened if you asked too much of a familiar, and let them have too much of you.

"Lamashtu! I demand that you stop."

Darkly shining eyes looked up at her, the expression disinterested. However, after a few more moments, the creature released her arm. Blood flowed freely over her skin, and she had nothing suitable to bind it with. She held the small wound closed and lifted her arm, waiting for nature to take its course.

"I need more," Lamashtu said. "You demanded a great deal of me."

"I can't give you any more right now," she replied through gritted teeth.

Eyes locked. She had a feeling this rapacious hunger was for more than just blood. Her control had slipped a long way, and if the familiar wished to take her over, it had good opportunity now. In the past, the entity had seemed like a friend and ally, but at this moment it looked like a dangerous opponent. Staring hard, she resisted the demand. "Tomorrow, or the day after."

Lamashtu hissed.

"Or you can break with me if you want." She had no intention of doing anything that would require this kind of help, for a very long time.

"I do not have that choice. I belong to you, until you die. You must feed me."

"I have fed you, and you look a lot better. I won't treat you unfairly Lamashtu, but I've been through a lot too and you will have to wait."

The cat smiled. It was not a comfortable effect, involving too many teeth. "You are not quite so foolish as your latest actions suggest. I can wait."

"Good. And I do know a thing or two. I'm not about to let you get control of me."

"You've lasted a lot longer than some. I like you, Annamarie. You are interesting. It would be a joy to consume your soul, but I would miss you afterwards." With that, he vanished, leaving her to deal with her pain and weariness alone.

Once the bleeding stopped, Annamarie dug her fingers into the ground, glad of the cold soil, and its solidity. Even being cold was nice, in an odd way. *Real.* There were no monsters visible. No writhing, hungry things. *Is that because I am unable to see them, or because there are no such things?* She drove the thought away, refusing to contemplate it further. The recent madness grew distant, as though she had shaken off the tatters of a bad dream. Looking about, she saw nothing but trees in all directions. There were no obvious paths. Annamarie knew the peripheries of the woods, and the area surrounding her home. She'd never gone deep into the wilder places of the island, although it had long been her intention. Hungry and exhausted, she could not go rambling about in the hopes of finding the way home. Her limbs trembled in the aftershock, and would not allow any serious walking, much less flying. The need for sleep gnawed at her, making thought difficult. Just for once in her life she wanted there to be someone who could rescue her, whose aid would not turn out to be expensive in the long run.

"You're on your own, girl," she said, hauling herself upright. "Might as well get on with it. Bit of a shortage of fairy tale princes round here, and far too many frogs." She set off, leaning on the broom for balance.

After a while, she came to the foot of an enormous tree. It looked like something from the few children's stories they had at the orphanage. It looked almost as though someone had set it there on purpose. The broad trunk and tangling roots looked more created than grown, to her eye. *Ah yes, of course exactly what I need now is a fairy tale magic tree with a pot of gold in it. I expect it fruits good looking men on a regular basis as well.* Thanks to her recent experiences, Annamarie did not feel confident about her perceptions, and had no inclination to trust anything that seemed too good to be true. *This however is probably just a tree. And it is better than sleeping under the sky, and it does look normal. Seems safe enough.*

The tree had a sizeable opening, leading into a dry looking, sheltered hole. *What could possibly go wrong? The hole could close over. The tree could turn out to be something other than a tree, and might then eat me. This could be home to something unpleasant.* Her head ached.

It started to rain. Gentle at first, the drops grew heavier, so she ducked inside.

"I'll warn you," she said out loud. "I'm not good to eat, so don't try anything, ok?"

The tree remained silent, much to her delight. *Talking trees I can't deal with. Not even if they sing cute nursery rhymes like that one in the book.*

She fell asleep almost at once, plunged into a quiet, oblivious state where even nightmares could not reach her. The passage of time did not touch her, nor did the cold trouble her body. Waking much later, she stretched and yawned. It surprised her that she did not feel hungry or uncomfortable from nesting in the tree. Clambering outside, she found the day bright and cheerful. An ancient, wizened, black clad woman sat amongst the tree roots.

"Hello," Annamarie said, genuinely pleased to see another soul. "I wonder if you could tell me how to get home from here."

"And where might home be?" the old woman asked.

"Jemima Kettle's cottage, on Fish Hill."

"Ah. Well, if I was you, I wouldn't have started from here, you've lost your way rather badly, my dear."

"I have. I'm not even sure where I am on the island."

The old woman smiled. "Or when you are no doubt. And I expect you've not given proper thought to why you are, either. Would you like an apple, my dear?" She held out a shining fruit.

Annamarie remembered Snow White and the poisoned apple. Tales of forbidden fruit in the Garden of Eden flooded her head. Apples could be dangerous, and smiling old women were not to be trusted. She reached out her hand. "Sure. Thank you."

"That's a good girl. Women's fruit, apples. Women's magic. You eat it up, and make sure you think about what it is, and what it means."

Taking a bite, she considered the sweetness. "What sort of an apple is it?"

"The sort that grows in my garden. If it has a name, it's never seen fit to tell me."

Eating the fruit cleared her thoughts. "So who are you, if you don't mind my asking?"

"Lorelei Nightshade, dear. You should think of me as your granny."

Annamarie stopped chewing. "Nightshade is a surname I made up. You are not my granny."

"What do you think happens when people go round making up new names? They get new selves, new histories, new grannies. That's just how the world works." The old woman chuckled, her laughter warm and infectious.

Making a conscious effort not to be swept along in this tide of good humour, Annamarie said, "No it isn't. What do you want?"

The old woman looked crestfallen. "There's no trust in you, girl. Although I will admit, it's not that simple. You might be my flesh and blood, you might not. But you've chosen my name and that makes a connection between us, doesn't it? In magic, these things can be very important."

"I don't know. I'm afraid there isn't much trust in me, and with good reason. I've seen the darkness behind things. I don't do trust. Everything wants something and fairy tale perfect grandmothers do not grow out of the ground like mushrooms."

Lorelei Nightshade rose to her feet. She wasn't very tall, even when she pulled on the pointed hat. "There's more to life than just the dark shades. Your familiar brought you here by accident, I think. It got confused, poor creature."

"Poor creature? It was talking about eating my soul."

"They're so vulnerable to where you take them, and that one has walked some dark roads of late. It would make anyone a bit evil, that would."

"Why should I believe you?"

"Because I would never do you any harm, dear girl. I'm exactly what you need and just what you've been searching for, aren't I? You are lost and I can help you. I've walked between the worlds myself, and I know how confusing it can be."

"Are we between the worlds here?"

"I don't think so, girly. But that depends a lot on where you came from. What's real to one is inbetween to another. Come along with me. Can you fly?"

"I think so."

Following Lorelei Nightshade, she took off over the woods, glad to have some guidance. When the smiling old woman landed on the top of a small hill, she had a feeling of uncanny familiarity. The cottage was tiny, made with stones that had been carefully slotted together. Were it not for the chimney, it looked far too much like the little outbuilding behind Jemima's home. Turning in a slow circle, Annamarie took in the wooded headland, the curve of valley, the line of coast. *Too familiar. But where are the roads? I should be able to see the church spire and the lighthouse. How long have I been asleep? This could be Hopeless in the distant past, or the far future. If there are dark and sinister layers, why can't there be good and beautiful ones as well? That would make sense.*

"Where is everything? This is Hopeless, isn't it?"

"What's hopeless, dear?"

"The island."

"This is Ynys Blodau."

"But it looks just like Hopeless only there's no town and no lighthouse and... " she grinned broadly. "I'm not on Hopeless anymore! Whatever Lamashtu said... he's done it! I'm not on the island!" she whooped. The feeling of triumph drove some of the shadows from her mind.

"You're on this island," Granny Nightshade said, smiling.

"It looks so clean, and peaceful."

"It is. There aren't many of us here. Just the few who survived the shipwreck."

Annamarie considered this. "So you came here by accident?"

"Yes. And there is no way to leave except for walking between the worlds. Some of my sisters have, but it is quiet here and my bones are too old. I shall stay here until I die. If you wish to stay for a while, I would welcome your company."

Annamarie had a vision of the old woman throwing off her skin and turning into something hungry and dangerous. Even with the warm sunlight on her face, she could not entirely shake off the fear of monstrous things hiding in the shadows. She did not trust the bright surface of this place. At home she could at least see where the rot was. Granny Nightshade seemed so nice though, so friendly and sweet. Before she even thought about it, Annamarie found herself agreeing to stopping for a while. Of course she would like some cake and a lovely cup of tea. It all sounded perfect.

Pretty Pink Corruption

For several days, Annamarie rested and explored. All the urgency she had once felt had gone, and she supposed this must be due to fulfilling her ambition. Having escaped Hopeless, she had no idea what to do next, and the time slipped by in a happy dream. She wandered without much thought or care. There were spots in the landscape that gave her a distinct feeling of déjà vu. However, each journey brought her back to Lorelei Nightshade with a stronger impression that whatever Ynys Blodau might be, it was not in any way the island she had known. Life with Granny Nightshade felt so comfortable. There was no work to be done, and good things came in abundance.

At first she enjoyed the absence of town and people, along with the feeling of having escaped. The novelty wore off after a while. It seemed safe here, granted. The trouble was, once she had shaken off the most immediate memories of horror, safe lost some of its appeal. The hunger that had sent her out into the world returned, gnawing at her from time to time, and making the perfection of Ynys Blodau seem flawed. Nothing changed here. Nothing happened. She could not be entirely satisfied.

"Could you teach me about walking between the worlds?" she asked Granny Nightshade.

"I can. But there's no hurry, is there? There must be other, nicer things to do. It's such a lovely day."

"It is nice out," she said, glad Jemima had taught her how to mask impatience. "But I would like to learn. I don't know much about it all and I was hoping you would teach me."

"There's other things I could teach you instead. How to make some of my special potions. I'm good at potions."

"I'd like that too. Let's do that today then." She smiled, hiding her feelings. Lorelei Nightshade had no desire to let her go, that much was obvious. Annamarie reasoned she might as well learn as much as she could, but had no desire to be trapped in this place. Bargaining with Lamashtu wouldn't work – the spirit could leave her in any number of unpleasant locations until she surrendered to it, and that wouldn't do at all. She needed to be able to leave by her own skill. It didn't help that she had no idea where she was.

They were gathering wild herbs on the hillside. "Have you seen many places, walking between the worlds?" she asked, casually.

"A few," the old woman replied. "All kinds of places."

"You must have had some wonderful adventures, Granny," the young witch persisted, trying to lure her companion into speaking.

"I'm not sure I'd call them that. This is the fairest place of all. Why would anyone want to go wandering when they could live contented on this beautiful island?"

Why indeed? The thought mingled with hers so readily that she almost didn't notice it. *Because it's dull and lonely,* she reminded herself. *This place is only perfection if your idea of a good time involves sitting by the fire and making your own socks.*

It's perfect here. It's lovely. I want to stay forever and be happy.

Annamarie bit her tongue, the pain giving her something to focus on. *No! This is not my life. Not what I want.* She fought the suggestions in her head.

"How about I make you something special for dinner, dear? Something nice with apples."

Forcing a smile, she nodded. "That would be lovely. Thank you very much. I do love apples." *I have got to get out of here.* With the smile still bright on her face, she continued. "Why don't I go and pick you some nice flowers to go on the table. That would be good, wouldn't it?"

Lorelei smiled at her. "That would be perfect, dear child. Thank you."

She missed Jemima's grumbles and growls. Back home, you picked flowers to make a tincture or a tea, but not because they were pretty. After days of nice little cakes and nice things to wear, little song birds coming to warble on the windowsill and fairytale sunsets, Annamarie hankered after lumpy stew, mud and honesty. Nothing here felt right.

"I'll find lots of pretty ones for you," she promised. *Just one more fucking cupcake with wings, just one more pink sparkly thing and I'm going to go mad.* She set off at a brisk trot.

Annamarie had no plan, other than the urge to get away. It had all become too much. The perfect sunny days, the perfect Granny, the perfect island – except none of it was what she wanted. Increasingly, the old woman treated her like a child. If it went on like this much longer, she feared she might accept everything. *There's more than one way to lose your soul and they aren't all ugly. They don't all advertise themselves with nasty looking teeth and the smell of sulphur.* She started running, needing to move and not caring where she went. *A cage is still a cage even if you tie brightly coloured ribbons to the bars.* But how to escape?

She slowed down, catching her breath. *Magic is will made manifest. Will is all that truly matters, that's what Jemima says. Clarity of intent, force of determination. So the question is, what do I want? And do I want it enough to make it happen?*

For a while, she thought about the island she had grown up on, with its frequently cold and windswept shores. The stark cottage where she had lived as a child, frequently hungry and forever being shouted at. Pallid Rock Orphanage, where the food had been better and the shouting worse. She considered a lifetime of not really fitting in, and frequently being alone. It had been unhappy, more often than not. It was, she realised, her loneliness as well as a hunger for adventure that had sent her out into the world.

It may not have been the best life, but it's what got me here. It's my life, my history, my island. Is that enough? How do I do this? Everything around her seemed entirely solid and real, not like the shifting unfamiliarity Lamashtu had carried her into. He had said there were layers of reality, realms overlapping each other, and that she could not go far from Hopeless. Assuming he was telling the truth, then all she needed to do was find the means to move between the layers. Granny Nightshade said it was possible – but there were no guarantees she'd been telling the truth either.

I got here, so it must be possible to get out again. If I have to beat a hole in reality to do it... well, I'm a witch, aren't I? What else is magic for but changing how the world works.

"Ah, there you are, my dear girl. You must have got lost!" Granny Nightshade smiled warmly, and everything seemed just fine.

"I followed a butterfly," Annamarie said, absent minded. "It was ever so pretty." She couldn't remember what else she had been doing, but it didn't seem important any more.

"You forgot to pick me any flowers, that's such a shame."

This, Annamarie felt, was indeed a very sad thing. "I'm so sorry. I must have forgotten. Can we pick some now, before we go back?"

"Of course we can dear. There should be plenty along the way. We can put some on the table, and some more in your room. Here.

Hold my hand." The old woman seemed bigger than Annamarie remembered.

Hardly thinking at all, she reached out and accepted the offered fingers, trotting alongside the old woman as they collected flowers together.

"That's just perfect, dear Annamarie. We'll pick some of the nice pink flowers and the lovely red ones, and I can put some in your hair for you as well. Everything's going to be lovely. All you have to do is listen to what I tell you, do exactly as you are told, and we're going to be so very happy."

"Yes Granny." *What am I doing?*

"Granny knows best. You trust your old Granny to tell you what to do." She sounded so warm and genuine. "And you'll never leave me, ever. You'll be my little girl always and we'll be happy, won't we?"

Annamarie felt something warm at her neck. Without really thinking, she reached up her fingers. Between her dress and underclothes, the amulet Durosimi had given her glowed with its own heat. Touching it through the fabric, her head cleared.

"I made you some darling little cupcakes for tea," Lorelei said. "You'll love them. I know you will."

Something inside her snapped, breaking the trance. She pulled the amulet loose, wrapping her fingers around it and concentrating. The web of enchantments around her shimmered, becoming visible. She raked through them, tearing the strands of intent that had nearly caught her this time. One by one the illusions fell away. The beautiful summer's day paled into mist and cold sea breezes. The flowers in her hand became bits of seaweed and narrow sticks. She half expected Lorelei Nightshade to turn into something vile. Instead, the old woman looked up at her with melancholy eyes.

"Did you have to break everything? We were doing so well."

Annamarie looked around at the small, rocky outcrop protruding from the sea. It supported a ramshackle house made of driftwood, and was home to a few crows.

"None of it was real," Annamarie pointed out.

"But it's all I had." The old woman looked devastated, as though she might cry.

Feeling more guilty by the moment, Annamarie almost reached out her hand. Durosimi's words returned to her. The amulet would protect her from malevolent spirits. Whatever her eyes might say, this was no lost grandmother figure in need of kindness.

"Why is it everything I run into these days seems intent on eating me?"

"Oh, I'd never do that dear. I just wanted to keep you and make you happy. That's not so terrible, is it?"

"It's not what I want." Annamarie decided it would be better not to ask what her fate would have been had she succumbed to the lure of the cupcakes.

"Then tell me, and I'll make it for you. It'll be perfect, I promise."

"I don't want perfect. I want real."

"Real is what you think it is, girly. I can be real."

"I don't think so."

"Ah well, suit yourself." The old woman melted back into the rock, leaving only shadows.

Nothing but Illusions

Time had no meaning here. It might have been days, or months that passed as she sat on the rock and contemplated the sea. The surrounding waters shifted slowly, revealing unhurried currents. Sometimes shapes emerged from beneath, suggesting that life moved in the depths. Nothing tried to eat her. This seemed like distinct progress.

I could sit here forever. There's nothing to eat or drink, no way of sleeping, but that doesn't seem to be a problem. I don't want anything. I feel odd, but who wouldn't in the same circumstances? Sometimes she talked aloud to herself instead, just to break the monotony. "So I have enough will power to ruin the whole too good to be true experience, but not enough to get myself off a lump of rock? What does this say about me, exactly?"

"It says you are perverse."

Annamarie looked at her suddenly manifested familiar. It seemed so very catlike and unthreatening, but she had not forgotten its recent behaviour. "I wondered when you'd show up."

"You could have invited me at any moment."

"I know. I chose not to." Folding her arms across her chest, she continued staring at the sea.

"I can take you home again, Annamarie, if that's what you truly want."

"And why exactly should I trust you to do that, Lamashtu?" When it didn't answer, she continued. "I have some idea what you are, and what you really want. You could leave me anywhere, again."

"Ah. That." The cat settled next to her and set about grooming fur it did not actually possess. "Yes, very much that."

"I have to do your bidding, if you feed me. That's my essence, my nature. I can only escape that if you die, I can only take your soul if you give it to me in exchange for something."

"Says you."

"Indeed. Or, you can sit on this rock until you die, and then I can find myself a new witch. I don't get to eat your soul, you don't get to leave, no one wins."

"How many souls have you eaten?"

"So far? I have consumed nine. They made deals with me. They were greedy, and sold their essence for worldly power and gain."

"That was very stupid," the young witch said. She thought of Durosimi.

"People frequently are."

"So why didn't you take me home when I told you to before?"

"I did, and you, like a fool walked straight into one of the weak spots and slept there! It's not my fault if you are an idiot."

She frowned at this. "I don't understand."

"What do you think reality is?"

"I don't know. I've never given it much thought. Reality is all the solid stuff, yes? All the things you can touch and taste."

"There is no 'solid stuff' as you put it." Lamashtu paused for dramatic effect. "Reality does not exist. There's only what we believe is real, and all the soft, flexible, uncertain places where even that doesn't work."

"Oh!"

"Hopeless is full of such things. I put you down nice and safely, and it took you minutes to get yourself straight back into trouble."

"How do I know you're telling me the truth?"

"Because I can't do anything else! It's the blood bond, I cannot lie to you."

"Yes, but if that wasn't true, then you could, and you could say anything, including that you're being honest with me."

"You are right of course." The familiar sounded amused. "So it all comes down to trust, and choices. You can stay here until you die. That will take a while, by my guess. You might perhaps work out how to walk upon the waves, shift between the layers of existence and make your way back to where you belong. Or something might eat you. Or you can ask me, and I will take you home."

"And then you eat my soul. I don't think so."

"We have not made a bargain that would allow me such feasting."

"Nor are we going to, so I'm stuck. I'll do this in my own time, thank you very much."

Some distance away, a large, sinuous form broke through the water. A vast amount of purple flesh came into view, and then sank back down. Annamarie shivered. She really didn't want to stay here, but wasn't about to sell her essence in exchange for temporary freedom.

"You assume I would demand your soul in exchange for taking you home."

"Yep."

"I have considered this. I have tasted you a little, Annamarie. I know you from your blood, and you are stubborn. Most of my witches were like you. Most died with their spirits unfettered. I only eat the stupid greedy ones, usually. I doubt they taste as good, though."

"So you would carry me home and not ask me for my soul?"

"That's right. I know you'd die before you made such a bargain so there's not a lot of point me offering it, is there?"

Annamarie looked at the monotonous grey sky above her. She considered the small rocky outcrop, on which stood a shack she didn't want to venture into, and which otherwise barely afforded enough room to lie down. Then she considered the sea, with its slimy-looking surface and hidden monsters. This was not a place she felt inspired to spend the rest of her life, moreover if she stayed, that life would be a very short one. *What are the odds that I can get out of here on my own without getting into worse trouble?* She looked at Lamashtu again. The familiar was doing a very good job of appearing both friendly and harmless.

"So you would take me home just for blood?"

"It will be a lot of blood. Not enough to kill you, I promise, but you will be weak and exhausted for some days, and it will hurt."

"Then it's not enough to take me back to Hopeless. You have to leave me at the door to Jemirna Kettle's cottage on Fish Hill. Understood? And no drinking my blood until I'm safely in and tucked up in bed, all right?"

"I accept. I will do exactly as you have asked, and in return you will let me feed until I am entirely satisfied."

"Agreed."

"In which case Annamarie, I will take you home. It will be as before, I will need to swallow you."

"Can I just make it clear that I'm agreeing to be swallowed for the purposes of being moved and that this is not me agreeing to you eating me in any other way, manner or form, yes?"

"Understood. You are not giving me permission to eat your soul."

"Let's do it. Take me home please, Lamashtu."

She watched the creature swell from comfortable domestic dimensions, becoming huge and disturbing as it grew. Heart racing, she fought back the fear this rapid growth inspired. Tired to the core of her being, Annamarie just wanted to go home and rest. Other things could be worried about once she felt awake enough to properly consider them. Lamashtu's open jaws did not seem quite so intimidating this time. She closed her eyes, and let the familiar consume her, wrapping its darkness about her weary frame.

Written in Dust

F alling hard against the front door, Annamarie thought she might be sick. After what felt like an age, her surroundings stopped spinning and the nausea passed.

"Delivered to the doorstep, as promised," Lamashtu said, rubbing against her legs like a normal cat.

She pushed open the door. "Hello? Jemima?" No reply came, so she entered. The kitchen looked a good deal tidier than she remembered, but a thick layer of dust coated every surface. The floor and table showed signs of very small footprints – from mice, she supposed. "Hello?" The cottage smelled musty and unlived in. "This isn't right." There were no bunches of herbs hanging to dry. All signs of life and activity had gone, aside from the evidence of mice.

"I have kept my promise," Lamashtu said. "It is time to fulfill your side of the bargain."

"But I don't know where Jemima is!"

"That can wait. I am very hungry, and you have a promise to keep."

Annamarie sighed. "All right. Let me fill a jug with water first."

She climbed up to the attic with a heavy feeling in her heart. The room was just as she had left it, but dusty. On the bed lay a rolled piece of paper, sealed closed with a blob of candle wax. It had her name on it. She fumbled it open, and read:

I, Jemima Mistletoe Kettle, being of sound mind, do hereby leave my cottage and all of my worldly possessions to Annamarie Nightshade, so that if she should ever return to Hopeless, she will have a home for always.

Annamarie stared at the document for some minutes, unable to take it in. "Does this mean she's dead?"

"It could do," Lamashtu said, jumping gracefully onto the bed.

"But I've only been gone a few days!"

"I doubt it's so short a time. You've moved backwards and forwards. Days bend and get lost along the way sometimes."

At this, Annamarie went deathly cold. "Have I been gone a long time?"

Lamashtu sniffed the air. "A few years I would guess. I cannot say how many."

She sat down on the bed, shaking her head and struggling to breathe. "I can't think. I don't know what to do."

"You must keep your promise to me. There will be time enough for thinking afterwards."

Annamarie pulled off her dress and climbed into the bed. It felt slightly damp, and in need of airing. She dropped back onto the pillow and stared at the ceiling, examining the familiar patterns of cracks. The bite at her wrist hurt, but she managed to ignore it as Lamashtu set about drinking her blood. *This is the last time. If I can't do a thing myself, I'm not doing it, ever,* she promised.

The drinking went on for a long time, until her head pounded. At least lying down, she didn't have to worry about falling.

There was nothing to eat in the house, so as soon as she felt able to move, Annamarie sought out some loose change from the tin on the mantelpiece and set out on foot for the town. Nothing looked quite how she remembered it, and with so many details out of kilter with recollection, she wondered if this really was Hopeless and not some strange echo. *I can't spend the rest of my life wondering if I'm in the right place. I'm here, I'm staying... but where on earth did that tree come from? There never used to be a tree here before, surely? And since when was there a barn over there? Or was I just not paying attention before?* She bought cake from the Swann Bakery. The new girl behind the counter eyed her suspiciously. Emerging, she saw a trio of figures on the other side of the street. He'd aged, but even so there was no mistaking Durosimi, with his gaunt face and unpleasant laughter. At his side walked Melisandra, as cold and unsettling as ever. Behind the pair trotted a third figure, a handsome child with bright eyes and a ready smile. *Surely not? Those two with a son? The world has changed indeed.* Durosimi raised a gloved hand and waved, crossing the street towards her.

"Annamarie Nightshade! Where have you been hiding yourself? I rather thought you must have died!"

"Nope, not so far as I noticed. Good day to you, Durosimi, Melisandra."

Melisandra glowered at her and did not speak.

"Hello!" The small boy grinned and waved.

"This is Drustan," Durosimi said, and offered no further explanation.

"He doesn't look very much like either of you," she couldn't resist saying. The comment won her a snarl from Melisandra and a raised eyebrow from Durosimi.

"Dear Annamarie. It must be... years! What on earth have you been doing? I called at the cottage, but you were never there, and then when Jemima died..."

"It was all very sad," Annamarie said quickly, not wanting him to suspect how little she knew.

"Of course. But you've kept very quiet. I had quite convinced myself you must have succumbed as well during that flu epidemic. I imagined you dying alone in the woods."

"How very romantic. I'm sorry to disappoint you."

"Nothing like sorry enough," Melisandra responded, her voice little more than a whisper.

"I thought there would have to be some very good reason why my dear friend had not been to visit me, did not even drop by to congratulate me on my wedding to my darling."

"There were reasons," Annamarie said. Her head reeled. So much seemed to have happened.

"We were just going along to the church. Couldn't face sitting through the entire ceremony of course, but it doesn't hurt to turn up and smile. I assumed you must be doing the same."

"Yes," Annamarie said, wondering what he was talking about. She walked alongside him, feeling like a sleepwalker who has surfaced from unconsciousness to find themselves in an unexpected place.

Bells chimed. They were a strange mix of notes, all but one having been taken from the wrecks of ships, and meant for alerting other craft in foggy weather rather than calling the faithful to prayer. Still, they created a cheerful noise. A small group had already gathered outside the main entrance to the building. Durosimi added their small party to this throng.

"I doubt Reverend Witherspoon will preside over many more marriages," Durosimi said, his voice low, lips uncomfortably close to her ear.

"No?"

"Something scared him very badly last winter. I've not found out what exactly, but he's a bag of nerves and his heart is certain to give out next time anything else shocks him. Given this place, he won't last long."

At that moment, the aged Reverend appeared in the church doorway. His hair had turned white, and he moved like a very old man. Soon the happy couple emerged from the church. Annamarie saw the bride first – a young woman with large, soulful eyes and an expression full of gentleness and compassion. Then the groom came in to view at her side, and the young witch felt her chest tighten. As though hearing the anguished cry of her heart, Emanuel Davies looked directly at her. His cheeks paled, lips parted slightly. The girl on his arm looked up adoringly, drawing his attention. He smiled, touched her cheek with his fingers, and then glanced once more towards Annamarie.

Part of her wanted to run away and hide, and never have anything more to do with anyone. *I told him to do this. She looks sweet and fair and good – very much what he needs. Not at all like me. Time to be brave.* She stepped forward, forcing a smile onto her lips. "Congratulations, both of you."

"Hello Annamarie," Emanuel said, his expression troubled.

The distinctive taste of magic filled her mouth, and the words flowed from her. "Your life together will be happy, and the child you have will be strong." She bit her tongue, managing to chew off the end of her prediction before it escaped. *There are things it is better not to know.*

"A friend of yours, Emanuel?" the new Mistress Davies enquired.

"Yes. We were at the orphanage together. Annamarie Nightshade, this is my wife, Sophie Davies."

"Pleased to make your acquaintance," Annamarie said.

"Likewise. I hope that we can be friends too."

Annamarie shook her head. "Not sure the world works that way, my dear. But it's good of you to offer."

"I don't really care how the world is supposed to work," Sophie said, conspiratorial.

"Well, we'll see then. I must be going. Make each other happy." Without waiting to see how her parting shot was taken,

Annamarie walked away. By the looks of it, Emanuel had picked a really nice girl, there could be no hating her. *That would be far too straightforward.*

Leaving the wedding party behind her, Annamarie made her way round to one of the little houses on Water Street. Much to her relief, the squint-eyed man she had seen there before answered the door and greeted her with a toothless smile.

"Can you get me a bottle of something medicinal please, Mr Jones."

"Will do lassy. I know just the thing."

Then, armed with a large quantity of homemade whiskey, Annamarie sought out the whores of Silver Street. Some things might change, but there would always be scope for keeping company with the other sort of girl, drinking spirits that might leave you blind, assuming you survived the hangover, and pretending that everything was just fine.

In the midst of her maudlin state, it occurred to Annamarie how much she had missed these things. It might not be any kind of happily ever after, but it was real, and hers, and she wasn't done with it yet.

PART FOUR
— GIFTS FROM THE SEA —

The Storm Crow

There were dark clouds chasing across the sky when he appeared. Annamarie had been standing at the window, watching the weather and contemplating the day. She could see the dirt track as it wound down the hill, and spotted the young man as soon as he emerged from the broader lane. He'd grown so much lately, although the last vestiges of boyhood still clung to him. Hands thrust deep in pockets, head angled towards the ground, he was a distinctive enough figure. She put a kettle on to boil and smiled in anticipation of her guest's arrival.

"Good afternoon to you, Annamarie," he said, voice soft as feathers. "I brought you something." He offered a bag, and she guessed it would be a fish.

"That's very kind of you, Seth. Feels like a big one. Why don't you stay and I'll cook it for both of us."

"I'd like that."

She could still see too much of the child he had been. The lost look that crossed his face sometimes. Although Seth had the makings of a very handsome man, Annamarie didn't feel entirely at ease flirting with him. He needed her more as an honorary parent, she felt. *A shame, because he's well worth looking at.* She set about cutting the already gutted fish, smiling to herself. Perhaps, many years ago, it had been like this with Jemima Kettle and Balthazar Lemon, she speculated.

"How are you keeping, Seth?" He seldom volunteered much if she didn't ask.

"Much as ever. There's dark things in the sea, hungry things. If I lived for a hundred years I wouldn't kill them all."

"Keeping to yourself, then?" She put a pan on the stove and threw a few herbs into it, watching them sizzle in the warming fat.

"Mostly. Durosimi's boy comes to see me now and then. Drustan. He's a good child."

"I've spoken to him a few times. That's a long way on little legs, though." She cut the fish up, hands working at speed.

"He's an old soul for his years," Seth smiled.

"Reminds me of someone." She stroked his cheek, feeling the first signs of stubble. "You were always old, as well. Still are."

"I know. Drustan reminds me of myself at that age. So serious, and alone. I'm glad he feels he can come to me."

"Can't be easy with those two for parents." Annamarie lowered pieces of fish into her pan, relishing the smell they made.

"There aren't many people I would willingly feed to the sea creatures, but those two..."

"Oh I know, Seth. His father was much the same."

"I do like the way you cook," Seth observed as they settled down to eat.

"I learned in self defence. Can't afford to live on cake all the while, and now it's just me up here... it was that or starve. I should keep an eye on the hiring fairs maybe, get a nice orphan girl to help me out in my dotage."

"Annamarie, you can't be thirty yet!"

"Not yet, no. I just feel very old sometimes."

"There's a storm coming tonight," Seth said. "That's what I came to tell you."

"I thought there might be, from the clouds." Her weather sense wasn't superb, but she could usually spot more dramatic shifts in the conditions, before they came.

"There will be a shipwreck."

"Ah."

"I don't know where she goes down exactly. Somewhere out on the rocks beyond the lighthouse, I think."

Annamarie nodded. "It can be treacherous out there."

"I'm taking the boat out, in case there are survivors. I was wondering if you would come with me? I could use your help."

"Alright. If we're pulling people out of the water, we'll need help with blankets and beds and hot food and all that practical stuff."

"Yes. Mister Lemon will be the closest, but I don't know how much use he'd be."

"I'll talk to him." She pondered for a while. "I'll have a word with Sophie Davies as well. She's a helpful girl." Annamarie had a feeling that in other circumstances, the Reverend's wife would have made a very good witch. She seemed to have all the right instincts, combined with a gentle, patient nature that won her considerable support. "Do you want to come in to town with me?"

"Not really. It confuses me. I get lost."

"You won't with me."

"I know, but even so, I'd rather not. I ought to go back and make sure everything is ready. There may be fighting. It depends on what the sea brings us."

"Understood. I'll be ready."

Seth smiled, his eyes seeming to look a little to her left. For a moment he seemed terribly young, making her want to cuddle him up and protect him from whatever dangers awaited them both. *No ulterior motives there Anna,* she mocked herself, silently.

Shipwrecks always attracted attention, and not always of a good kind. Broken boats often strewed goods onto the beach, and all manner of things might be salvaged. The islanders depended on such accidents for new goods. Ships arriving intact and of their own choice were so very rare. She had heard stories, of how the fight to claim goods often led to violence, of islanders who had died in the surf thanks to their neighbours. People from the ship might be left to die in preference for taking whatever was of value. If word got out that a wreck was expected, the beach would be heaving with the least helpful people Hopeless could provide.

She could tell Sophie Davies, and trust that the young woman wouldn't breathe a word. It meant a visit to the orphanage, but she didn't mind that. Since Emanuel and his wife had taken over, the place didn't seem quite so grim. They at least tried to be kind to the children in their care.

Approaching Pallid Rock, Annamarie saw her quarry cutting rosehips. There were a lot more flowers at the orphanage now.

"Hello Sophie."

She rose, the movement very slightly awkward. "Hello Annamarie! How lovely to see you."

"Can I have a quick word?"

"By all means. Would you like to come in for a cup of tea?"

"I don't really have time." She went on to explain about the anticipated wreck, watching Sophie's face cloud with concern.

"I'll do everything I can to help, be assured of that." She rested her palm against her stomach, in a gesture Annamarie had seen a lot of women make over the years.

"Ah," Annamarie said, and nodded. "How long?"

"A little over a month." Sophie blushed. "I've not told anyone."

"Wise. It doesn't always work out. Three months and you'll start to show. Tell people then."

Sophie smiled. "I'm a little nervous."

"Of course you are. Everyone is. If you need any help, you come to me."

"I will. Thank you." She turned large eyes towards Annamarie. "Do you have..."

Sensing the form the question would take, she interrupted. "I know more than enough, don't you fret."

"I'll see you at the lighthouse then. What time do you think?"

"After the storm breaks. And make sure you wrap up warm, Mistress Davies."

"I will."

Annamarie set off to warn Balthazar Lemon. A melancholy mood descended on her as she headed out to the coast. There were things she had long ago chosen not to have in her life, but they still gave her pangs of regret now and then.

Riding the White Horses

They sailed from Seth's beach, where a gentle slope between land and water meant the breakers weren't so insane.

"You can't do this in a frock! Let me lend you some pants," he protested.

"I do everything dressed like this. I'll be fine. Don't worry."

Even here, the wind drove wild breakers into the shore and by the time they were afloat, Annamarie was soaked to the skin. Gusts tore her hair loose from its fastenings, and every wave sent water into the small craft. She bailed, and left the rowing to Seth. The light was fading fast, storm clouds hastening the end of the day. Balthazar's lighthouse sent a golden beam of light across the bay, offering some hope in the encroaching darkness.

"There!" She could just make out the ship, its sails torn by the gale.

"I see it."

Further out the swell was enormous, plunging the boat down and throwing it high.

"They've no control over her," Seth shouted. "Even if they see the lighthouse, it won't help them."

"It's a long way out. Can we make it that far in this little thing?"

"No, not in this weather. I'll go as far as I can, but further out the waves would turn us over. Unless you can do something?"

"I can try." She considered the boat. It was larger than anything she normally moved, but was floating well enough by itself. "Tell me what you need the boat to do, I need to understand."

"We have to ride the waves, and not take on too much water, or roll."

"I'll see what I can manage."

Shutting out the sounds of wind and wave, Annamarie closed her eyes and tuned in to the motion of the small fishing craft. She could feel the way the waves moved beneath them, lurching more dangerously as they approached more open waters. Thinking about the relationship between wood and water, she focused her mind and magic on keeping the little vessel the right way up. It made her head hurt. The waves fought against her, but did not manage to swamp them. From somewhere behind her came the ominous crack of wood splintering against rock. For a moment she thought they had grounded on something, and as she panicked, the boat floundered.

"They've hit," Seth called out.

She bit her lip and willed the boat to stabilise. "Can you tell if there's anyone to rescue?"

"No! Not a soul. I can't feel anything." He paused. "It's not a big ship, but even so, there must be someone. Would take at least half a dozen. Maybe they're dead already. I've no sense of them."

Annamarie risked a quick look. Waves dashed the ship into the rocks, wood splintering under the assault. One of the masts came down, and the next wave turned the vessel onto her side. "I don't see anyone. We should go back."

"No wait, there's someone in the water. I can feel it now. I'll try and get nearer."

The storm tore into them. It was as much as Annamarie could do to keep them afloat, and the continual rocking motion made her feel sick. Seth stood, with poise and balance that surprised her. He lifted a coil of rope from the bottom of the boat, and cast one end into the waves. Annamarie could see nothing through the wall of rain. "This is mad. He's never going to make it to us."

"No, he has the rope. I can feel the drag. I just need to pull him in. Keep the boat as steady as you can."

The waves caught them, tilting them up at an angle, despite her efforts to resist. She could not tell how the young man kept on his feet or avoided being thrown into the spray.

"Lean out to your left, as far as you can!" Seth shouted.

The boat lurched, tipped by the weight of another person. Annamarie leaned, and willed, and prayed to whatever gods ruled the waters that they would get out of this alive. A thud and gasp told her their passenger was aboard, and she retreated inside the profile of the boat again.

"Is there anyone else?" She asked.

"I don't think so. Let's get him ashore." Seth sat, reaching for the oars. "Either we fight the currents, or I try and beach us here."

"Which is safest?" she shouted over the wind.

"No idea, but this is quickest."

"Quick is good."

"Help me then."

The storm carried them, each wave pushing the boat back towards the island. This bay had a lot of rocks in it, some protruding, others hidden beneath the waters and doubly treacherous. It wasn't an easy place to bring a boat in safely when the weather was fair. In these conditions, the odds were very much against them. Annamarie had no idea what she was doing, or what would help. The boat groaned.

"We've hit rock!" Seth shouted.

Annamarie lifted the small craft. It took all the strength she had to raise it an inch, but the grinding noise ceased, and the bottom of the hull did not splinter. Gasping for breath, she peered into the darkness, wondering how much further they had to go. The lighthouse seemed close by, but heavy rain made it impossible to tell.

"Steady there!" came a cry from somewhere ahead.

"Hello there!" Seth hollered back.

They crunched against gravel as lanterns appeared out of the night.

"I'm amazed anyone could survive out there," Reverend Davies said.

Annamarie heaved a sigh of relief.

"The sea's angry tonight. Very angry. Hungry as well. She'll have her fill of flesh, you can be sure," Balthazar Lemon said.

"Well, she's not taken us," Annamarie said. "And we got one of the crew from the ship."

"Annamarie? What on earth are you doing here?" The Reverend sounded shocked.

"Helping," Seth said as he jumped from the boat. "We need to get him into the warm."

Between them they hauled the sailor out of the small boat and onto the beach. Seth and Balthazar took him, and headed off into the night, leaving her alone with Emanuel.

"Here, take my hand."

Annamarie accepted the assistance. Her legs trembled as she clambered out. Sodden, exhausted and no longer buoyed up by the adventure, she was glad of help.

"You turn up in the most unexpected places," Emanuel said. "Sophie is waiting at the lighthouse; we had best get you there as well."

They walked up the beach together, neither speaking.

Sophie had worked her own domestic magic. The stove glowed cheerfully, filling the kitchen with warmth. She had a kettle boiling, blankets at the ready and a pot of broth bubbling as well.

Balthazar Lemon hopped from one foot to the other, clearly as perplexed as he was enchanted by the woman who had transformed his domain.

"Oh you poor dears!" Sophie exclaimed. "You're soaked through as well. We must get you out of these wet things before you catch your death of cold."

Annamarie stripped off her saturated jacket and handed it over. The rest of her dress followed. A stunned silence filled the kitchen – she knew full well just how improper it was to have stripped to her undergarments in mixed company, but there were advantages to being a witch. The usual rules did not apply in the same ways. Sophie handed her a blanket and she wrapped it round her shoulders, rendering herself decent.

"Well, that was a sight to rouse a half dead man."

She hadn't given much thought to the sailor. Wrapped in a blanket and propped in a chair, she guessed he too had abandoned sodden attire. Warm enough to be able to think, Annamarie looked him over. Dark eyes. A dangerous smile. There was something feral and hungry looking about him. It made her shiver in a most unfamiliar way.

"Emanuel, let me hold this blanket up for you." Sophie set about parting her stunned husband from his waterlogged attire. "And you too, young man."

"I'm well enough," Seth said. "My coat is oilskin, I am not overly wet."

"Then you can make tea and give the broth a stir," the young woman instructed him.

Annamarie settled in a chair, enjoying the sight of someone else organising everything for a change. Quiet she might be, but Sophie Davies clearly knew how to get her own way. Casting a sidelong glance at the rescued man, Annamarie found him staring in her direction. Caught staring, he didn't look away, but continued to watch her.

"What's your name, stranger?" she asked.

"Oh, I get called all sorts of things, depending on who you ask."

"Yes, well, I am asking you," she said, sharply.

"You, my pretty, can call me Joshua."

His tone irritated her, but she liked the compliment none the less. Rounds of introductions followed as Emanuel Davies took it upon himself to try and make the situation more socially normal.

"Mistress Nightshade," Joshua said, chewing her name over between his lips. "An unusual name, for a most unusual woman."

"I should be going," she said.

"Your things are still wet!" Sophie protested.

"I'll live."

Putting them on was unpleasant, but she had the overwhelming urge to be somewhere else, and on her own.

Beachcombing

The storm blew out during the night, and in its wake came a warm and gentle day. Annamarie felt like walking, so she ambled up to Seth's cottage. He had his boat out of the water and was working on its battered hull.

"Nice day," she said by way of a greeting.

"This will take some fixing," he replied. "It was a close run thing last night."

"I thought I'd see if anything's come in. Everyone else will be round by the lighthouse I expect." This quiet stretch of beach sometimes had things wash up; the currents sweeping across the bay from the lighthouse deposited odd items there.

"I picked up a lot of wood this morning. There may be other things. I've not looked far," Seth replied.

Annamarie set off along the beach, whistling to herself and scanning the shore. A small wooden box caught her eye, and she waited for the small waves to bring it in. According the words painted on its exterior, it contained tea. Whooping with glee, she raced up the beach, hair blowing around her face. Seth lifted his head towards her approach. For a moment it seemed like he was the old, sensible one and she barely out of childhood, not the other way round.

"I don't think the water's got into it!" she called out. "I've got a whole box of tea."

He smiled at this. "You can stash it in the cottage if you wish. I'll keep it safe for you."

"Bless you lad! We can open it together, later." She raced off again, enjoying the freedom to move and the sea smell in the wind. There were days when she felt skittish and carefree.

She saw a hat bobbing in the water, just the crown breaking the surface. Thinking it might dry out and be of service to someone, Annamarie stepped into the shallows to retrieve the item. It felt heavier than she had anticipated, and at first she assumed this was due to its waterlogged state. As she pulled it free, the head gear parted company from the weight within it, dropping a bloated, blood drained head neatly on the sand at her feet. It looked wan and slimy, like a dead fish. Annamarie swore. She wasn't especially squeamish, but even so, severed heads were not her idea of a cheerful find. She'd been prepared for the possibility of corpses, but they tended to come up whole, if they'd drowned. Sometimes the dead arrived having been chewed, there being plenty of things in the sea that would enjoy human flesh. Even that she could stomach. Something about the head disturbed her, but she could not place where the discomfort came from. Lifting it by the hair, she moved the remains above the high tide mark for someone else to deal with.

The sea had other grim offerings for her that morning. Three feet. Two with shoes that did not match, and another without. Two left hands, one of which was missing the fingers. A mess of innards that could have been human, but might just as easily have belonged to something else for all she knew. A lump of flesh and splintered bone that could have been someone's thigh. She'd never seen anything like it. Once the nauseated woman reached the beach's far end, she could hear foragers in the next bay, shouting to each other. Annamarie climbed the rocky outcrop to see over the top. As she had anticipated, there were plenty of townsfolk out scavenging. They had discovered body parts too by the looks of it, and Reverend Davies seemed to be in charge of collecting up the pieces. She waved to him and set about scrambling over the seaweed encrusted stones. When the tide was high, you couldn't get from this beach to the next without going inland.

"Good morning, Annamarie," the Reverend called out as she dropped down onto his side of the rocks.

"I see you're attending to the dead."

"I am. Although not one of them has come in whole, I do not know how many poor souls we have to bury."

"There's more back there. Severed parts, and a head."

He nodded, expression grim. "I'll send one of the Jones boys round with a wheelbarrow. I think we will have to make one grave for them all, I cannot sort out what belongs to whom." He shuddered, the work evidently having taken a toll.

"It is peculiar," she said. "I wondered what happened."

"I have no desire to know. I've sent my poor Sophie home, she was quite sick."

"Seems quiet enough now, at least."

"I think our more gruesome finds have reduced people's hunger for material things. Although some of the children are taking far too much delight in it all, I think."

"Some children are like that."

He shook his head.

Realising the extent of his discomfort, Annamarie changed tack. "How is the survivor doing, do you know? I suppose I ought to look in on him."

"I've not spoken with him yet today. I should ask him the names of his crewmates so that we can say prayers for all of them."

"I'll come with you, then."

"Doctor Willoughby and Doctor Bentley both came to have a look at him this morning, I gather," Emanuel said as they walked along the shore.

Annamarie sighed melodramatically. "Well with a bit of luck he'll still be alive in spite of them."

Balthazar appeared to have collected every scrap of rubbish from the beach. A heap of broken, unidentifiable and otherwise useless objects stood outside his abode. The lighthouse owner was nowhere to be seen, his door left slightly ajar. Emanuel Davies knocked.

A recognisable voice responded. "Hello? Come in, it's open."

Joshua was in the same chair as the night before, but dressed now. He had breeches that came to his knees, showing muscular legs, dark from sun tanning and thick with hair. Bare feet stretched towards the fire. A yellowed shirt covered his body, the open collar revealing the dense growth on his chest. Annamarie swallowed hard and tried not to stare.

"Good morning both of you," Joshua said. "I'd offer you a drink, but I'm half afraid to touch the old man's contraptions. They all look dangerous to me."

"Most of them are, although I don't think that's his intention when he builds them." Annamarie took a seat. "How are you feeling today?"

"Much better for seeing you, my lovely. You're a far better tonic than anything the Doctors could suggest."

"Quacks," she muttered.

"Anna," Emanuel cautioned. "They are professionals."

"Professional my arse. I don't know where they get their ideas from. When they've finished making a mess of folk, I'm the one who has to sort things out. Don't tell me they are professional."

"I do like a girl with spirit," Joshua said, evidently amused.

"Don't you start either, Mister. Flattery won't get you anyplace at all with me. Save that for the girls in town. I'm sure they'll be much more interested in your exotic good looks and smooth tongue than I am."

"Oh, it's a very smooth tongue, you should try it."

Annamarie blushed scarlet, and was glad to hear Emanuel clear his throat. "Mister Sullivan, as you seem to be recovered, I was wondering if you could tell me the names of your comrades so that we can pray for them."

"They're all dead then?"

"All but you it seems. I'm sorry."

"Will you bury the bodies, Reverend?"

"We will, at least, what we can find of them."

"Ah."

Annamarie studied his face. The man seemed distracted. "What happened out there?" she asked.

He met her gaze with eyes so dark she though the pupils might actually be black. "I don't remember anything much. The storm, fighting to keep the ship going, the mast breaking, being in the sea. It's a bit of a blur after that." He spoke calmly, but there was something else in his eyes.

"When you are ready to find employment, come and see me, and I will make arrangements for you," the Reverend offered.

"Very kind of you, but it won't be necessary. Just put me on the first boat out of here."

"Ah," Emanuel said.

"Oh," Annamarie echoed. "There are no boats out of here."

"What? Then I suppose I'll have to wait for the next one to stop by. Don't you have a ferry to the mainland?"

"We don't," Emanuel confessed.

"Ah well, no doubt there'll be something along in a week or so."

"I'm sorry Mister Sullivan. The only boats that usually come here are shipwrecked, like you. People don't leave. I'm sorry, that's just how it is." He twisted his hat in his hands, gaze turned away.

"I see. Then I guess we'd better find me a job and a place of my own."

"I'll talk to some people, see what I can arrange," Emanuel promised.

"I'll be off then," Annamarie said.

"Wait, Mistress Nightshade. I didn't get to thank you or the boy properly. You two saved my life. I won't forget that."

"I hear you, Joshua," she said. "Or should I call you Mister Sullivan?"

"Joshua's fine. Perhaps I'll stop by and see you some time."

"Fish Hill," she said, and departed before the intensity of his gaze could make her feel any more uncomfortable.

Death Patterns

There wasn't much to do at the Jones' farm. Hester had given birth aided by her husband, who had brought a lot of other things into the world. "And babies aren't so different from piglets when you get down to it," he had pointed out. It was her second child, and she had the kind of hips for shelling them out every few years.

"So what are you calling this fine fellow?" Annamarie asked, having checked the new arrival over.

"Perseverance, I thought."

Annamarie grinned. "Percy for short."

"I thought so. I wish I'd thought about that a bit more with Politeness. He doesn't abbreviate well."

"If he'd been a girl you could have shortened it to Polly."

"Hindsight is a wonderful thing." The new mother smiled and gazed adorningly at her sons.

"You might not want to think about having another one right off. I'm guessing you must have caught with Percy just as soon as Politeness stopped breast feeding, yes?"

"About then, yes."

"Well if you don't want another right away, I can get something that will help."

"I'm not sure about it." She looked uncomfortable. "I'm not sure if that's right. Wouldn't it be a sin?"

"You wouldn't be harming anyone, just pacing the babies a bit so that you can really look after them well."

"Well, now you put it that way..." Annamarie smiled. That usually did the trick. Jemima had felt very strongly about women having options, and had passed the philosophy along.

"I'll bring you something. Now, try and get as much rest as you can, although I think you should be fine. He's nice and quiet that one, isn't he?"

"He's a pet."

As she was leaving, Authenticity Jones stepped up to her.

"Anything the matter, Mister Jones? You look troubled."

"Well, there is something I was hoping you might have a look at."

"Of course." She supposed it would be another three legged chicken, or a cow that had 'gone strange' – a problem the Jones farm frequently encountered.

Following Authenticity out into one of the fields, she yawned heavily. It had been a busy few days and sleep kept evading her.

"Now, I don't reckon it was an animal, it just doesn't look right. I know it's not the sort of thing you'd do at all, but I was wondering if it might be some kind of dark magic. What do you think?"

Annamarie studied what remained of the cow. Horns, bones, sinews, hooves and the tail. Blood stained the grass, and there were flies buzzing over a pile of entrails. Two things occurred to her – firstly that it all looked rather too tidy, and secondly, a feeling that the animal had been pulled apart. It reminded her of something, but she couldn't quite think what.

"Happened last night. Didn't hear a thing or see any lights. You'd think, if someone did that to a cow, well... you'd expect to hear something."

"But you didn't?"

"My old Dad found her this morning, right upset he was."

"I should think so."

"What do you reckon it is then, Missus? Is it bad magic?"

"I don't think so. Not that I'm any expert." *But I really can't imagine Durosimi in a field much less touching a cow, so that's our most likely source of evil magic ruled out straight off.*

"It's times like this make me wish there was someone to go to," Authenticity Jones said. "Someone with authority who could sort things out and fix things up right."

"Ah. Has Doc Willoughby been talking to you about his council?"

"How did you know?"

"Just a lucky guess. Think about it, what can anyone do? Doesn't matter how much authority you give a person, they still can't put the bits of a dead cow back together in any way that's going to work." The image of a zombie cow floated across her mind. *If you can do it with people, no doubt you can do it with cows, but no one in their right mind...* She paused. There were people who would, just to see if it could be done, she feared. "Don't worry about it," she said. "I don't reckon it's black magic. Might be someone's idea of a joke."

Walking home, she pondered this latest mystery. In hard winters, people had been known to steal each other's livestock, but traditionally you took the whole thing. It wasn't like times were difficult, so need couldn't be a motivation. It was a very odd thing to do as a prank – a lot of trouble to go to. *If dismembering mammals is your idea of fun, why not leave the bits somewhere a bit more obvious? And what happened to the flesh and hide?* She considered the torn skin, and her impression that no blades had been used to break up the carcass. *And there's another thing. No one walks into a field and tears a cow apart, that doesn't make sense, so I must have misread things.* She growled to herself. *Bloody stupid island. There's always some damn fool thing or another to deal with. I'd like to see Doc Willoughby come up with a council that could sort out this one.*

She cut through the woods, approaching the cottage by a small track. As she reached the edge of the trees, Annamarie saw there was someone loitering by her front door. Pausing, she studied the figure. Tall. Broad. Leaning against her wall like he owned the place. *Joshua Sullivan.* She growled and retreated back into the trees. *And what on earth does he want with me? Nothing good. No doubt come round to pay me more compliments so he can have a laugh at my squirming. I don't think so, thank you very much.* She stopped walking. *It's my bloody house! Damn him if I'm going to let him keep me from my own front door.* Turning, she headed back.

"Did you want something?" she asked, coming upon him from behind. Seeing him jump gave her no small amount of satisfaction.

"Well, you did invite me over, so I thought I'd be neighbourly and come by."

"I did not invite you over, I merely mentioned where I live. But, since you're here, and since I was going to make myself a cup of tea anyway, you might as well come in for a moment."

"Are you always this friendly?" he asked.

"This is me being extra specially nice, being as how you are a stranger to these parts and friendless and whatnot."

"I wouldn't want to get on the wrong side of you then."

"No, you wouldn't." She put the kettle on to boil and fed more wood to the stove. "So, have you found something to do with yourself?"

"I'm still asking around. Mostly what I'm good at is sailing, but there's not much call for that, I'm finding."

"There are fisher folk, perhaps one of them would take you on."

"I've asked, but no one has so far."

"Or perhaps one of the farms could use your labours. You look strong enough."

"No luck there either."

Annamarie sighed. "Well I'm sure I don't know what to do with you."

"Can't you think of anything?" The tone of his voice was playful, and struck her as being suggestive.

With fists on hips she stared at him, obliged to look up, which slightly undermined the effect she'd been aiming for. "Mister Sullivan, what exactly is it you want from me?"

He grinned. "This."

Before Annamarie had time to object, Joshua swept her up in his arms, bent her over backwards and kissed her until she could barely breathe. She thumped him repeatedly, but it made no odds. When he let her up, she kicked him in the shins. "What do you think you're playing at?"

"Ah, you're irresistible when you're angry," he said, and kissed her again. This time she didn't fight quite so hard. "And I think you want this."

"I most certainly do not," she said, but somehow her arms had found their way around his broad shoulders. "I hardly know you."

"Then get to know me. There's wildness in you. I can see it in your eyes."

"Hmm." This time she was the one kissing him.

The Ill-Fated Creatures

This is very peculiar, I'd agree," Annamarie said. She considered the horns, hooves and entrails of what had once been a goat. "No idea how it happened, I suppose?"

Herb Chevin scratched his head. "No idea. Can't think what would do that to a goat. Mighty peculiar. That's why I thought I'd have a word with you."

"There was a cow over at Jones's farm last week. Very much the same."

"Oh." Herb Chevin considered this. It appeared to be a difficult thought. "Same thing done it, you reckon?"

"It would seem likely, yes."

"Some sort of wild animal I suppose. I'll get my bow out. If it shows up again, I'll shoot it."

"Whatever it is," Annamarie said, dryly.

"Yeah, well, whatever's doing this, it isn't normal... it's got to be funny looking, right? So if I see anything that looks a bit odd, I'll shoot it, and that'll be just fine."

"You be careful, Herb, anything that can do this to a goat, has got to be dangerous."

"It won't have a bow though, and I will, so I reckon it won't stand a chance."

Annamarie knew better than to argue with him, so she smiled and said her goodbyes. Taking her broomstick, the troubled witch flew from this farm to the Joneses, then over the woods. The whole mutilated animals business bothered her enormously. She could understand Authenticity Jones wanting there to be some kind of authority to take such issues to. Right now she could fancy handing over the problem, but who was there? The ostensibly great and good of Hopeless were an underwhelming bunch: Doc Willoughby, seldom sober and far too self important. Elderly Percival Jones with his printing press and newsletter. Elgar and Vortigern Frog, last vestiges of a founding family. Durosimi, who might possibly have summoned the goat-eating beast. Reverend Davies. *Oh yes, the community pillars of Hopeless. The only one who might know anything useful is the one I really don't want to talk to.* With a sigh, she turned the broom south.

These days, Durosimi's crumbling house smelled wrong from quite a distance away. She'd loathed the place in his father's day, but it was worse now. Landing, she almost fell over a boy with leaves in his hair. "Hello Drustan."

"Hello Annamarie. I've built a den. Do you want to see it? I'm going to live out here. Then when I'm bigger, I shall go and live with Seth."

She crouched down next to him. "I think that's a really good plan."

"Don't tell mother. She'd be cross. She's cross about everything I do. And everything I don't do. That's why I'm going to live out here instead." He was terribly serious.

"Seth likes you."

"Mother doesn't like me going over to see him, but she doesn't like me being under her feet either," he sighed. "Sometimes I wonder why she had me in the first place." He looked so forlorn, Annamarie wanted to hug him.

Instead she opted for offering a distraction. "Shall I tell you a secret?"

"Yes please."

"I can't stand your mother either."

He grinned at this. "I don't think she likes you very much. Mind you, I don't really think she likes anyone apart from herself."

"You might be right there." Annamarie dug about in her pocket and retrieved a pair of hard sweets wrapped in brown paper. The boy's eyes lit up as she passed them to him. "I need a word with your father," she said.

"Good luck. I'll let you in."

The hall was full of smoke. Annamarie coughed, shouted "Hello?" and wiped her streaming eyes on her sleeve. There were feathers in the smoke, and sharp things that raked at her skin. She flailed arms, trying to push them away, but made contact with something more substantial. Durosimi yelped and swore.

"What are you playing at now?" she asked, making no attempt to hide her irritation.

The air cleared at little as Durosimi opened the door further. "Just an experiment. They should die in a little while."

There were forms in the unsavoury air. She could see them now, all sharpness and anger. "So this is how you pass the time, is it? Playing with unnatural things."

"I'm getting rather good at shaping them," he said, evidently too pleased with himself to notice her tone of disapproval.

"I'll come straight to the point, Durosimi. Have you made anything lately that's got out?"

"Oh, one or two things no doubt. Why, have you caught one?"

"Not yet. Anything that could tear a goat apart?"

He chuckled. "I have yet to shape and summon the kind of thing that would tear goats. I will admit, the dismembering of domesticated animals had not been one of my priorities."

"Right. So you don't know anything about this, then?"

"About what, dear Annamarie? You really aren't making sense."

"Something tore up a goat on the Chevin's farm this morning."

"Ah, I have never taken much interest in animal husbandry, I'm afraid. For all I know, goat tearing could be one of those charming rural practices that you country folk do to while away the monotony of long evenings."

She stared at him, hands on hips.

"I jest, Annamarie."

"I'm not laughing. This is serious."

"I'm sure it's very important to you. Forgive me if the subject does not inspire any enthusiasm whatsoever."

"What if there was some kind of creature, a powerful, perhaps demonic one at large on the island. Would you be interested in that?"

"Ah, now you have my attention. Yes, that would interest me."

"Then you can help me find out what it is, and catch the thing."

Durosimi's eyes gleamed. "If I catch it, I get to keep it."

"So long as it's not rampaging about, you can do whatever you please with it."

"Then I think we have a deal."

Flying home, she chewed over an uncomfortable theory that had been developing in her mind. She thought about the goat, the cow and the shipwrecked bodies and wondered if there might be a connection. What if there had been something else on that ship? Something hungry and dangerous that had slaughtered the crew, and now roamed free on Hopeless? The timing was suspicious. Bad enough to think there might be something killing the livestock, but if it had a taste for people as well, this could get very nasty. She contemplated warning people – assuming anyone believed her ideas. But would that make things better, or worse? There would be others like Herb Chevin digging out bows and improvising weaponry, and then shooting anything remotely unfamiliar.

By the time she reached the cottage, Annamarie had settled on keeping this to herself. As yet she had no plan for finding or stopping whatever was at large. If it was striking once a week, that gave her some time to think and make plans. *Oh for an apprentice! This would be so much easier with a few extra hands.* She sighed. Although she'd been keeping an eye out, there hadn't been any suitable young folk that she'd seen. *Just me then. Better come up with a good plan.* Whatever was out there could no doubt tear her apart as easily as it had the cow. She didn't at all fancy that sort of demise. *No wild heroics. Whatever it is, it does not get to eat me.*

A Seed of Suspicion

I f he had turned up carrying flowers, Annamarie told herself she would have turned him away. She'd seen enough – men who bought favour with pretty things of no real value, and who would treat their women with no more respect than those pretty, useless gifts. Men with flowers were not good news. Joshua Sullivan had a whetstone in his hand when he knocked on the door.

"What do you want?" Annamarie said.

"To see your sweet face and bask in the warmth of your greeting," he said with a leer.

"Either you've gone mad or your jokes are getting worse. I don't think there's much hope for you whichever it is."

"I've come to sharpen your knives, axe blades and anything else in need of a keen edge. So your tongue won't need any help from me."

A flush blossomed on her cheeks and she turned away in the hopes of hiding it.

"Not for sharpening," he added in a lower tone.

"You do take some liberties, Mister Sullivan."

"Only because you want me to." He kissed her, stealing away all thoughts of anything else for a while.

"I thought you were here to sharpen things," she said, one hand on his shoulder, the other at his waist.

"I'm working my way round the island, seemed as good a reason as any to drop by and see you. Although I'll not charge you for my services."

"I should think not. Right, let's find some blunt things for you to sort out then, shall we?" She let go of him reluctantly, and followed him to the bench outside when he went to work.

"I'll just keep you company awhile. There's some things I've been meaning to ask you, Joshua."

"In which case the answer is, yes, I'd be delighted to stay tonight and warm your bed for you."

"Joshua!" She slapped his arm. "That wasn't what I was going to ask at all."

"That's a shame. Can't blame me for trying though."

"It's about your ship. I want to know what happened to the crew."

He started working one of her kitchen knives over the stone, turning the blade. "They all drowned, that's what I heard. I don't remember much about that night."

"We didn't find whole bodies. Only pieces. I picked up some of them myself, and it was grisly work." She watched his face, but no flicker of response showed there. The only sound was the swish of metal on stone. "They didn't drown, I don't reckon. I think they were torn apart."

"What makes you say that?"

"In the last few weeks, we've had a cow and a goat torn apart on the island. Never heard of anything like that before in all my life. It's very queer. And the more I think about it, the more curious it seems. The timing, with your ship, and all those dead sailors."

"I don't see how that adds up at all. You could make a good story out of it to frighten the young ones, but that's about all."

"I've seen a fair few things in my time, Joshua. Dark and terrible things. I know when there's something odd going on, and it most certainly is now. I'd lay good money there was something on that ship of yours, and now it's on my island. I want to know what it is, and I don't want it causing any trouble or killing folk."

He stopped sharpening the blade and looked up at her, expression impenetrable. "It's an interesting story, Mistress Nightshade."

"How long were you at sea, before the wreck?"

"That time, a couple of weeks."

"Anything unusual about the boat, or the voyage?"

"Not that I recall."

"Anyone die before you hit the rocks?"

He looked down at the knife, examining the blade. "Nope."

"You're not a terribly good liar, Joshua. I can see you're hiding something from me. You could save us both a good deal of trouble and tell me what you know. Don't worry if it sounds crazy. I'm used to crazy."

He met her gaze again. "You're a very strange woman and no two ways about it."

"I'm a very persistent woman, and I'm going to find out what's happening here."

"It'll just be some wild animal, I expect," he said.

"What sort of wild animal, would you say, turns up on an island where it's not been before and starts tearing goats to pieces? I expect you know a lot more about the world than me. So you tell me what kind of animal does that, and how it got here. I suppose it must have swum, or flown. You'd think something new and that big, someone would have seen it."

"I don't know. I'm just a sailor."

"Our local magician is very interested in demons," she said, making her tone conversational as though this was the most natural thing to mention.

"I don't believe in demons," Joshua said.

"Neither do I. Don't need to. I've seen a few. I don't believe in this table, or that window. They don't call for much believing in either. I trust what I see." She fell silent for a while, wondering how much to say. "Durosimi O'Stoat summons them, I gather. Has done for years."

"So maybe you should be talking to him about your goat problem."

"Have done, and he doesn't think it's anything of his making though. He's interested, mind you, and on the lookout. He'd love to catch whatever came off your ship, and subject it to his will, or whatever it is he does. I'm no expert."

Joshua put both knife and whetstone down. He didn't look at her. A thought crept across Annamarie's mind. It was so wild and alarming a notion that she almost put it aside. The broad shoul-dered man turned his head towards her, and for the first time she saw something vulnerable in his face. Fear, perhaps, or uncer-tainty. She couldn't tell exactly what.

He spoke slowly, head turned away as if he was addressing someone else. "I'd imagine, a creature like that wouldn't survive long on an island this small. Someone would be bound to catch it and kill it."

"I expect so." Annamarie kept her voice carefully neutral.

"Even if it was very clever, didn't strike in the same place twice, didn't kill with any kind of pattern."

"That's the one," Annamarie said. "Something that strong and dangerous would frighten folk, and they'd hunt for it, and if they could, they'd kill it."

"And if for some reason it killed a person..."

"They'd look a lot harder and find it a lot faster."

"And there's no way to leave?"

"No."

He fell silent, gazing intently at his hands. "Sooner or later then, someone's going to catch your creature and kill it, and that'll be the end of the problem for you."

"That seems the most likely outcome yes, but not inevitable. I think there might be other ways of resolving this."

"I doubt it. I'd better get this lot sharpened and be on my way."

"I'll leave you to work, but don't go without saying goodbye."

"I won't."

She went back into the cottage, and paced the kitchen, picking over his words to see if they might have other meanings. "Bugger." She repeated the word a few times, but it didn't help in the slightest. "What is it with me and men? Why don't I like the nice quiet sensible safe ones?" Part of her wanted to ask him to stay, but the implications were daunting, and he was definitely hiding something. Until she knew what, keeping him at a distance would be a lot safer. She went back outside and offered him a mug of tea, saying nothing until he'd consumed it. "Stay with me tonight."

His eyes widened.

"Don't you dare tell me you were jesting before. Stay here tonight, with me."

He growled. "I can't. Believe me, I want to, but I can't."

"Are you seeing someone else then?"

"No it's not that... it's just not a good time for me... I..."

She watched him flail. "It wasn't a question, it was more a statement of fact. You are staying with me tonight. That tea's going to kick in any moment now and..."

There was a flash of surprise on his face, then Joshua Sullivan toppled off the bench and landed face down on the ground.

Sleepless

Even with a little magic to smooth the process along, Joshua Sullivan took some moving. Annamarie dragged him to Jemima's old room. She kept the bed made up in case of visitors, although no one had previously used it. Just to be on the safe side, she tied him to the bed, and then dragged a chair through. She would sit up through the night and see what happened. By her reckoning, there ought to be another attack that night. Worst case scenario he would wake up fine and tied to a bed. The possibilities sent a flush of heat through her.

"Right then Mister Sullivan, let's see what happens," she said, making herself comfortable in the chair. "Of course it may all be in my head, but I'd like to be on the safe side, if it's all the same to you."

She read for a while, then wandered in and out of the kitchen, finding apples and biscuits to eat. The night dragged along slowly. Tired eyes and flickering candles made the watching difficult. Her vision blurred, causing Joshua's face to seem fuzzy and less than perfectly real. "Why do I put myself through these things?" she asked aloud, talking to herself to try and stay alert. "And what on earth is he going to think of me when he wakes up tied to the bed?" She laughed. "Probably better to think I had deviant sexual intentions towards him than let him know what's actually on my mind."

Joshua shifted in his sleep, arms tugging against bindings. His back arched, and he growled. Something twisted his features, making him look entirely unfamiliar. Annamarie stood up, wide awake now. *Here we go.* With no idea what might be coming, she could only hope to be adequately prepared. Her broom stood by the front door. If all else failed, she could run for it, and fly.

On the bed, her prisoner writhed, pulling against the knots that held him. Eyes snapped open, burning with malevolence and rage. The face looked more animal now than human, but not like any kind of living creature she had seen.

"Let me go!" The bellowing voice shook her.

"I don't think so. Tell me what you are."

"I am hungry. When I break these ropes, you are mine." She could see nothing of playful Joshua in that face now.

"I don't think so." *What is this?* She kept her distance, staying near the door in case it looked like the ropes might give. "Joshua Sullivan, can you hear me?"

The bound creature on the bed roared with anger and continued to fight against its restraints.

Annamarie drew a deep breath and tried to be calm. None of the books she had read, nor any of her mentor's lessons had prepared her for this. Lamashtu might be able to help, but she had not called on the creature in a long while, and preferred to keep it that way. In such circumstances, Durosimi would no doubt try and bind the creature to his will. *That's not the way either. What on earth do I do? What would Jemima do?* The answer came: Open a bottle and wait for things to improve. As a plan it had some definite merits. It might be possible to try and subdue him without taking him over completely, but she didn't feel equal to such a task.

Through the long hours of darkness, she watched him toss and struggle. Knots and ropes held true. Eventually he grew quiet and still, some time after which, Annamarie fell asleep in the chair. She woke disorientated, to find her captive watching her nervously. For a long time, neither of them spoke.

"What are you going to do with me?" he asked.

"Now that is a very interesting question. You're entirely at my mercy."

From the look on his face, he had probably worked out that she didn't mean to kill him. She experienced a rush of power, seeing that she could indeed do anything to this man. His life was in her hands.

"Annamarie, if you untie me, I swear, I won't hurt you."

"All right, but on the condition that you stay for breakfast."

"Done."

She undid the bonds, thinking how easy it would have been to take advantage of his prone body. She hadn't as much as undone his shirt. *Desdemona and Cassandra would be ashamed of me. Some bad girl I am!*

"So now you know," he said, tone resigned.

"I have some idea, yes. Something takes you over and you become violent, dangerous."

"I crave blood. Afterwards, it's like a bad dream, I remember fragments of what I've done, but it's like it was someone else, not me."

"You killed your crewmates."

"I think so, yes."

"We don't exactly have any laws round here, Mister Sullivan. We have habits, and conventions and people who see it as their job to dish out justice now and then. There are people who would hang you for what you've done, and other folk who would shrug and consider it none of their business, seeing as you hadn't harmed anyone they cared for."

"And what sort are you?"

"I'm more the second sort. But I think you're dangerous, and I don't want to find you've done something that turns me into one of the first sort."

"I can't control it. I try to, but I last a few days and then it breaks out of me. I move around a lot."

"But you were out at sea longer than you'd expected, am I right?"

"That's about the size of it, yes."

"And you lost control and started killing people."

"Most of them were dead before the storm hit us. I should have thrown the remains overboard before then, but I couldn't control the ship and I didn't know what to do." He buried his face in his hands. "Sometimes I think it would be for the best if someone just killed me and put an end to it."

"It would certainly be a straightforward solution. I could poison you."

"You'd do that for me? Let me go quietly and easily?"

"I could, yes. It's something to consider."

"Everything you said yesterday, you were right. I won't be able to hide it forever, and I can't leave. Whichever way you look at it, I'm dead."

"Oh, there may be other ways."

"I doubt it."

Annamarie smiled. "I don't believe you killed anyone last night."

"No, but what about tonight, and the night after? You can hardly drug me and tie me up every night, can you?"

"Why not?"

He raised his head and stared at her intently. "You're serious?"

"Absolutely. If it doesn't work, we may have to think about doing things differently, but it's worth a try."

"You're a remarkable woman, Annamarie Nightshade." He shook his head. "You're taking a lot of risk doing this."

She took his hands. "You've torn people apart with these," she said, examining them. They were large, strong hands but by no means abnormal.

"I can't explain. It burns in me, and my head fills up with fog. I have to make the blood flow."

"And if you lose control, you'll kill me?"

"Very likely, yes."

She considered this. "Does it only happen at night?"

"So far, but I don't know if that would change, if I didn't let it run free. It might happen more often if I didn't satisfy it."

"Understood. It's a risk I think I can live with."

He squeezed her hands. "I don't want to hurt you. I don't want to wake up one morning with your blood on me."

Annamarie flushed a deep crimson, her thoughts having turned to an altogether different way by which she might leave her blood on his skin.

Hunters and Prey

For two more nights, they fought against his nature. By day Joshua plied his new trade around the island, sharpening knives and implements. At night he came to Annamarie's cottage, to eat and flirt, trading hungry kisses. It was easier tying him up when he co-operated, and she drugged him afterwards. The monster in him rose with the falling light, making him flail and sweat, growing ugly and abusive in its thrall. Morning found him a man again, paler than before, and exhausted.

On the third morning he said, "I can't do this. It's driving me mad. I can hardly think in the day."

Weary to the core of her being, Annamarie nodded. "I don't know what else to do."

"Let me hunt tonight, let me sate it. I'll be fine for a week or more then."

"Please be careful. Don't get caught, and try not to kill anyone."

He smiled. "I could almost believe that you care about me, that your witch's heart isn't all rock after all."

"I..." She shook her head, unable to express her feelings. "I just don't want any trouble, alright?"

"Then you should never have pulled me out of the sea."

"I don't regret that." She kissed his brow. "Tonight... afterwards... what will you do?"

"Once the madness has passed, you mean? I hadn't given it much thought."

"Come to me."

Joshua closed his eyes and sighed. "You'd have me then, with blood still on my skin and my heart half wild?"

"Yes."

She slept through the afternoon, her dreams full of running and hiding. As night fell, she lit a fire and waited, unable to occupy herself for more than a few minutes at a time. *How long will it take?* For a while she felt angry that he was being so slow. Then anxiety set in as the hours passed. When dawn began to lighten the sky, her certainty that he had got into trouble grew. Unable to wait any longer, she pulled on her jacket and went out with the broom.

With no idea where he had planned to feed, Annamarie could do nothing but search from the skies, and hope for some signs of Joshua. She had visions of him having been caught, wounded, or killed even. Several times, she had to land the broom in order to pull herself together. Lamashtu would be able to find him, but she disliked seeking help from her familiar. The birds were singing. A new day had begun and every moment she wasted increased the risk that her man was going to die.

My man. Oh bloody hell! Is he? Not if I don't get him out of this mess, he isn't. Shit.

She landed. "Lamashtu? Come to me. I have need of you."

The catlike familiar appeared before her, and set about licking a paw. "Yes?"

"I need you to bring Joshua Sullivan to me, right now."

"Gladly."

Better than asking where he was, she reasoned. Whatever chaos Lamashtu caused by stealing the man, they could deal with later. Her familiar appeared again, and beside him appeared the bound and bloodied form of her goat killer.

"Blood."

She offered her hand and let Lamashtu help himself. "Are you conscious, Joshua?"

He grunted.

"I'll take that as a yes." Once the blood drinking was done, she took out her penknife and cut him free.

He stretched and groaned. "I thought I was done for."

"I take it you were caught."

"Three or four big lads. I was unlucky. But they weren't sure what I was, or what to do with me, so they knocked me out, tied me up. Last I heard they were going for the Reverend."

"Well, that's something. At least they didn't go for Durosimi. That would be much more of a problem."

"How did you rescue me?"

Annamarie pointed at Lamashtu. "I had help."

"It's as well."

"Yes." She considered the matter. "But it was luck. If someone pulls a crossbow on you, I won't be there in time. Unless..." She paused, uncertain that she wanted to be suggesting this. "Unless I go with you when you feed."

"I can't promise I wouldn't hurt you."

"I know. But I can fly. If you can't reach me, you can't hurt me, yes?"

"That's very good of you."

"It's the only way I can think of to stop you getting into trouble. I'm not going to spend another night at home wondering who or what you've killed, and whether anyone has killed you."

"You keep on surprising me, Annamarie."

Worried that she had given too much away, she folded her arms and glared at him. "Good. Wouldn't want you getting bored. Can you walk?"

"I should think."

"Let's go home."

He grinned. "It'll be a while now, at any rate, before I'm too much trouble again. That's something."

She took his arm. "Are you telling me you aren't dangerous to be around, Mister Sullivan?"

"It depends on whether you're worried about being eaten alive."

She ignored the innuendo in his voice. "I'm sure I can find you something for breakfast."

"You, Annamarie. I'm not especially hungry for anything else right now."

She shivered.

Afterwards, Joshua held her with more tenderness than she had imagined any man could be capable of.

"You never said you were a maid. It never crossed my mind."

"You never asked," she laughed. "Usually I have this conversation the other way round, with Lamashtu. There's a great many things I've not told you."

He kissed her cheek. "I want to know everything."

"We'll see."

A volley of knocks on the door shattered the moment. Annamarie jumped from the bed and pulled a shawl around her shoulders to cover herself. Opening the window, she leaned out. "What is it?"

There were half a dozen people clustered around her door. At the sight of them, her heart sank. She couldn't put names to any of them, and they all looked angry.

"We need to talk to you, Mistress Nightshade. There's some sort of demon loose on the island."

"Have you talked to Durosimi O'Stoat? He knows far more about that sort of thing than I do. I expect he summoned it."

There were surprised mutters from below. Diverting their attention to Durosimi might buy her some time, but she didn't much like what was in the air.

"So you didn't call it then?" one of the men shouted up.

"Do I look like someone who consorts with demons? I'm a witch! I make potions, I deliver babies, I tell people where to find things they've lost. I don't deal with demons."

There were mutterings from beneath, then more words directed at her. "Reverend Davies says there is evil amongst us, and that we must unite and fight it."

"I'm sure he knows best." She closed the window and stepped back from it. "Drat. Damn and blast it."

"They could turn against you. They could blame you for what I've done."

"Yes they could. But with a bit of luck they'll go after Durosimi instead, and give us some thinking time."

"I owe you my life," he said, more serious than she had ever seen him before.

"In some traditions, that means I'm now totally responsible for you," she said. "How big a thing do you need to kill, to ease your bloodlust?" she asked. "Has it got to be a cow, or would a chicken do?"

"I've no idea."

Annamarie nodded. "Then we'll have to experiment a bit."

Devil's in Detail

Heat from the talisman woke Annamarie from sleep. She clutched the item, pulling it away from her neck as her eyes accustomed to the gloom. The reason it wasn't completely dark turned out to be perched on the end of the bed, glowing in sickly green and yellow tones. She had an impression of beak and bone, sharp scraping things, deadness and malevolence. It shrieked and flapped towards her, only to smack into something she couldn't see.

The sight of it filled her with rage. She rose from the bed, letting the anger build inside her. Jemima's lessons on the subject of demons had been few, and purely theoretical. However, they had been very much about dealing the messes other people made. *Don't fear them, not ever. Give them anything except your fear.* There was a demon in her bedroom. It would be easy to be terrified by this.

She pulled the rage into a tight ball, and then released it. "Get out of my house!"

The thing on the end of her bed jumped and skittered, filling the air with hideous noise. Again it lunged towards her, but failed to make contact.

"You can tell Durosimi to bugger off," she spat. "I'm not going to be intimidated, you hear me?" She stamped her bare foot on the floorboards. "Be gone from my house! You pitiful excuse for a demon. You're a joke, you know that? You don't frighten me with your bones showing and all those pointy bits. What are they supposed to be, anyway? Have you any idea how silly you look? Small children could imagine worse demons than you." It took her a while to find out how to laugh at it, but once she began, it rolled from her. Mirth shook her body, and she giggled at the foul manifestation. "Ah, you're too funny. Tell Durosimi his jokes have improved. You're a hoot. Get it? No? Never mind."

The demon looked increasingly ill at ease. It backed away from her towards the window. Annamarie kept laughing, pointing at the demon, her sides aching with it. The eerie light it had given off faded somewhat. "You've not been eating your fish then. Balthazar reckons eating fish makes you glow in the dark! Demon want a fishy?" She whipped tears from her eyes. "Now piss off out of my house."

The demon shook, uttered a final shriek and faded out of existence, leaving only a noxious smell. Trembling, Annamarie sat down on the edge of the bed. Joshua was still asleep, oblivious to the drama. "You were right," she said to the house. "I didn't believe you at the time Jemima, but you were right. Laughter. I'm going to kill Durosimi when I see him."

She was halfway to Durosimi's house when he appeared on foot, heading her way. They met in the middle of the lane, the air between them crackling with anger.

"How dare you?" she began.

"You ask me that? When you've been telling the plebs that I summon demons?"

She glared at him. "Well you do, and I don't. I'm not about to be blamed for something that isn't my fault."

"I heard about the thing on Meadow Farm. My demons are under my control, and I would not waste my energies on something so.... petty and pointless."

"You sent one of your blasted demons round to my house!"

"You needed a warning. I will not have you making life difficult for me, Annamarie. Is that understood? You do not want me as your enemy."

"I've got better things to do with my time, agreed. Don't waste your demons on me. I know how to see them off."

A subtle shift in his expression indicated that she'd touched a nerve with that remark. "How did you do that?"

She grinned. "Just because I don't summon them, doesn't mean I can't control them." Durosimi might be able to do dangerous things, but he could be thrown off balance all too easily. There were flaws in his character that kept him ineffectual and she had a fair idea how to exploit them. "Really, was that the best you could think of?"

His expression darkened further. "Do not meddle in my affairs."

"Do not send demons round to my house, thank you very much."

Durosimi rolled his shoulders, pulling himself up to full height. "I've been doing a lot of thinking lately," he said. "On the subject of demons, and timing, pondering what exactly might have come ashore from that last shipwreck."

Annamarie set her jaw and hoped her face revealed nothing.

"It is an interesting coincidence, don't you think? The shipwreck, and now a strange beast on the loose. I haven't mentioned this little theory of mine to anyone else just yet, but I might. And of course if I can think of it, there are a few others with some intellectual capacity and they might be able to draw similar conclusions."

It was supposed to be a threat. She heaved a sigh. "It's hardly any great act of brilliance to notice that the attacks on livestock happened after the shipwreck. I'm sure everyone on the island has managed that unremarkable bit of thought. Why don't you talk to Joshua about it some time?"

"I might just do that. Such a shame that he was the only survivor, don't you think?"

"Of course. But then, the wreck before this one didn't have a single survivor. The sea is harsh."

"Just one survivor. And now this business with something marauding the wildlife."

"As far as I know it's domesticated animals that have been killed. Could just as easily be kids trying to summon demons. Young folk take it into their heads to do all kinds of things."

"You know there's gossip about you and Joshua Sullivan."

"I didn't know that. Always nice to be talked about, I think, especially if it's complimentary."

"If it happened to be the case that you were lovers, and if it also happened to be the case that he's the one causing all the trouble, your situation could rapidly become a very unhappy one. You need me onside, Annamarie. You need me to feel benevolently disposed towards you. These are things I suggest you bear in mind."

"You have a remarkable imagination," she replied.

"If it was just animals of course, folk might tolerate it, but a boy got hurt the other night, and Doc Willoughby says he might not pull through. That changes things, don't you think?"

Not wanting to continue the conversation, she straddled the broom and took off. He had rattled her, and she wondered if anyone else was thinking along the same lines.

If he's killed someone... I can't think about that right now... I've got to think about that. It's a whole lot different from killing animals. He has killed people before, but this is more complicated, this is here. The slaughter of Joshua's shipmates was something she had managed to ignore. It hadn't seemed entirely real, even though she had seen the remains. The man who shared her bed had killed people before, and might have done so again. *I ought to be horrified. I ought to be handing him over so that what passes for justice around here can be done. I should be running to Emanuel. I absolutely should not be going home and trying to work out how to protect him from the consequences of his nature. Under no circumstances whatsoever should I do something stupid like falling in love with the man. Definitely not.* She looked up at the sky, and spoke aloud. "Alright world, here's the deal. I'll do everything I can to make sure he doesn't kill anyone else, but in exchange for that, I get to keep him. How does that sound?"

There was no answer, but she hadn't expected one.

Crying for Blood

The days passed, and Annamarie watched for signs of the change coming in her lover. The easy playfulness faded from his demeanour, replaced by a hunger in his eyes that she had no way of answering.

"It's coming, isn't it?" she asked him as they sat on the floor together beside her hearth.

"I can't fight it for long. A day perhaps. Then if you drug me, what, two, three days?"

She held him close, resting her head on his shoulder. "And then the need to take life."

"It's more than that. It's not enough to kill. This thing inside me... I don't know how to explain. It's brutal, full of the need to destroy, to rend and ruin."

"So it wouldn't work to arrange for you to help the butcher out once a week?"

"Not if you want anything left, no."

"Ok, think again then."

He stroked her back. "I can't run forever. If that boy had died... I'm not even sure I should be running any more. I've killed people."

"Hey, so has the Doctor," she laughed, but it was forced.

"I didn't used to think about it much, before I came here. I didn't care about what I did so long as I didn't get caught. But being with you, I am so afraid I'm going to lose control. I'd die rather than hurt you. But the one thing I cannot protect you from is me."

"Don't think about it, don't worry about it. We can find a way."

"What if we can't, Anna?"

She could hear the pain in his voice. "Is it you, this thing in your skin that goes mad and has to kill, or is it something separate that takes you over?"

"Would it make any difference?"

"It might."

"And what if I say this is me, my nature. This is what I am. What then?"

She held his head between her hands and kissed his brow. "It won't change how I feel."

Hands gripped her waist, a little too hard to be comfortable. Fingers dug into her skin. She could feel the rawness in him, and the ferocity. Reason told her to back away, but other, deeper feelings kept her on the floor beside him.

"I don't know how to do this," he said.

"We work it out together," she replied, with no idea of what to offer him. "We'll see what happens with a chicken, yes?"

"We can try." He squeezed her. "I just have a feeling it won't work."

Before night fell, they went outside together. Annamarie had bought a few chickens, intending to raise them herself. She had cleared out Jemima's outhouse, removing relics from countless witches passed, and washing away years of dust. With its flagstone floor and stone walls, it wouldn't be too hard to wash away the blood. She picked up a squawking hen, shushed it and then cast the bird into the outhouse along with Joshua. A couple of strong wooden slats held the door in place, but to be on the safe side, she resolved to wait outside. The last thing she needed was her lover escaping and causing havoc.

Above her, the stars came out one by one. The moon rose, fat and heavy on the horizon and still a few days from being full. From the outbuilding came growls and frightened bird shrieks, cut short suddenly. Then sounds of tearing and crunching. *So far, so good.* She leaned against the door frame, breathing in sweet night air and listening to the wind. *We can do this. I can keep him safe, avoid him killing anyone.* Elated, she hummed to herself, dancing in her tangled garden with moonlight shining on her hair and skin.

Once the sun crept over the horizon, Annamarie pulled the wooden bars from the door and threw it open. "Joshua? How did it go?"

He came blinking into the sunlight, smeared with blood and feathers. "It was enough," he said. "For now at least. I might need something bigger now and then, but chickens will do."

"Yes!" She threw her arms round him, not caring about the mess. "I'm not going to kiss you though, not until you wash the blood off your mouth."

He laughed. "The feather's don't taste so good either."

"You're on your own there. I am not plucking live chickens for you."

"I can live with that!" He lifted her up in the air, twirling her round. Annamarie had never felt happier.

"What a charming scene, don't you think? Shades of Beauty and the Beast perhaps."

Durosimi's voice stole every ounce of joy from her heart. Joshua lowered her to the ground and she looked about. There were two of them, and they had evidently hidden in her garden.

Doc Willoughby was brushing leaves from his coat. "A most informative night, I must say. Thank you, Durosimi. I think we've seen enough."

"What are you talking about?" Annamarie asked, hoping to bluff her way out of it.

Durosimi smiled nastily. "We've had people watching you for a while now. We know everything, Mister Sullivan. We've had our suspicions, but last night proves everything and with two of us to testify... it won't take long to sort this little matter out."

Behind her, Joshua growled. "You can't prove anything."

"We can prove enough. Run if you want to, but the island isn't that big, and we will hunt you down in the end," the doctor said.

Durosimi produced a length of rope from his bag. "Or you could save everyone the trouble and come with us now. Co-operate and we'll make sure your death is a quick, clean one."

"No," Annamarie hissed. "Get out of my garden, both of you, now." She watched them exchange looks and stand their ground. Rolling up her sleeves, she drew on her anger, filling her voice with power and menace. "Go! Leave or I will remove you both from my land." Her words landed like blows, and the pair took a step back, then retreated further.

"We'll be back," Doc Willoughby promised. "And there will be more of us. We can starve you out if needs be. Or torch your house." With that, he and Durosimi headed off down the hill.

"I should give myself up. They'll hurt you as well, and I couldn't bear that."

"If you go with them, there will be a noose, if you're lucky. And we're not talking a quick drop to break your neck; they'll hang you from a tree until you suffocate." Tears muddied her words.

Joshua caught her, holding her firm as she heaved sobs against his chest. "I thought we had it figured! I hate him. I'll kill him one of these days."

"I wish I had answers for you, but I think they will be back, and there will be more of them next time. I'd rather not have them find me here. I don't mean to drag you down with me."

"I'm in this, come what may. There's no point making it easy for them. Let me grab a few things and we can run together."

He touched her cheek, the smell of blood strong on his hand. "And then in a week or so when the bloodlust takes me? What will you do then?"

"Sit in the top of a tree if needs be. A week is a long time. I'll think of something. I'm going with you. Go and wash the blood off, and get rid of the feathers."

"I can see there's not a lot of point me arguing with you."

"Good, you're starting to get the hang of this! Now, let's get moving before they rouse up every idiot who can wield a farming implement. There's plenty of wild places. It's not such a small island. We can give them a run for their money."

"Alright then. Let's do it."

It's no different from demons. Give them anything except fear. Would that I could get rid of Durosimi just by laughing at him.

From Whence We Came

There was an abandoned cottage, deep in the woods. No obvious path ran there, and Annamarie had found it years ago, from the air. The roof had few holes, although the one window had long since lost its glass. Once she had settled on running, it seemed the logical place to go. Finding it on foot and without creating an obvious trail presented challenges, but she figured out ways around those fast enough.

Following the stream, she took them in completely the wrong direction for half a mile.

"I'm going to have to carry you for a bit," she explained.

Joshua snorted in amusement. "I doubt you could even get me off the ground."

"You might want to close your eyes, this could be unsettling. Whatever you do, don't wriggle or resist me in any way or I'll drop you. I'm staying low but even so, a mistake could be painful."

"I'll be good."

Wrapping her arms around his waist, Annamarie concentrated on lifting them both a few feet off the ground. It was radically different to using a broom, although she could not help but picture herself straddling him in the same way. Suppressing a giggle, she took them in amongst the trees, moving as fast as she dared in such a confined space.

"Whoa! Bloody hell!" Joshua gripped her tightly.

"I can't do this for too long, my arms are getting tired. But, if they use dogs this should make us harder to find, and there are no footprints for any bright spark to track. They'll assume we've walked in the stream bed and with a bit of luck will spend a long time looking for where we came out."

"People know you have a broom, won't they think of that?"

"I'm not in the habit of giving lifts, they will be looking for you on the ground, be sure of it."

"It's worth a try."

She dropped, and made a mess of landing, bowling them both over on the woodland floor. Lying together a bit tangled up, she thought this fugitive lark might not be so bad after all. They walked for a while, not talking much. Eventually the cottage came into view, with its tumbledown garden wall, and small well.

"This should do us for a few days. It's going to be bottom of the garden stew for the foreseeable, but we'll survive."

"Never heard of that kind of stew," he said.

"It's a local tradition. It's how we hide the bodies," she grinned. "So not entirely inappropriate!"

For two days, Annamarie walked the small paths near the cottage, and listened to the soil beneath her feet. She contemplated the wind, and the shapes of branches, paid attention to the fire in the hearth, lit only after nightfall. Townsfolk were searching for them, she could feel it. Every day they pushed deeper into the woods and soon they would break with the trails and risk the wilder places. They were hungry for blood. There were other things abroad too. Darker, malevolent things whose names could make a person's ears bleed. Durosimi sent them out, searching for signs of the fugitive pair. She had seen them pass overhead.

It took time and effort to make this shell of a cottage look uninhabited. She spent hours at it, shaping and reforming her illusions so that even questing demons would not find them. Never in her life had she worked magic so intensely, and it took a toll. She could not keep this up forever, which made being caught an inevitability. *The more time I can buy us, the more scope we have.* These last days had been precious beyond words, despite her weariness. *We have this, if nothing else. No matter what the future brings, they cannot take these days from us.* She looked up, finding Joshua watching her intently from nearby.

"What do you want most?" she asked.

"To be alive and with you."

"And how far would you go to make that possible?"

"I would do anything, give up anything, whatever it takes. Have you thought of something?"

"Yes. I don't know if it can be done, or what would happen if I didn't do a perfect job. I've done a lot of thinking and I don't reckon we have all that many options."

He came and sat nearer, taking her hand in his. "I can't think of any. I feel like a rat in a trap."

"I'll see if I can get you one," she said with a smile. "There may be ways, but there will be risks."

"It's not like we have much to lose, is it?"

"That's what I figured. We need to hide you where no one can find you, and where you can kill when you need to."

"So we're leaving the island then?"

"I've tried that before. It doesn't work. There's only one thing I can think of, and that's to hide you in the sea."

"I'm not a great swimmer, Annamarie, and it's bloody cold. Might work for an hour or two, but that's the best you can hope for."

"It all depends on what you are. The best of you is purely man, but what the other things are, I cannot say. I've seen enough of your monstrosity to know I can't drive that from you, but perhaps we can harness it."

"I haven't a clue what you're talking about, sweetheart."

She laughed. "I'm not sure I know either, but that's what we stake our lives on if we try this."

"You can try anything you like."

"In which case, when the sun sets, we're moving."

The stretch of beach near her family home was about as far as you could get from the town without actually getting into the sea. The tiny stone house she had once lived in lay dark and empty. Abandoned. She supposed they were all dead now, but felt little sorrow over it. The full moon bathed the duo in light, as they entered the cove.

"Take off your shoes love, and stand where the waves lap the sand."

He did so, silent and trusting.

"When you are on the land, you'll be a man, with a man's form, but when you are in the sea, you will be the creature of your blood hunger. You will never forget yourself, never become lost in your other self. This I promise."

"I accept."

She felt the flow of magic in her, growing strong on the intensity of emotion this night inspired. She took his hands, reaching into him for that which killed. Magic coursed between them, shaped by her words and feelings, and aided by his willingness. "The sea will be your hunting ground, and all that dwells beneath the waves will be yours to feed upon. Your heart will be true and your own, no matter what skin you wear."

He trembled, the monster within him rising towards the surface. Annamarie could see it there and she crooned to it, calling it out and inviting it to find its own shape.

"When you want me, come out of the water and onto the land, be your own human self again. When the hunger calls you, the sea is your home and you can hunt there in safety. I call to the shape of your dual soul. I call to what lies within you, to the need you can only answer with blood. I call the demons into your skin so that their true shape may be known." On she went, building layer upon layer of magic, wrapping it around his form and singing it into his bones. His body changed, twisting and elongating, sprouting new and startling protrusions.

"Joshua my love, hide yourself and be safe. Come to me at the next full moon."

He had nothing left resembling a human mouth with which to answer her. The face staring back at her had lost all trace of humanity.

"I'll be here on this beach when the moon is full, and I will miss you every day between here and there."

He touched her face, and what he had become felt cold and sharp against her skin. Shape did not matter. The heart inside that form was hers, and she had no doubts. "Go now, love."

He slid into the water, and she watched until every last ripple had gone.

Annamarie turned her back on the sea and headed for home. No doubt there would be questions and difficulties ahead. She meant to tell Durosimi and the others she had killed Joshua herself rather than letting them do it. With him hidden from sight, they would believe her, and there the matter would end. Her thoughts turned to the next full moon, when her lover would find his other skin and emerge from the sea. She smiled. It would be worth the wait.

THE ODDATSEA

The Prospect of Joy

LADY ALISON TIFFANY HEMPTON ADDLEBY PETTIGREW had a very long name, a very long head of hair, two very long legs and came from a very long line of somewhat eccentric English explorers and adventurers. Her grandfather, Allan Tiffany Addleby Pettigrew, had crossed the Arctic by balloon and one of her distant ancestors, Wilfred Addleby Pettigrew, had discovered the fabled Isle of Black (which subsequently disappeared in a rupture of the ocean floor sometime in the sixteenth century). Although Alison shared her surname with her illustrious, intrepid and inspired ancestors, there was one important aspect about her that was thoroughly different—her sex. She was the first of the Tiffany Hempton Addleby Pettigrew women to take up exploring.

She was a very determined young lady and despite it being unfashionable and ill-advised, she was heroically determined to outdo all her masculine predecessors, or at the very least, equal their dauntingly impressive list of achievements.

To this end, she spent her formative years pursuing all those pursuits that admirable, well-prepared, professional explorers should. She learnt about geography, navigation, survival, baritsu, fencing, horse riding and more. She mastered several languages from both European and Eastern cultures, and a number of classical writing systems. She also kept herself physically fit through hill-walking, cycling and workouts with dumbbells, medicine balls and a fitness instructor named Henry. (She always smiled when she mentioned him—I'm still not sure why.)

As you might imagine, all this was wildly unusual for a lady in society, and it was regularly remarked upon with tuts being muttered almost constantly when she occasionally mingled with the country's social set. Partly because of this, but mostly because she had little time for her fellows, she withdrew early on and kept herself to herself. This was easy enough to accomplish, given that she lived in a large mansion in the English countryside surrounded by servants, landscaped grounds and a certain air of mystery.

As I was her nephew and perpetually intrigued by this "mad" and possibly dangerous lady, I visited her often. I found her neither mad nor unfriendly; she insisted I called her Auntie Ally, which amused her—probably because she considered herself far too young to be an auntie. (Her brother, my father, was considerably older than she and had married, and then fathered, young.)

She liked to tell me of all the activities she had planned, the trips she had been on, the strange people she had encountered and the effective use of a garotte. I was captivated by her.

One hot June day, she told me of the strange rumours she had heard of a mysterious island. No-one was quite sure where it was, but the few scattered accounts she had managed to put together had indicated three things. Firstly, that it was always surrounded by a strange mist. Secondly, that a handful of tales told of people and ships disappearing near the island—but remarkably—not one of anyone actually returning. Thirdly, a solitary scrap of parchment from a fifteenth-century, fire-damaged collection of books briefly mentioned a mist-covered island and then one other discernible word had been shakily scrawled in the margin: Hopeless.

Whether this was a comment on the search for the island, the chances of returning from it or more poetically perhaps, the name of the island, Auntie Ally really didn't know. But she became irrevocably intrigued by the possibility of its actual, physical existence.

She was planning an expedition she told me.

"Can I come?" I asked.

"No" was the simple but firm reply.

And that was that.

I was at college by this time and at a crucial stage of my education. So, most unfortunately, it was quite a while before I could find the time to visit again, and by that time Auntie Ally's disappearance was in all the newsheets.

The following are the collected accounts from her personal papers, recovered from her exploratory vessel. I have omitted the more routine entries and those of a personal nature.

I, Alison Tiffany Hempton Addleby Pettigrew, depart now on a great adventure. I do so in the spirit of my many illustrious fore-fathers and the greats of exploration: Columbus, Polo, da Gama and others of their ilk. I would be modest—but modesty has no part in a great exploration; I have studied them all and I know that only through a steadfast will and an iron determination did they manage to succeed in their endeavours.

And so, I set off now, my quest fixed firmly in my mind. I was fortunate that a relative owned a number of merchant ships, and a suitable vessel was hired for the conveyance of my very own transport of delight—the submersible *The Prospect of Joy*. It had taken three years to build and was designed by the finest submarine builder in Europe, Monsieur "Eau" Cousteau. Whilst I had supervised its construction at Chatham and had insisted on some modifications of my own, I cannot claim responsibility for its magnificence. And although it was a one-woman vessel, it was quite large—for I had ensured that plenty of fuel and food could be stored onboard. It incorporated a number of truly revolutionary devices, the most impressive of which was the atmosphere recycling unit. This patented and highly secret apparatus cleaned the air and allowed the submarine to stay in its natural environment under the water for weeks at a time.

I am looking forward to seeing if its endurance would be matched by its captain. For in maritime tradition, I was now Captain Pettigrew—yes, that has a certain ring to it, almost heroic, I think!

We have been asea for many days now. I have finally become accustomed to the roll of the ship and the nature of the changing seas. The Captain tells me we are about halfway. Of course, he doesn't know exactly what we are halfway to, he only has a longitude and a latitude to work with. Indeed, there may well be nothing there, but the clues I have pieced together point to that spot if they point anywhere at all.

Why a submarine I hear you ask? After all, it would surely be easier to discover an island in a boat? Well, the tales I read spoke of many shipwrecks, some quite ancient, and I wanted to see if I could find these and use the submarine's equipment to recover whatever treasure was still extant. And the number of shipwrecks suggested treacherous waters for a surface vessel, and likely hostile natives. It was a matter of record that savages in war canoes had caused the fateful end of many a sea-going expedition. I shiver now even to think of it—tall, strong, muscular, dark-skinned natives attacking the ships and dragging the helpless passengers into their canoes and then doing who knows what to them, whilst fires rage, native drums beat and strange substances are inhaled. I often lie awake at night thinking of it...

A submarine, on the other hand, may well be able to investigate the seas around the island whilst remaining undetected by local miscreants. And there was yet another reason—the sketchy accounts I had read spoke of strange sea creatures like none seen anywhere else on God's Earth. Perhaps I could become the first to discover a new species, to document them and classify them. I must admit, the prospect filled me with an almost sensual feeling of anticipation. But the final reason I chose a submarine was simply childish fun – travelling under the water like Verne's Captain Nemo would be immensely exciting!

Finally, oh finally, we are here, as much as an empty patch of ocean can be a "here." There is nothing on the Captain's charts. I am suddenly reminded of Melville's *Moby Dick*: "It is not down in any map; true places never are." But there is a curtain of mist in front of us halfway to the horizon. The Captain has become quite agitated and is insisting we turn back. "There is nothing here!" he protests, but I assure him the mist is the sign that I have been seeking. He refuses to lower the submersible into the water citing my womanly frailty and delicate beauty. Why, I do believe he is sweet on me! I remind him of his contract, the money accorded to his account, and afford him a kiss on the cheek. With that he orders his men to do the work whilst hiding his slowly reddening face from their gaze.

At last, it is time and I climb down, through the hatch and into my new temporary home, waving cheerily to the assorted sailors watching bemusedly from the rail. I reduce the buoyancy, throw the lever to disconnect the cradle and drift off into the unknown free of all restraint and feeling a truly unique freedom to explore.

It's the end of the first day in the submersible, a routine day. I have been spending most of it ensuring I was fully familiar with all the submarine's systems, equipment, layout and living arrangements. It goes without saying that I had trained for this; I am not a foolish person and proper planning was a topic close to my heart. But truly nothing can prepare you for an actual expedition no matter the circumstance or mode of transport.

I surfaced to signal to the ship that had so recently been my home and that I had now left a short distance behind to let the captain know I was fine and everything was as expected. I took the opportunity to prepare a simple meal and sat carefully on the deck of the *Prospect* to eat it under the darkening sky. Later, I submerged, anchored the vessel in the currently placid depths and repaired to my cosy berth.

Today, I had planned to skirt the mist-covered area to look for any signs on the ocean floor or in the undersea fauna that the environment was changing and that an island might be nearby. I rose early and manoeuvred my craft to run parallel with the edge of the mist. And here was my first surprise. The water in the distance was noticeably darker than what I was currently travelling through. Ahead of me the visibility was good, here a shoal of small fish, there a solitary squid below some modest coral. To my right side, starboard if you will, there was only an inky black greenness with occasional swirls of lighter grey-green water. The difference was striking.

I had travelled around the misty area for three days and I had not been able to discern a shape to my path. By always keeping the mist on my right, I imagined that I would circumnavigate the area in two days at most. Given the lack of any landmass on the charts of the area, any island would surely have to be correspondingly small.

It is now the fourth day of my trip around the island. I am now convinced that an island does indeed lie at the centre of the mist, although truth be told, I cannot place a finger on why I feel that so strongly. Navigation has proved difficult. At first, I thought only to circle the area of mist, feeling sure that I would return to the start and find the ship waiting for me. And although I have steadfastly kept the mist on my right, I have not returned to the ship's position, or if I have, then the ship is no longer there. Perhaps an emergency has compelled them to return to the nearest port. I was not worried for I believed the ship's captain was beguiled enough to return for me. I had plenty of supplies, and if I was in real trouble, there was always the island...

Waking up this morning, I found to my astonishment that the misty area was now to my left. I checked my instruments, but there were no signs that my little underwater craft had been turned around in the night. My compass had long since proved useless, which would help to explain why so many vessels ran aground in this area. I resolved to surface that evening and check the stars.

I had been inching closer to the edge of the darker waters and occasionally I would catch a glimpse of a mast or a fragment of broken hull. Indeed, as I am writing this, I espy a piece of rudder just visible in the murk. It seems I would have to leave the safety of the clearer waters and venture beyond if I wanted to seek out ancient treasure. I would not be long, just a quick dip in. But I probably shouldn't, something there... is not quite right.

Night-time. I have surfaced but the night sky is full of constellations I do not recognise. Admittedly, there are wisps of cloud—or is it mist?—obscuring parts of the sky. I tried to force the stars into shapes I knew but they did not oblige. I could not explain this and I was struggling with it, but then... The Plough! Yes, a constellation I recognised, the first I learnt as a child. I hang on to this, despite the lack of other signs. I let the familiarity of The Plough reassure me, and I now retire to my berth to sleep.

It's the morning and I realise that I still don't know where I am exactly. It was strange. Part of me finds that disconcerting, almost frightening, and yet a part of me finds it exciting. After all, I could always land on the island and gain directions. And yet, another part of my mind sincerely hopes it will not come to that.

There were things moving in the dark. Curious things. Strange things. There was a flash of serrated fin or a brief sighting of a split tail, and even now a dark mass, which as it came closer, was revealed to be hundreds of small fish... I think. Yes, fish. Let's say fish. I was very close to the dark water now, and as the fish turned, I saw a rippling glitter that I thought most beautiful. That is, until I realised that it was hundreds of sets of wildly angled teeth that caused the effect. I wanted to see more, to know more. They looked dangerous. But you must take a risk to learn, must you not? Surely the risk is too great? But science! I should venture in for science. No, no, I should be cautious; history tells us that many an expedition failed through rash decisions.

I feel I must learn more, the tantalising impressions of wrecks and strange, odd, well weird really, marine life seem to be exerting a strange pull on my intellectual self, my curious self. I was suddenly reminded of a cat one of the servants had many years past. It was forever chasing and catching frogs, and one day it had decided to investigate the well in an exploration that did not end favourably for the poor cat. Yes, my feeling self is ill at ease in these waters. I sense a sadness, a foreboding, a dark presence. But that's just nonsense. I must investigate. After all, I've come all this way...

I realise I have lost all track of the days that have elapsed since I launched from the ship. I can't even bring myself to surface to gauge the time of day.

The Prospect of Joy is touching the darker waters now on the starboard side, creating weird little eddies in the murky wall of water, water which seems physically different, exerting a greater drag on that side of my craft, so much so that I am having to compensate in the trim and the heading to keep the *Prospect* from spinning around. I am strangely torn: half wanting to end the suspense and sink into the velvet green-black darkness, and half wanting to run away, although there is precious little space in the submersible to get very far on foot.

I have not slept well. Strange dreams have been visited upon me and haunt my waking hours too. I am not a religious person, but I found myself praying last night. Praying. Preying. Preying on my mind. I am writing everything down now, every thought. It somehow seems important.

I need to pull myself together and be the great explorer that is my destiny... or else leave. Yes, I must leave. I don't want to be the cat.

My mind feels so woolly. What is wrong with me?

Leave, immediately....

...Or soon at the very least...

...But not before I examine, capture, erm... take a sample of the water. It is in my head I think, therefore I am Ishmael. Sorry? Who said that?

Is it too late? Can I still go? In. Out. Where is my hat?

Onwards. Away. To the island or to my home? Where was my home?

The sea is only the embodiment of a supernatural and wonderful existence.

I must anchor, go full speed, dive, surface, swim, relax. Oh, I just don't know anymore? So difficult to think. In two minds. To decide. Today. Too much.

I must get a grip.

A moment of clarity...

...So, can I escape?

Or is it hopeless?

That was the last entry in my Aunt Ally's notebook.

At around the same time, I had received word she was missing, and I immediately mobilised the family's resources to find her. There was no trace of the ship that had transported her submarine, but by chance, they had encountered another vessel the day before my aunt had launched into the sea, so we managed to determine a start point for our search.

After three days of looking, we found *The Prospect of Joy*. It was bobbing on the surface just in front of a wall of mist. I am a naturally cautious person and so I arranged to have the vessel grappled from a distance and then reeled in. Once we had lifted it on board, I wrenched open the hatch expecting the worst. And the worst was what I found.

At this point, you may be forgiven for imagining that we found a ravaged body, some inhuman horror or no body at all. But what we found was far worse.

Aunt Ally was lying in her berth apparently asleep, the picture of peacefulness, not a mark upon her. We brought her out and laid her on the cot in the Captain's cabin. It was a while, but eventually, she opened her eyes and I breathed a sigh of relief.

That feeling quickly drained from me and became deep dismay as she turned to look at me. Her face was entirely blank, her eyes devoid of the normal human spark. She sat up and we fed her, but she said not a word.

It has been six months since that fateful rescue, and Lady Alison's condition has not changed. She breathes, eats, sleeps— the basic movements of life, but there seems to be no-one there. I cannot look her in the eye for the emptiness chills my soul. Her body is physically present, but there is no Aunt Ally. She is simply not at home.

Having read her account and being close enough to that mist to feels its power, I have my own fanciful ideas of what has happened. I am no scientist, and I fear if I fully state my thoughts out loud I would be laughed at. But even so, I will say that I just have this feeling that Aunt Ally was left behind that day we rescued her. Where she is, I do not know. What form she now takes, I can only fantasise.

I am having *The Prospect of Joy* refitted to my own design for I am resolved one day to return and search for her no matter the personal cost.

But whatever has happened to her, I just pray it's not Hopeless.

The Journey of Faith

You may have heard of the disappearance of the explorer Lady Alison Tiffany Hempton Addleby Pettigrew and the subsequent rescue expedition organised by her nephew, Jason Hercules Pettigrew Johnson. At the time the papers reported it a great success, a wonderful story of a family reunited. But the few who knew the truth were aware that it was anything but.

Auntie Ally, as she was known to her devoted nephew, had launched an audacious subaquatic expedition to observe new species and explore ancient wrecks around a mythical island. But she had returned from her ill-fated expedition little more than a husk of a human being. Despite her nephew's best efforts, as the months passed, that truth eventually came out and poor Auntie Ally's fate was news again. She was even described in the parlance of one of the more fanciful penny dreadfuls "reporting" the story as a revenant or zombie-like creature, albeit one that did not shuffle, threaten or hanker after the meat of humankind.

It seemed a sad tale, and soon the public started to lose interest in even reading about the more sensational, and let me say, entirely fictional versions of the story. So poor Auntie Ally eventually moved from being a passing concern to a forgotten tragedy. But there was one person who never gave up hope, never lost his faith in an eventual solution to Aunt Ally's lamentable condition: her devoted nephew, Jason.

Jason had grown up into a determined young man, a man who, by virtue of a series of circumstances, had inherited a considerable fortune and a number of residences. Since Aunt Ally's return, he had become obsessed with returning to the spot where her submersible was found, to investigate and to find some way of returning Aunt Ally to normality. (Let me point out, dear reader, right here, right now, that although he was obsessed with his Auntie, it was an entirely innocent obsession; this is not one of those stories.)

Jason had few friends, but one, in particular, seemed to put up with his single-mindedness and adored him for his pureness of heart. Homily Williams was a singular young woman who had known Jason from his college days. They had met at an evening science lecture on the talking cure and had long discussions over coffee afterward. She was an intelligent and pragmatic lady and had remained a faithful friend when his fixation with his aunt took hold. Although when she learnt of his plan to return to the seas and dive in that fateful craft, she urged him to reconsider. After all, she argued, one soul had been lost to those hopeless waters, why lose another? And particularly why lose his, she thought to herself.

But Jason was not to be swayed. He spent time, money and a great deal of thought on planning a new expedition using *The Prospect of Joy*, Lady Alison's revolutionary underwater craft. He made sure the finest English mechanics and engineers had checked the entire vessel more than once for faults or possible weaknesses in construction or design. But the craft's famous French marine designer had done his job well, and Jason was reassured on that score. He did, however, add some new elements. He fitted bigger, stronger windows, five lead-shielded compasses, added a more powerful periscope, several inches of armour, multiple torpedo tubes, and mounted a waterproofed machine gun of radical design to the front deck. He even fitted a device based on Tesla coils that would pass an electrical current of great magnitude through the outer hull at the throwing of a knife blade switch.

As originally conceived, *The Prospect of Joy* was purely an exploratory vessel, the product of an inquiring, innocent, peaceful mind. But in Jason's determined hands, it was turned into a most potent weapon of war. To transport it, the expedition utilised as its floating base an old steam cruiser retrofitted to suit Jason's more single-minded requirements which he renamed *The Journey of Faith*.

A week before the scheduled start of the expedition, the Admiralty caught wind of the submersible and its militant new capabilities. This forced Jason's hand, and he slipped port in the dead of night having checked that Auntie Ally was being looked after, but without the chance to say goodbye to faithful Homily.

The journey to the area of sea where Lady Alison had met with her singular fate was largely uneventful. It is true that when they left port, they were hastily followed by navy ships, mustered as quickly as they could manage, but Jason's expedition had a decent head start and soon outdistanced them.

They arrived at the most likely spot to start their search for... well, to be honest, Jason wasn't sure where to start. Although Alison had written of an island, she had never seen it, it wasn't on any charts and there was simply no evidence of it. What he had seen with his own eyes was a wall of mist, beyond which human vision could not penetrate, but which seemed to have a definite influence on the psyche. If there was an island in the mist, he was determined to press ahead and find it, for he was sure it would be there that he would find the means by which to save his aunt.

It took them several days to locate the mist, and to his credit, Jason had been prepared for this, sending out no less than six steam launches in a complex, scientifically developed search pattern that covered an enormous area of ocean in a short space of time.

Once located, they recalled the launches and sailed to the relevant spot. Jason viewed the swirling mist ahead of him and remembered the last time he had witnessed it. Lady Alison was always very fond of quoting literature, but all Jason could think of at that moment was Dickens: "There are strings in the human heart that had better not be vibrated." He pulled his jacket tighter against the slight chill that had crept up on him.

"Well," he said out loud, grabbing at another quote: "Carpe diem, quam minimum credula postero."

"What's that?" asked the captain of *The Journey* who had quietly pulled up alongside Jason on the ship's rail.

"Oh, sorry, it means to pluck the day, time for action. Launch stations, Captain, if you please."

"Aye, aye sir!"

Jason felt a strangeness as he lowered himself into *The Prospect of Joy*. He must be experiencing some of the same emotions and sensations that Lady Alison had felt as she set off on that fateful undersea voyage. He had left strict instructions for *The Journey of Faith* to withdraw at least twenty leagues from this spot. He did not want them becoming yet another disappearing victim of the mist.

Unlike his cautious Auntie, Jason set his teeth together, strapped himself in and set a course directly for the water under the mist. As he advanced, he could see the water getting darker, seemingly heavier and the pace slowed. Almost immediately he noticed strange sea creatures in the murk around him and the vague shapes of masts and funnels of wrecked ships beneath. Despite the upgraded engines, he was making slow progress, and weird, dark, twisted shapes that resolved into loathsome, many-eyed creatures began to investigate this mechanical interloper. They were small creatures, but threatening nonetheless, for Jason detected a maliciousness in the way they twisted and turned around the craft.

Suddenly one darted forward in a flash of fins and teeth, but at the last moment, it was propelled unnaturally sideways as one of its brothers, snared it between hugely out-of-proportion jaws. Jason shivered and checked all the weapons systems, although truthfully, these small creatures would be no match for the submersible's thick iron hull. And almost as he thought that, Jason noticed a darker shape off to his right, just too far into the gloom to make out its proper form. After observing it for a minute or so, it became obvious it was of a magnitude larger than the other aquatic beasts inhabiting these dark waters. Indeed, Jason realised that there were no other creatures near it, as if they feared to be in its very presence. At the back of his mind, Jason felt an unnatural fear, a strange contradictory wave of emotions urging him on and yet at the same time compelling him to leave. But driven by his fondness for his auntie, Jason's will was resolute. He quelled the rising feelings and pushed on.

The submersible swayed as something tugged against it, and Jason took a moment to swing the vessel around. Swirling purple tendrils writhed up from the sea bottom, the monstrous fronds of some huge marine flora. Trimming *The Prospect of Joy* to rise to a higher level, Jason resumed his course.

Something ahead in the distance caught his eye, a slight iridescence in the gloom. It was getting closer and brighter. To Jason's eyes, it resembled an underwater waterfall somehow catching the light as it tumbled down to the depths below. But this was a waterfall that was moving, and not composed of water. Jason realised at the last minute that the iridescence was caused by an electrical discharge and that he was witnessing the lower part of what could only be described as a gigantic electric jellyfish. Or more like, a Portuguese Man 'O' War of unparalleled size and stunning beauty. Jason slammed the controls hard to port as he broke the spell of the creature's dangerously enticing glamor.

The Prospect of Joy was a fine example of the best of French marine knowledge and English engineering and manufacturing. It responded fast to helm control, and its powerful engines and streamlined shape helped it speed through the water at an unprecedented rate and with fine manoeuvrability. It was designed to cope and excel in all waters known to man. These waters, however, were not known to man. And here, alas, *The Prospect* was a little slower, a little less powerful, a little less manoeuvrable, and in this case, found a little wanting. Jason had almost evaded the threat, but at the last possible moment, a single tentacle lightly caressed his iron craft.

All the lights in the cabin went out and there was a sudden silence. To his credit, Jason did not panic and scrambled to the wall on his left and a huge bar attached to a rotary switch. He grabbed the bar and wrenched it counterclockwise for a count of three, then clockwise for a count of three... nothing. As the submersible sank slowly lower, he tried again: left, one...two...three..., right, one...two...three... This time there was a loud buzz of electricity and a massive clunk as the engines started up again and systems returned. Lights came back on and Jason threw himself back in the chair. He had regained control. Nervously checking the windows all around him, he could see nothing.

Would this reassure you? It did not reassure Jason. After witnessing an ocean teeming with deadly ravenous life, the absence of it seemed to be by far the more frightening outcome.

It was not long before those irrational fears proved entirely legitimate. Shapes in the dark distance, movements in the murk. Darker water now moved around *The Prospect of Joy,* and the feeble light that was fighting its way down to the depths was fading.

If Jason could see above him, he would have found the surface roiling with violent waves, rocks awash with huge spumes of spray, and a mere few hundred yards away—the cliffs and chines of Shipwreck Bay, the most notoriously treacherous feature of all those that made up the hazardous coastline of Hopeless, Maine. At the surprising depths below the bay, all was calmer, well, the current anyway. This was of no comfort to Jason however, who now found himself surrounded by a veritable menagerie of misshapen aquatic beasts, monstrous miscreations of teeth and spines and eyes and claws and tentacles and… unidentifiable vicious appendages. Jason did not suffer from nightmares, nor did he read "gothic" fiction, but here was the very embodiment of the most exaggerated form of night horror or ghastly, obscene, bestiary become life.

He could feel them somehow calling to him like he had ants crawling through his mind. He ran his fingers through his hair, scraping his skin sharply with his nails as he sought to get a grip on his sensibilities. Oddly, it seemed to help, and he gained a moment to assess his predicament.

Jason heard their freakish forms grinding against the outer hull, teeth scraping on metal, tentacles trying to find gaps to worm their way insidiously into. The submersible was not moving forward now, and Jason saw a wall of rock ahead of him. Even if he could proceed, there was simply nowhere to go. Jason considered his options as unseen brutish forces rocked *The Prospect of Joy*.

There was no point in the torpedoes, there were simply too many creatures and only one was conveniently lined up with a firing tube. Hitting it point blank was likely to cause an explosion that might do as much damage to the submersible as to the creature. The Tesla shocker came to mind, but Jason wondered if it would still work after the earlier encounter with the electric behemoth. He reached for the switch, paused a moment and threw it. An extremely satisfying arc of wild blue electricity surrounded the craft, an intense crackling, buzzing sound, a boiling of water and a nauseous burning smell that was so intense, Jason felt it assaulting his nostrils even through several inches of iron, however, improbable that might seem.

The end result was not nearly so satisfying. The shock merely drove the creatures outside mad with rage, and they buffeted Jason's vessel with renewed vigour. Some swam away and then back again at high speed to ram the sides, the bottom or the top of the submersible. Jason was thrown out of his chair and anything not tied down was to be found rolling around on the floor. The Tesla shocker was efficient but intermittent; it would be a while before it could build up enough charge to be used again. Several more times the creatures buffeted the iron ship. Every time Jason managed to stagger to his feet, he was thrown down again, and new bruises were added to his pain-wracked body. Throughout this barrage, the ants in his head were getting worse. They felt like small mammals now, noisy rats talking to him, murmuring, muttering, urging him to leave the safety of the craft.

Just as he felt he would surely be pummelled to a pulp, the pounding stopped and things went dark again. But it was not the cabin lights that had failed, they were soldiering on, still illuminating the small metal cabin although much dimmer now. No, this was a darkness from outside. Two or three huge forms enveloped *The Prospect of Joy*. There was a sudden brighter shape in the forward window. Jason made out the form of a mighty tooth the size of a man, and a tall man at that. It was vaguely ivory in colour, but with much green mould around its edges and a yellowy-red vein running randomly across its side. That was all Jason could discern before it was gone.

But then, seconds later, there was an ominous grinding noise. Jason was no longer sure that the armoured iron would be enough. Should he try to swim to shore? How deep was he? Would he survive the swim to the surface? He could feel the island calling to him.

―――◖●◗―――

Out of the three, it was Gertrude who was inevitably the most observant, so whilst Ludmilla and Mildred were often wrapped up in the latest gossip, Gertrude still managed to keep one of her three eyes trained upon the seas around the island. The three were known as Agents of Change, or The Ocular Ones. Those who had perhaps encountered their influence in some way, or knew them better, called them The Aunties, a name they rather liked. But whatever you named them, they had been around since, well, let's just say it's a very long time.

"Look," Gertrude said, "Stop your fussing for a moment. There is some sort of commotion over there."

"Oh yes," said Ludmilla, "the pets are getting obstreperous again."

"I don't know why you call those nasty creatures that," responded Mildred. "And stop using silly long words. You know it irks me."

"I'm sure it's nothing, just some simple shipwreck. Their ship will break up and the silly humans will die. That's that," responded Ludmilla.

"Oh, don't be so trite, Ludmilla. This is different. It seems to be happening underneath the waves," pointed out Gertrude.

"Oh yes, why there is some sort of tin can with some poor dear stuck inside," observed Mildred.

"Well, they will soon open that and he'll be pet food for sure!" exclaimed Ludmilla.

"Stop it with the pets again. Can't we help him? I sense he has come a long way in search of something... or someone," reasoned Gertrude. This statement piqued their curiosity and they all turned their many and varied senses toward the trapped submersible.

"Oh, he's searching for that nice young lady who arrived here a while ago. She was in a tin can too. Most interesting, not at all like the others," said Mildred.

"Oh yes, she was a lot more ethereal, a strange one that. Still, she's lost like the rest," stated Ludmilla in an off-hand way.

"I think we should help him to find her," decided Gertrude. "He is resolute and determined to find that lady. He is devoted to her."

"Oh, not another tale of lost love, how pathetic," said Ludmilla petulantly.

"No, it's not that sort of love. She's family. And family is important," Gertrude said firmly.

Despite her general reluctance to agree, Ludmilla nodded, as did Mildred. Family was important.

"Besides, we have to help," affirmed Gertrude.

"Why?" asked both Ludmilla and Mildred in unison.

"Because, dear ladies, she is an Auntie, just like us!"

The Fate of Rapture

J ason was trapped in a relentless nightmare. Perhaps you would consider that description too strong? Well, consider this. He found himself inside a submersible, surrounded by huge monstrous creatures who were clearly devoting all their energies to get at him and who seemed to be making excellent progress on that score. The submersible was at the bottom of a weirdly dark ocean, faced with a wall of rock that defined the edge of a mysterious island that no-one had ever returned from.

Above him, the waters boiled with raging eddies and whirl-pools as enormous unnatural waves smashed violently against jagged outcrops and hidden rock pools. Below, nameless horrors awaited, their poisonous fronds and clutching tentacles writhing in anticipation of a feast to come. That surely would seem to fulfil the definition of a nightmare would it not? And that was but the external torment. Not content with physically assaulting his body, strange forces were inside his head, too, stretching his sanity, urging him to swim, urging him to make it to the shore.

He was at the point of going for the hatch when a deafening screech made him cover his ears. It was like the sound of chalk scratching a blackboard, or perhaps metal on glass, or more likely, impossibly large teeth running through several inches of solid iron. The panic triggered Jason's training and he went aft, out of the cabin into the next chamber, his eyes darting around to locate his diving suit. If the hull was to be breached, then the procedure was clear, diving equipment was mandatory.

He pulled the thick one-piece suit on roughly, grabbing gloves and the helmet from the rack, all the while fighting the inner demons urging him to forget such nonsense and just swim fast. As he held the helmet above his head, the urgings reached a crescendo… and then… abruptly ended as the helmet dropped into place. Jason felt a strange peace he hadn't felt in days. Something in the make-up of the metal helmet was acting to stop the pervasive thoughts that had been edging him toward lunacy.

For the first time, Jason realised he wasn't going mad, that he was being influenced by some dark outside force or forces. He didn't know what it was about the diving helmet that was acting as a sort of mental shield, in truth, he didn't even know what it was made of, but he resolved to find out its particular composition and buy the inventor an inn-full of drinks when he got back.

When he got back. He laughed somewhat hysterically. The creatures were still outside. The situation was still dire, and he had yet to even start his quest for some cure to his Auntie Ally's condition. When he got back. The hull was about to be punctured and the creatures would have him. He knew it was hopeless.

Now, some of you may recall the fate that befell his Aunt Ally who was the first to pilot the submersible *The Prospect of Joy* toward the mythical island that we now know to be Hopeless, Maine. The island was surrounded by mist, and somehow Alison's mind was lost while exploring the very edge of the island's strange influence. Jason had recovered his aunt's still living body some time ago, but had then set out on this fateful mission to locate her spirit, which he believed… no, which he felt sure, would be found in some form, somewhere, somehow, on the island.

Jason found himself praying to the fates, and whilst we know not whether the Moirai heard him, an intervention from an altogether more ancient trio of meddlers was about to take place. Making his way back to the main cabin, which seemed the appropriate place to meet his fate, rather than an ignominious corridor, something compelled him to look out of the front viewing window. And he saw something, or rather, he saw a patch of nothing—an absence of teeth and claws and tentacles and jaws. A distinct area of blackness in the jagged wall of rock ahead of him.

Jason blinked inside the helmet and comically tried to rub his eyes, bashing the glass of the helmet as he did so. He grabbed the controls and gripped tightly, forcing them to obey his will. Gradually the submersible inched forward. Yes! Yes! It must be a cave of some sort, an opening in the undersea cliff face. Why hadn't he noticed it before? After all, caves don't appear out of nowhere, do they? And yet, there it was. The entrance was now so obvious.

The Prospect of Joy juddered forward, still impeded by the tenuous grips of countless small creatures and the more powerful jaws of the harrowing leviathan that had been the cause of the deafening screech. He was close now, the looming blackness spread across his forward vision. Was it a big enough hole to hide in? It was going to be tight, Jason thought. He pressed on. As his only hope, he wasn't about to stop and measure the cavern's capacity.

But something was wrong. He checked his eyes, was it receding? "Damn it!" he shouted. His doughty vessel was being pulled back. "No, no, no!"

He checked the gauges. Maybe, just maybe…

He rose from his chair and frantically turned some dials and threw some switches. All the lights went out and the engines fell silent. He stood at the knife blade switch for the Tesla Shocker. I hope it's enough, he thought as he threw the switch. Although he had used this one-shot device on his trip already, he had now diverted what little electrical power still remained in the rest of the submarine, so when he triggered it, he was rewarded with... well... a slight humming and a small burst of wild, blue electricity. In all likelihood, it was not enough to do any real damage to the creatures assailing *The Prospect of Joy*, but it was, if you will pardon the intentional pun, somewhat shocking.

For mere moments, the submersible was free and Jason wasted no time. Moving like a mad man he reversed all the switches and dials and threw himself into the chair, yanking the controls forward with as much speed as he could muster with his movements still restricted by the diving suit. And then... the blackness engulfed the submersible and it was out of that accursed, demon-infested ocean.

The thought occurred to Jason that given recent events, he could now be in an even worse position. What was the saying? "Out of the frying pan, into the fire." And he noticed that not only thankfully, but worryingly, too, the creatures had not followed the submersible into the cave. But he no longer cared; frankly, a different horror would be a refreshing change from the torment of the depths. Now he was away from the creatures. He ventured to switch on the outside lights. Their dim, flickering illumination revealed not a cave but a tunnel. "Maybe an old smuggler's tunnel when sea levels were lower?" Jason theorised. In his scientific mind, some believable, logical rationale for the existence of the tunnel was in some way important.

It was a while before it dawned on Jason that the tunnel was rising imperceptibly, a few feet every hundred yards, and some minutes later, he realised the submersible was about to surface. After it broke the water with a smooth whooshing sound, Jason opened the hatch, still wearing his full diving gear. He had a powerful revolver clutched in his right hand; although given the thickness of the glove, he was not sure how effectively he could use it.

He found himself in a cavern the size of a small hall, with no light other than that of the submersible's lamps. A rock shelf running the length of one side formed a natural dock so Jason manoeuvred *The Prospect of Joy* alongside. He found two rock pillars and tied up the vessel. It was all very convenient, but Jason found himself not wanting to think too much about that.

For a long time, he simply sat on the rock shelf, still in his diving suit, simply recovering and thanking whatever forces of providence had led him here. (Which, incidentally, said forces approved of. Politeness was always appreciated in any creature.)

In time, his sensibilities recovered, and he ventured to take off his helmet. As he drew deep breaths, he realised with a great sense of relief that even with the helmet off, the voices were no longer calling to him, no longer inside his head. He took off the rest of the diving suit and began to look around. In the corner of the cavern, he discovered a small passageway leading upwards. Returning to *The Prospect of Joy* he gathered a number of items and laid them out on the deck.

When planning this venture, Jason had been viewed with much derision and scorn from the many suppliers he had dealt with; for he had, in their eyes, gone quite overboard in the range and depth of supplies, provisions, equipment and weapons. They were quite happy to take his money, however, and the result was a huge inventory of items that Jason could now choose to outfit himself with. And whilst he chose carefully, Jason was of a typical Victorian mind that generally felt there was no such thing as overkill.

He packed a large carpet bag with various items, among the more interesting of which were explosives, rudimentary grenades, ammunition and some flares. Rope, tools and other expedition essentials also ended up in the bag. A cause of some of the most vocal derision was in front of him. Several carefully laid out pieces made up a suit of what could only be described as armour, although it bore little relation to any that fabled knights of old might have worn. It was made up of a series of leather pieces to which were attached linked metal plates. Jason considered it for a moment and, remembering the creatures in the waters around the island, then proceeded to strap it on.

Complementing his ensemble was a frighteningly large elephant gun over his shoulder, an ammunition belt across the other shoulder, and the revolver, which he kept reassuringly in his right hand. Satisfied that he was as prepared for anything as he could be, he set off up the passageway.

He considered using a torch, but there was a faint blue bioluminescence emitted by occasional lumps of otherwise filthy green slime. It was enough to light the way. Jason would have preferred the passage to have been eerily silent. Perhaps it would have been had it not been for some distant rumblings, a low consistent murmur, skitterings in the distance and some percussive sounds he could not even begin to describe. Thankfully, after a short climb, the nature of the light changed and he emerged on the side of a hill. Although elevated, there was not much to see, for the mist that heralded the island's presence in the ocean was as pervasive here as elsewhere.

Now I know that if you or I were there, standing alongside Jason at that moment, we might well have questioned him as to his plan. How was he to proceed with the business of locating Auntie Ally's missing spirit, for example? Well, it was certainly something Jason was unclear about. He thought to find some signs of civilisation or inhabitants. Once again, Jason felt there must be some people living hereabouts, and once again, he couldn't lay a finger on why he should think that it must be so.

As he walked down into a valley, various creatures shadowed him. Some were creatures of the air, some moved amongst the strange, twisted vegetation, and a few scuttled underfoot, but all had far too many eyes, Jason thought. He found it difficult to make out their exact shapes in the swirling fog. Most seemed curious, or playful even, but one or two were definitely stalking him.

Given the creatures' relative size, Jason did not see them as much of a threat, but when one came too close, he thought to fire a warning shot just in case. He aimed casually in the creature's direction and pulled the revolver's trigger. The creature was not impressed, and neither was Jason, for nothing happened.

He checked the revolver's chamber and firing mechanism. All seemed sound. Experimentally, he dropped the elephant gun from his shoulder, aimed skywards and pulled the trigger... again, nothing. For some reason, Jason wasn't entirely surprised. Despite their proving ineffectual, he shouldered the gun and hung on to the revolver, he still felt more comfortable having them on his person.

As a diverse range of potentially aggressive creatures began to approach a little bit too close for comfort, the mist suddenly cleared a little and he came across a modest house with an impressive gateway that had a column on either side. The metal ironwork connecting the columns and the nearby trees were festooned with bells. Despite a slight breeze, the bells did not ring with any sound that he could hear.

Jason espied a light behind one of the leaded windows and walked up to the front door. As he raised his hand to knock, he suddenly felt as if he were being watched. He noticed the intense gaze of a black cat upon him, but in that manner of cats, there was a distinct element of disdain to the stare. It turned and slipped away. As it did so, the door opened and a hooded lady of some beauty considered the visitor to her abode.

"Why you're a strange one, but they said you would be weird."

"I'm not weird!" exclaimed Jason before he could stop himself. "It's everything else that's weird."

"Oh, they all say that," stated the lady gently. "Come in and have some herbal tea. I've something for you."

"How did you know to expect me?" Jason asked, bewildered.

"Oh, you are a lost soul, aren't you?" replied the lady in the hood. "I've been asked to help you, by agents it would be unwise to refuse."

She led Jason into a room with a long table and a tall chair at one end. Just one chair. Jason surmised she received few visitors. In a corner he noticed a broom; obviously she was house proud, thought Jason, and he took that to be a good sign. She beckoned him to sit down.

"Who are you?" asked Jason, "What is this island? Why is it always so foggy? What's that thing with too many eyes in the corner?"

The lady in the hood waved her hand toward the "thing" and it faded.

"Now, now, that's too many questions at once. Just relax. I'll bring you some tea."

Despite Jason's burning desire for answers, her voice was soothing and the idea of tea sounded very comforting.

The tea was... strange; not unpleasant but he was unfamiliar with the blend. It was warming and tingled slightly on the way down. His fever for answers subsided and he felt very calm. The room swirled around him slowly, but he did not feel dizzy. The lady was smiling at him, waiting expectantly.

He found himself smiling back and began to say something...

He awoke sometime later in a simple bed. Thinking he had been drugged for some nefarious purpose, he quickly checked his surroundings. He was not bound. He was whole. Furthermore, he felt completely refreshed and invigorated. He sat upright and took in the room, which was plainly decorated and sparingly furnished.

Thankfully, he spied his clothing over and around a chair. He got up and quickly donned his clothes. He did not want to start any encounter at an embarrassing disadvantage. He cautiously made his way downstairs and back to the room with the long table and the single chair. In the centre of the table was a rolled-up parchment tied with a ribbon. Next to it were his armour, weapons and carpet bag. He untied the ribbon, unrolled the message and began to read:

"I am so sorry I am not around to wish you good morning as I have had to go out to undo something which should not have been done. I did want to give these instructions to you in person, but this cannot wait, and I did not want to wake you. You must go down to the sea west of the lighthouse and root out the beachcomber, Edgard. He will have the answer."

Jason paused. What did she mean by the answer? He dared not hope. Did she know of his quest? She knew of his coming, so anything seemed possible. He read on:

"I have forced an invocation over your guard wear and laid certain runes over your firesticks. You should find them effective enough, but do not venture near the mines or swim in the sea—miracles are absent there. The invocation is a strong one. It should also keep the fog from troubling you."

Jason regarded the armour and weapons laid out on the table. They looked the same, but after mere moments of staring at them, they seemed to shimmer, and he found it both uncomfortable and difficult to focus upon them, so he quickly looked down and read the last of the scroll:

"I doubt you will see me again, for that I am grateful. You are decidedly odd and do not belong here. I have a great deal to do and you ought to be long gone by the time I return if you wish to succeed. My future lies with a myth of fire, yours with the fate of rapture."

Jason struggled to make sense of it. The details were confusing but the overall message was clear. He needed to leave now to find this Edgard fellow.

As he left the house, he realised he had no knowledge of the island's topography. Where was the lighthouse? And which direction was west? He had little faith that his walking compass, safely stored in the carpet bag, would be of much use, but he dug it out anyway.

He opened it and noticed a mark on the rim. It was a blood red line, and Jason could not remember it being there before. It was too deliberate to be a random scratch, and besides, the compass had been folded up for storage. He found north and aligned the bezel. The line pointed off to his left.

As you may have deduced if you have read this far, Jason possessed a logical, scientific mind. He was not want to speculate, to indulge in flights of fancy or to put his faith in irrational religion or augury. And that was certainly true under normal circumstances. But, and again if you have read any of our humble tales, you will have also noticed that these were far from normal circumstances. The island of Hopeless, Maine, appears to be on the very edge of the rational plane.

In these abnormal circumstances, Jason was inclined to follow instinct, to favour a gut feeling, and specifically to follow a path in the direction indicated by a mysterious red line that had inexplicably appeared on his compass. (Other, more sceptical observers might also credit the after-effects of a certain herbal tea as a factor too.)

Jason cut a path across the island toward the coast. This simple sentence implies that it was an easy route with little to remark upon, but the same denizens of the dark shadows followed his footsteps. The same curious critters bedevilled his progress and the same sinuously secretive shapes came-a-stalking. This time his hike was different however, as at the first sign of trouble, Jason fired his revolver in the air. Unlike before, there was a satisfying crack of black thunder and everything within earshot scattered and reconsidered where their next meal might come from. There was also a lot less of the dolorous fog swirling around him, indeed, he could see for a short distance, enabling him to avoid a number of otherwise hidden perils.

They left him alone for a while, and although Jason still sensed the larger beasts shadowing him, he was more confident in his step and more relaxed in his demeanour. Back in England, Jason often walked the moors and enjoyed a stroll around the estate on Sundays. Now he found himself beginning to settle into a long walker's lope whilst at the same time, curiously appreciating the warped landscape around him. With the mist lifted slightly, it had exposed spiky, gorse-like bushes, twisted trees, dark pointy flowers and writhing ferns. Even here, thought Jason, there was a strange dark beauty in the warped vegetation and singular scenery.

Now, this would not be much of a tale if we talked about trees and bushes and flowers for too long. And so it was just as Jason was starting to enjoy the walk that the next dramatic trial revealed itself.

The footing had been getting rocky for a while now, and the perennial damp of the ever-present mist had made the path slippery underfoot. Jason had stout footwear upon his feet, made by a renowned London bootmaker, but he lost concentration for a second as he tried to learn the nature of a strange flying shape in the mist, and that was all it took for him to tumble down a previously unnoticed slope to his right. He scrambled to get a grip, but there was so much loose shale and rock that his gloves could not gain a purchase. He tried digging his boots in, which slowed his descent but did not halt it completely. Suddenly, the ground gave way, his feet found nothing, and he fell into a dark hole.

Now, Jason was an intelligent sort, possessed of an excellent memory, so his first thought upon recovering and getting to his feet was not, "Where am I" or even "How do I get out?" but "Is this a mine?" He remembered the hooded lady's warning: "Do not venture near the mines or swim in the sea." Jason feared he had not only ventured near, but had actually fallen into, one of those two proscribed places.

He made out tool marks on the walls of the small dark chamber. Much to Jason's dismay, it was clearly an abandoned mine working with a passageway braced by sporadic timber leading off to his right. Up above was a jagged circle of faint light—his ignominious entry to the mine. The walls were black, damp and slick. He very much doubted he could climb the short distance up the shaft to the breach above.

It is common in stories of this sort for characters to think when in such a situation that things couldn't possibly get any worse, at which point it inevitably, remorselessly, almost mechanically, does get worse. Jason, however, did not think this. His thoughts were entirely along the lines of: "How is this going to get worse?"

A distant sound answered him. Jason gritted his teeth as he took his elephant gun from his shoulder and rummaged around in his bag. Now, a not quite so distant sound reached his ears. Somewhere in the bag was a clever grappling hook device that fitted the gun.

There was a slight scuffling nearby. Jason spared a moment from his exploration of the carpet bag to look up. Then he rather wished he hadn't, as he clearly saw several sets of glowing eyes regarding him from the shadowy recess of the passageway. Menacing though those eyes were, they were standing their ground, and Jason realised he was standing within the tiny pool of light cast by the newly created hole. So, he thought, they were afraid of the light. Interesting.

As soon as Jason thought this, his mind uncharacteristically commenced imagining all sorts of creatures, but his thoughts returned to one.

It was not his fault. Many years back, a friend had tried to introduce him to fiction but Jason had resisted. His friend was insistent and lent him a horrendous, penny dreadful. Jason found no entertainment in the volume and vowed never again to read such frightful nonsense, but it did mention a race of beings that lived underground, did not like the light, and preyed on humans for food, or more specifically, craved their blood.

It was a ridiculous thought. But then, so was his entire adventure on this island. "There are more things in heaven and earth, Horatio, than are dreamt of in your philosophy." Jason usually found quoting Shakespeare a great comfort, but not at this moment and certainly not that particular quote.

He knew it would be dark in a couple of hours and the piercing eyes were not going away. He renewed his scrabbling about in the carpet bag, and his hands alit on the device he wanted. Carefully he pulled it out of the bag and unfolded the three prongs. Pulling out some rope he tied it to the hook and then loaded the hook into the gun.

Whilst doing all this, the creatures with the eyes had crept closer. He could make out vaguely human-like shapes in the gloom, shapes that were not quite human. He quickly cocked the big elephant gun and took careful aim at the patch of light above him.

When the gun went off, it was loud. Not just loud, deafening. Jason recoiled, even though he knew what to expect. The explosion of black powder reverberated around the chamber and there was a panicked scuffling for a few seconds as the eyes retreated hastily.

Jason pulled on the rope, hoping that the grappling hook at the far end would catch and hold. Hope was not to be found on this occasion, and the hook came crashing down, followed by chunks of rock and shale and vegetation. Whilst initially dismayed, Jason noticed that he had made the hole bigger, and the light was a little stronger now. He smiled for the first time since he had found himself below ground. He examined the enlarged hole for any clue as to his next move. Through the opening, he thought he spied a large rock.

Suddenly, without warning, a large dense dark cloud drifted over the void above his head. He heard loud murmurings, and the creatures in the dark started moving forward. He switched to his revolver and aimed for the densest clump of black inching forward from the shadows.

Again there was a loud bang, and again everything stopped for a moment. Jason realised to his horror that the weapon seemingly had no effect on the advancing shadows. Their eyes now glowed with greater intensity and they were near enough that Jason could make out vague humanoid shapes along with a strange sweet sickly odour. What were they?

Whilst Jason was undoubtedly curious, he was more interested in self-preservation. He loaded the grappling hook and took aim with the elephant gun once more. The hook sailed upwards again, and this time it caught. Sensing their prey was about to make a bid to escape, the dark creatures rushed forward, the light not enough to deter them now that they had latched onto the scent of him. With no time to test the line, Jason grabbed the rope and climbed up as fast as he could manage.

Halfway up he heard a scraping above him, and the rope dropped… but thankfully it descended by just a few inches. Managing to hold on, Jason wasted no time in recovering and climbed up the rope with an impressive show of speed. His physical fitness instructor from his old school would have been proud of him was the thought that came to Jason unbidden.

He felt the creatures below tugging at the rope and he prayed it would hold. He hadn't fallen far, and so in a few more moments, he reached the lip of the opening. At that moment, the rope was wrenched away from him, but not before he had a hold of the rocks around him.

He ducked as the grappling hook flew past his head into the depths below, eliciting a loud shriek from whatever unfortunate devil had been underneath it. He pulled himself over the edge and onto solid ground. Grabbing a moment for breath, Jason considered throwing a few large rocks down the hole, but he realised that he couldn't bring himself to hate those denizens of the dark. Despite everything, he felt pity for them and their dismal existence.

Rooting about in his pockets he retrieved his compass, and checking the direction, he set off again, this time being a little more careful of his footing than before.

As he headed downwards, his nostrils were assaulted by a far from pleasant, musty, salty odour.

The going was a little easier now, and soon the path wound down to a gap in the rocks. A small stream ran to his left and he followed it for a short while until it splayed out across a grim beach and onwards into the sea.

Jason paused and took in the scene. Behind him were dark sheer cliffs with the only chink in that wall of rock being the crack where he and the stream had emerged. Littered about the beach were rocks of all shapes and sizes, strange, twisted rotting trees, congealing seaweed in strange misshapen clumps, and here and there decomposing fish and weird shapes that perhaps were once animals.

An English pleasure beach it was not. No self-respecting deckchair peddler would ever set up here.

To the left of him he spotted two strange birds in amongst some reeds where a second stream flowed down the beach. He had trouble making them out as they seemed almost transparent. They were beautiful in form and reminded him of the magnificent herons that lived around the lake back home.

He walked toward them... and then something made him stop. They were bigger than he had assumed and had nasty looking hooks on the end of their long beaks. Suddenly, they did not look beautiful anymore, they looked decidedly dangerous. Whilst he crouched as low as he could get, unmoving and not quite behind a rock, they turned in his direction, their fierce eyes searching him out.

Then one curved its neck and playfully batted the other, and they resumed whatever it was they were doing. Jason exhaled carefully, first moving fully behind the rock and then backing away, carefully keeping the rock between the herons' line of sight and himself.

Underneath his feet was what looked like black sand, but on closer inspection, it was grittier in texture and appeared to be mostly ground up bones, shells and other organic deposits. The sea smelled. Of course, it is true that all seas smell, but usually, they exhibit a healthy, invigorating odour. The seas around Hopeless, Maine, were very different in their aroma.

The compass was pointing up the beach to his right now, and Jason made his way through the rocks and the remains. In the distance, he could just make out the lighthouse on a distant outcrop.

He had not gone far when he noticed a dwelling, if that was not too grand a name for the ramshackle arrangement of wood, sailcloth and other material that was tucked up in a ledge about halfway up the cliff face. Just the place for a Snark, thought Jason. The rock wall turned at this point so as to form a natural haven against storm and tide. A ladder of wooden rungs and rope woven from some organic matter hung down.

At the bottom, sitting on a rock, was one of the strangest men Jason had ever seen. He was hunched over in the manner of Quasimodo, his arms sticking out of several jackets worn one over another in a haphazard manner. He wore shorts and his feet were bare, although those "bare" feet were larger than average and covered in copious amounts of hair. Or possibly fur. His arms were strong and long and resembled the branches of trees with impossibly long fingers on their ends. He wore at least three hats and a number of ropes finished his ensemble, not for decorative purposes but literally to tie it all together.

He looked up, head cocked to one side and regarded Jason curiously.

As Jason approached, he noticed the man's face was rough, his eyes were mismatched, his nose twisted, his mouth curved and his cheek was embellished with a large red lump. Jason found himself muttering, "My father and mother were honest, though poor..." but then stopped.

"Good afternoon," greeted Jason in as civil a manner as he could manage given the oddity he was addressing.

"Afternoon, good. Yes. Maybe," replied the hunchback.

"Are you Edgard by any chance?" asked Jason.

"By chance? Yes. Lucky, I am, Spearman I am."

Jason decided to take that as a yes and carried on. "I am looking for something."

"Something? Plenty of something here. Monsters mash, waves crash, killer eyes, tides rise and fall, leaving it all," commented Edgard.

"Are you a beachcomber?" asked Jason slowly in the British manner of talking to foreigners.

"Hair too scraggy to comb," said Edgard and paused. Then he laughed raspingly and loudly for a few seconds, ending in a colossal spate of coughing that shook every bedraggled item of clothing attached to him.

Jason realised Edgard had made some sort of a joke. "Can you help me?" he persisted.

"No," said Edgard. "But I may have something you need. Can you climb a ropey ladderey?" He grinned in a way that was both fearsome and yet strangely endearing all at the same time.

"I'll try," said Jason.

"If you try, you will fall. If you succeed, you'll be fine," was the reply.

In a surprising show of agility, Edgard leapt onto the rope ladder and was up it like a monkey up a tree. Jason followed somewhat slower.

At the top of the ladder, Jason could see that the natural ledge ran back under the rock for quite some way and Edgard's shanty home looked larger than it first appeared. It was hard to describe the space as a home, it was more of a nest really. There was no obvious furniture, but plenty of places to lie on, or perch.

Edgard ushered Jason to the back where a large area was set aside for a number of piles of detritus. One pile appeared to be bits of wood of various shapes and sizes, mostly all rounded by the action of the sea. Another, slightly smellier pile was bones, some old and sea-worn but others less so. Yet another, smaller pile was metal objects, pewter plates, bolts, small sections of hull, various unidentifiable machinery bits and some chunks of metal so corroded they were little more than rusty pebbles. And at least one pile seemed to be just seaweed.

Around these Edgard nimbly tip-toed, showing great reverence to his "treasure" as he led Jason to a small pile near the very back covered with an old tarpaulin.

Edgard grinned. "Grail. Holy," he stated as he reached down under a corner of the tarpaulin and produced a goblet riddled with gashes and dents.

Jason smiled at that one.

"Most valuables of mine." Edgard waved his hands over the pile. "Mine," he repeated in case anyone had missed that. "Trade maybe."

Jason imagined that Edgard lived a lonely existence and met few people, so language was clearly not needed and was now mostly forgotten.

Edgard removed the tarpaulin with an unnecessary flourish, and Jason gasped. Over the years many, many vessels had run aground on the shores of Hopeless, Maine. And those vessels had contained many, many things. And many of those things had washed ashore and ended up in the hands of the most assiduous beachcomber on the island. Whilst Edgard was by no means the only beachcomber hereabouts, he was the best and the most successful.

There was a veritable trove of items in this small pile, some gold, some silver, some simply shiny. There were scientific instruments, musical instruments, medical instruments and more. Glass items, jewellery, books and articles of clothing of a very high quality.

"You don't want this do you?" stated Edgard.

"Actually, no," answered Jason. And truthfully, back at home, Jason could have bought any of those things.

"I know!" exclaimed Edgard. "I know," he repeated gleefully and dug around at the bottom of the pile.

"French! Voilà, that is!" Edgard was brandishing a peculiar glass vial encased at each end in ornately worked metal.

Jason looked closer, something indefinite was swirling inside the vial.

"Alison," said Edgard, a look of triumph on his face. "Trade?"

Well that caught Jason's attention. How did Edgard know that name? What was the vial? Who had created it?

For half an hour Jason tried to get any sort of comprehensible answer out of Edgard, but all he said was "Trade" and "Can't tell." Jason gave up and went through his carpet bag with Edgard to see what he might want. Finally, it was simply Jason's ornate pocket watch that Edgard settled on as the price for the vial, and Jason surrendered it happily, taking the vial off Edgard's hands and placing it carefully in his bag.

"Stay now. Night not good. Things eat," affirmed Edgard.

"Well, that's very kind of you, I am hungry," said Jason.

"Ha ha," laughed Edgard. "Night things eat you if you go out there!" He pointed down at the beach. "But I cook. Recipe book. No ingredients though. Stew. Pot luck. I, Edgard, Lucky Spearman." That seemed a long sentence for Edgard, and he caught his breath and then disappeared to one side.

Much to Jason's surprise, Edgard prepared a very palatable fish stew, which if you ignored the heads, eyes and tentacles, actually tasted very fine. Of course, Jason was very hungry, so that may have had some influence on his sense of taste.

Now that his hunger was assuaged, Jason realised he was incredibly tired. For some reason Jason trusted Edgard, and he found an area of old cotton bales to lie upon and sleep.

Jason found himself dreaming of the strange glass vial. In his dream, he was in a shadowy place, possibly a cavern. The light was eerily tinged with green and any walls were frustratingly out of his reach. There was a small modest altar in front of him, seemingly always there and yet unnoticed by him before, in that manner of dreams.

The glass vial was laid out on a piece of soft red fabric on the top of the altar.

As Jason approached, the swirling inside the vial became more agitated. He picked it up and held it in front of him. Whatever the vial contained, it was indistinct, always moving and strangely hypnotic. As Jason studied the object, wisps of the ethereal substance curled around the outside of the glass. He was not the slightest bit surprised, however, this was a dream after all.

But as he started to enjoy the strange sensations of the dream, he was suddenly taken aback by his aunt's voice calling to him.

"Jason, Jason, you have come for me." The voice appeared to emanate from the vial. "You foolish, wonderful man, I thought I was forever lost."

What a weird and unsettling dream, Jason thought. Seemingly unable to respond to his aunt's gentle chiding, he looked around and saw a single black feather upon the altar.

"You have to break the spell, Jason, the spell that kept me safe but trapped me. You have to break it to free me."

Jason looked around again, the space was completely featureless. He could have been hanging in faintly green air for all he knew. How could he break the spell? Was he supposed to break the vial? But the only other item here was a feather.

He thought he would check his clothes for anything useful and it was only then he realised that he was completely naked. Once again Jason accepted this as part of the dream and even when his aunt spoke to him again, he did not feel uncomfortable.

"You have to break the spell," she urged.

Jason wrestled with the logic. The only item here was a feather. He knew a feather could not break glass, and yet the only thing in the room was the feather, therefore he had to use the feather to break the spell.

Holding the vial in his left hand, he picked up the feather in his right. When he brought the two together, the feather gently passed through the glass of the vial, melting it wherever it touched.

Finally free of the vial, the smoky tendrils that had been the vial's contents seemed to explore their surroundings. After a few moments, they turned and approached Jason.

He observed them moving this way and that in front of his face, and then suddenly they flowed directly toward him. Before he had time to respond, they were circling his head. Then, again without warning, they flowed into his nostrils, his mouth, his ears and his eyes.

Staggering backward, Jason prepared for the worst. But after recovering his balance, he felt fine. He was still in one piece and thinking rationally. The space around him began to fade and the dream began to fray at the edges and become intangible as Jason fell back into a deeper sleep.

In the morning, Jason awoke with an incredible sense of refreshment. He felt somehow cleansed, that in some way a great weight was lifted from his mind.

He headed out of Edgard's ledge home and down the ladder and walked to the sea's edge, breathing in the strange but fresh scents of the sea.

"Good morning, Jason."

Jason spun right around at the sound of his aunt's voice.

"I trust you slept well?"

He turned a full circle, but there was nobody within sight. He started to panic. Had he succumbed to some strange foodstuff, been bitten by a weird flying pest or maybe something in the sea air was affecting him?

"Yes, Hopeless is a strange place, isn't it? I don't think you realise quite how strange, Jason. And I don't think you are prepared for all of its surprises."

"A-li-son?" Jason managed to utter a single word falteringly into the slight breeze.

"Yes, Jason. You have found me and set me free. Well, at least, free from that small vial. Now I am trapped in another place entirely."

Jason couldn't understand how she was talking to him. "So, so where are you?" he wailed.

"It might be a little difficult for you, for you see, I am inside your head I'm afraid."

"Hah," Jason half laughed and half gulped. "In...my...head?"

"Why yes, when you freed me, I had to go somewhere."

"Right, yes, okay...No, sorry?" Jason struggled with this new information.

"I am still rather incorporeal. I can't exist outside a body. You have to get me home."

"You are in my head?" Jason repeated somewhat dumbly.

"Yes, oh do keep up, Jason. We've still a long way to go and it will become very tiresome if you struggle with every little fact."

For a while, Jason was conflicted, but if his short stay on Hopeless, Maine, had taught him anything, it was that he really shouldn't be surprised at any occurrence or happenstance. By far the easiest way to proceed was to accept things exactly as they were.

As he was resolving his thoughts, he headed back to Edgard, who was cooking breakfast, a breakfast not like any Jason had experienced before, but palatable none the less. The yellow eggs with their green yolks were actually quite tasty and only sighed a little as they went down. He gathered his things and said a final goodbye to Edgard.

"Tin ship, cave entrance. Lighthouse head for," was Edgard's advice, and Jason's compass faithfully pointed in the same direction as Edgard's stubby, stabbing finger.

"You brought my submarine!" his aunt's voice in his head exclaimed.

"Your submarine?" Jason responded without thinking.

Edgard looked at him funny. "No sudarine here?" he half asked.

"Sorry, Edgard. Thank you for everything."

"No thanks. Good trade. Edgard happy!" He attempted a smile that surely would have scared young orphans.

Despite the challenge it presented, Jason shook Edgard's knobbly, furry hand, and set off down the ladder.

As he walked along the desolate beach in the direction the compass was leading him, he considered that he really didn't know where he was on the island, he just had the notion that his submarine was in a completely different direction. Logically, he thought, he should not be heading this way. But then he sighed, he was getting a little fed up with logic and rationality, for it clearly had no place on Hopeless, Maine. There were different rules here, rules which he was slow to learn, but which he was increasingly open to. So he stopped questioning and followed the compass.

As much as he loved his aunt, and as much as he had a thousand questions for her, he was still grappling with the idea of her being inside his head. Thankfully she stayed quiet whilst he walked. Perhaps she was getting used to the circumstances as well.

The compass suddenly changed direction, and as Jason checked the landscape ahead, it was easy to see why. A massive wall of rock faced him and headed out some considerable distance to sea. The sheer vertical feature was a black shiny rock with loose shale on the few wafer-thin ledges that sporadically appeared on its face. There was simply no climbing it.

The compass was pointing inland, and Jason's eyes picked up a small zig-zag path up the less formidable muddy dunes to his right. He set off up the path and soon reached the top. The rock was now to his left and not quite as dramatic. He could see it sinking slowly into the ground some distance ahead. The path led on, but curved to the left...

"Who is Homily?" his aunt asked from inside his head.

Jason started. He had momentarily forgotten about the strange presence of his travelling companion. "She's just a friend. Are you looking inside my head now?"

"I'm bored," answered Aunt Alison. "You know, you have quite a fascinating mind, I had no idea that..."

"Stop it!" Jason demanded. "Stop that right now. My thoughts and dreams are private. It's making me feel most uncomfortable."

"My dear boy, you have nothing to worry about, your thoughts and dreams concerning Homily are perfectly natural and as far as I can tell, quite honourable."

"I don't have any feelings for Homily, other than friendship," asserted Jason.

"Hmmph," snorted Alison, which was even more unnerving given her location.

Once again, they travelled in silence.

There was a slight rise ahead, and when Jason reached it, he had a good view over that part of the island, or rather he would have had not the ever-present mist been its usual ever-present. A bit closer to hand he noticed the path touching the edge of a forest on its way around the black rock and back toward the coast.

As he passed, Jason peered into the forest and caught sight of a clearing. In it, there was a man to one side, who must have just finished digging the shallow hole next to him. Curious, Jason walked quietly and carefully toward the clearing and stopped, still some way off behind a wide tree. He could now see that the man was dressed like a priest or a reverend maybe? He appeared to be burying something that Jason could not quite see. Was it books? It could be, but then again it could have been a small animal.

"Or maybe part of a larger animal?" suggested Alison, giving Jason another start.

Jason didn't want to think about what sort of large animal the part may have come from. He suddenly became aware of a mumbling coming from the man in the clearing. Were they words? They didn't sound very religious, more like an incantation. Although perhaps it was just Latin. Latin can sound strange when read out loud. The man in the clearing made a peculiar sign with his hands over the little grave and then shuddered. He looked around quickly, picked up his spade, and then walked off through the forest.

"Well, that was strange," said Alison. "Let's go see what he buried."

"Yes, it was strange," Jason agreed. "But I have no desire to investigate, we need to get you home." He realised he was speaking the words out loud even though he was not sure he actually needed to when conversing with Alison. "We can't risk any..." he tried to think of the words.

"Any what?" asked Alison innocently.

"Erm, unforeseen circumstances," was all Jason could answer. And he set off down the path at a newly determined pace.

Soon the path traversed the black rock where it disappeared into the ground and started heading downwards again. Ahead, there was the merest suggestion of a light, low in the sky. As the path reached the beach, Jason made out the shape of a lighthouse, a tall substantial building with gantries and stairs around the outside. The main light was on, but there were other lights too. It was all quite indistinct, and Jason's eyes began to ache and his head filled with vagueness as he looked in that direction. Tearing his eyes away, he focussed on the compass.

"We have to hurry," stated Jason, knowing that it was true, but not knowing why. "I don't think we have much time."

The compass swerved violently, pointing toward a group of rocks jutting out across the beach. Jason marched quicker now and with the help of the compass, soon discovered a cave entrance otherwise hidden amongst the rocks. As he headed toward the back of the cave, he noticed an unnatural light, the same faint blue bioluminescence he had encountered when he first arrived on

Hopeless. It led him to a passageway heading off the back of the cave and down into the depths.

After a few minutes, Jason found himself in another large cavern, half-filled with water. And there, a sight that filled his heart with gladness—the submersible, *The Prospect of Joy*.

Had he been the introspective type with time to spare, he may have wondered at how fortuitous an event this was, at how wondrous was the fact that the vessel was in one piece just as he left it, and at just how odd it was that his sense of direction remembered *The Prospect of Joy* in a totally different location on the other side of the island.

But Jason was not wasting any time. He hastily stowed his belongings, untied the submersible, closed the hatch, grabbed the controls and dived.

There was an underwater tunnel leading seawards, and Jason powered the submarine forward as fast as it would go. The strange light that the lighthouse was emitting was visible even at some depth, and the waters appeared mercifully clear of the rabid sea creatures that had so plagued his approach to the island.

Just as the submersible was leaving the island behind, Jason caught a glimpse of the underside of a small sailing boat on the surface above, and then it was gone.

Somewhere else on the island, three entities of a decidedly singular nature observed the departures with a growing number of eyes.

"I do love a happy ending," said Gertrude.

"They're not home yet," retorted Ludmilla.

"That's true, but we have done all we can," replied Mildred.

"And she still isn't whole," pointed out Ludmilla.

"She will be," said Gertrude firmly. "You just wait and see."

The Triumph of Hope

I t is an entirely queer experience being a passenger in someone else's mind. Despite my natural optimism and adventurous nature, it was not something that I relished or would have chosen. Traversing vast oceans, trekking across deserts, ascending mountains of great altitude, even embarking on lengthy polar journeys—these I would have commenced without a second thought. But this unnatural travel arrangement was beyond unnerving.

But do forgive me, I haven't introduced myself, and it would be very remiss of me if you attended this evening's talk without any notion of its presenter.

My name is Lady Alison Tiffany Hempton Addleby Pettigrew, which I admit is quite a mouthful, so please refer to me in your notes simply as Lady Alison. There cannot be many in this illustrious gathering that have not heard of my ill-fated journey to discover the island of Hopeless, Maine, my subsequent disappearance, the first rescue mission mounted by my nephew, Jason Hercules Pettigrew Johnson, and the retrieval of my body. Likewise, most of you will no doubt have read Jason's account of his second quest, as serialised in the newsheets under the dramatic moniker, *The Journey of Faith*.

So, in today's talk I am going to tell you the untold story of what happened when Jason returned, which I will tell from my point of view, as I know no other way of telling it.

It is a strange, possibly unbelievable tale that starts in the most unbelievable way. I care not whether you believe it, it is not a requirement of listening. I would, however, very much like to think you would be entertained by my tale, or I might be wasting a very pleasant June evening!

I said my tale may stretch the bounds of the credible, and so it does, for it starts with my incorporeal spirit trapped in the mind of my nephew, Jason, this being the only way I could escape that hopeless island.

I am sure there are scientists and doctors of the mind who would want me to describe all aspects of this experience and how it all worked. It is with regret that I must state here and now, I have not the slightest interest in this subject matter. For me it was unsettling, and I would rather forget the whole experience, were it so possible. I bore it with fortitude and put on a brave face, as any Pettigrew would have done.

Yes, the temptation was strong for me to explore Jason's mind, and whilst this may seem outrageous to some, he was my nephew and I am an explorer. However, he objected when I named a certain lady that seemed to be in his thoughts, albeit subconsciously and seemingly set aside. So, respecting his wishes, I ventured no further beyond my own ethereal domain.

As we journeyed back to England, Jason and I had plenty of time to reflect on our reunion. Our conversation was of an odd character, as I talked to him in words and sentences that only he could hear, whilst he replied, out of habit, out loud. There may have been other more direct ways to communicate, but that was not something I cared to think about.

"I have never really thanked you for rescuing me," I said as Jason stood at the starboard rail staring out to sea.

"You don't have to," replied Jason. "You are family and deserved saving," he added awkwardly.

"Well, I am glad that you think so. Do you have a plan for what happens next?" I asked.

"I'm not sure," said Jason honestly. "We have been caring for your body, and I had rather hoped it would just be a case of putting the two of you in the same location."

"It's a good thought, but somehow I don't think it will be that simple."

In truth, I was most doubtful. The journey to this point in time had been far from straightforward and never easy.

"I will save you, Auntie," stated Jason, as if it were the last word on the matter.

I admired his confidence but reserved the right not to share it. Some intangible, malevolent unseen force had separated me from my physical form. I had to assume that some equally powerful conjuration would be needed to unite spirit and body and make me whole once more. The thought of living the rest of my life inside another's mind did not bear thinking about, even if it was my good nephew.

It is true to say that we both felt a sense of tempered elation as we approached our home port. As we moored on the dockside, there was quite a collection of humanity waiting for us. There was the press furiously scribbling in their notebooks trying to capture the moment. There were friends and well-wishers, including staff from Jason's household, and, not entirely unnoticed by Jason, Homily, the girl who seemed to be most often in his thoughts.

Finally, there was an impressive military presence—a highly decorated naval officer, an aide, two armed sailors, and four men dressed in plain clothes, but clearly either soldiers or law enforcement. And one more thing that did not escape my notice: a small unit of armed sailors hovering in the doorway of one of the nearby warehouses.

As Jason made his way off the gangplank and tried to traverse the crowd, the admiralty group pushed their way through and confronted him.

"Welcome home, Mr Pettigrew. I am Admiral Thorne. Now please come with us."

"Why? I need to go home, to refresh myself and to see my family."

"I am sorry, sir, you will have to come with us." The man gave the slightest nod toward his armed escort, implying some consequence if Jason did not agree.

"Very well, lead the way then," Jason instructed, resignation in his voice.

Well, that's one way to avoid getting mobbed by the press, I thought. As Jason (and I) were led away, I saw a number of people trying to get past the unit of sailors who had formed a line and were preventing anyone from following us. The press were furiously waving notebooks, a footman was remonstrating with them, and in the middle, a lone figure, forlorn and standing quite still. It was Homily.

Admiral Thorne's little troop had taken over some offices near the dockside, and it was in a simple office chair that we now found ourselves. Facing us, across a substantial desk and flanked by two sailors was Admiral Thorne. Behind us by the door were two of the plain clothes types.

"I am sorry it has come to this, but you built an unauthorised, highly-armed naval vessel, with unknown capabilities and sailed off to who knows where."

"This is England, Admiral. Surely a man has the right to build what he pleases, go where he pleases?" questioned Jason.

"Legally, perhaps. But the Queen's Royal Navy is entrusted with the security of the Empire, and we cannot have private, heavily armed submarines loose on the seas without some supervision, without knowledge of its plans and its intended use. For all we know, you could be aiding a foreign country."

"I was doing nothing of the sort!" exclaimed Jason.

"That's as may be," returned the Admiral. "But I need to know your future intentions for the craft, and you will not be allowed to leave this port again without my personal authorisation, is that clear?"

The Admiral was clearly used to getting his way, and Jason knew there would be no winning this argument. An idea formed in his mind, and sensing it, I silently approved.

"How about we cut this conversation short? I hereby donate the submersible, known as *The Prospect of Joy*, to the Queen's Royal Navy."

The Admiral was visibly taken aback by this turn of events. "Err, yes," was all he could manage. "I think that would be most equitable." Recovering his composure, he continued, "And that would save the unnecessary unpleasantness of having to seize the vessel, should it prove necessary."

"Think of it as my contribution to this great empire of ours," Jason said magnanimously as he smiled.

"So, your mission, it was a success? You found Lady Alison?" the Admiral asked.

It was my turn to be surprised by Jason's answer, as he smiled somewhat disingenuously and replied, "No. No, unfortunately not."

Quite why Jason felt he had to lie to the Admiral, I did not know, but maybe he was just too tired to explain. In any event, the Admiral seemed content with the discussion and waved us to go. As we left, we heard him making arrangements to move the submersible to a secure Navy warehouse.

After a brief search of the nearby streets, Jason found his footman and the waiting carriage.

As he approached, a strident voice hailed him, "Jason. Jason Hercules Pettigrew Johnson, just you stop right now!"

There was no need for Jason to look around to identify the voice, he knew full well who it was, and he turned to see Homily, red of face but as beautiful as ever.

"Homily…" he started.

"Just you tell me why you left without a word. Why you traipsed off on some boy's adventure without a thought for me! Why, I was worried beyond all reasonable feeling."

"I am so sorry, Homily. You see the Navy was…"

"Balderdash!" she blushed as she blurted it. "I thought you were my friend, and friends say goodbye, no matter the circumstance."

"I am truly sorry. It was poor judgement on my part. I would never want to cause you distress…"

It wasn't clear that Homily was listening as she continued, "And friends do things together. Why did you not take me?"

"Take you?" Jason blustered, taken aback. "Take you? It was dangerous!"

"So?" Homily challenged.

I sensed that Jason was just about to say something like, "It was just too dangerous for a lady," which, being a lady myself, I knew would simply enrage Homily further, so I decided this nonsense had gone on quite long enough and I spoke two words to him.

I saw the brief conflict in Jason's mind, but he had been through a lot, and his logical, cautious, sensible mind had been battered, bruised and generally proved to be of little help to him on Hopeless. So it was with a great deal of delight and no little pleasure that I watched from Jason's eyes as he took Homily's hand, brought her close and kissed her.

I somehow managed to place my attention elsewhere at that point, but I could tell that the kiss was reciprocated and that their relationship had changed forever.

As they entered the carriage together, I felt Jason say a silent "thank you" and the carriage was off.

The journey was a long one, and as they tentatively held hands, Jason recounted the whole of my tale from the start to the present.

"So, she is in there now?" Homily inquired.

I went to answer "Yes", but of course she would not have heard me, so Jason was the one who supplied the answer, "Yes, yes she is."

"Oh, so is she in control? Is she doing all this?" Homily withdrew her hand from Jason's.

He took it back gently, and said, "No. I am very much in control. She is just, well, a passenger so to speak."

Just a passenger? I wanted to kick him, but it was one of many little pleasures currently denied to me.

"Does it hurt?" she asked in a concerned voice.

"No, but it is strange, and a little unsettling... for both of us I imagine," he replied.

"Yes," considered Homily. "My goodness, yes. Poor Lady Alison, why, it must be terrible with no body."

I warmed to this girl. She clearly felt for me, which I appreciated.

"And trapped in your silly head too!" she laughed.

My appreciation somewhat lessened.

"We must do something," Homily avowed. "Poor Lady Alison must be returned to her body."

"Yes, she must," replied Jason. "I must help her." Homily briefly glared at him, but gently. He saw and quickly corrected himself. "*We* must help her"

They spent much of the rest of the journey deep in thought, but still holding hands.

I will relate this section of the story now, as it has a relevance to my part of the tale which will eventually become clear. It was only much later I gained the opportunity to read the Admiralty accounts of what had transpired that same night. The *Prospect of Joy* had been hoisted out of the water and taken to a warehouse, which was slightly away from the main dockyard. The building was secured, along with other offices and a small barracks, within a fenced and gated perimeter.

There were just a couple of sailors on duty outside the warehouse during the late evening, the rest of the men being asleep in the barracks, with a couple patrolling the fence and one in the gatehouse.

At just past midnight, one of the two reported hearing a scratching sound from the building they were guarding. At the time, he dismissed it, as rats were common hereabouts, and what else could it be? Nonetheless, he remarked that he felt uneasy, and his fellow sailor agreed. There was "something in the air" as he put it.

A bit later they heard a faint banging, again seemingly from inside the warehouse.

This time they thought it enough reason to investigate. Holding their rifles at the ready, they opened the side door. They saw pretty much what they expected to see.

A big, empty warehouse with the submersible sitting on wooden supports in the middle. It was what they heard that was unexpected. A banging. A banging that was clearly coming from *The Prospect of Joy*.

"Ere, maybe one of lads fell in and got accidently trapped?" suggested one of the sailors.

"I don't fink no-one's missin'," replied the other.

"Well, there's definite banging," said the first.

They shouldered their rifles and climbed up the ladder that had been set up on the side of the submersible and then walked the few steps across the deck to the hatch. The banging was louder, and there was that scratching noise too.

"You first," said the senior of the two.

"Fanks a bunch," the other responded grumpily and went to unscrew the hatch.

In the empty warehouse, every turn of the hatch-wheel reverberated as metal ground against metal. The sailor paused. He listened, but the banging had stopped. He resumed the task.

They then became aware of a faint hiss, growing louder, and a sort of eerie low moan... then the hatch suddenly flew open, throwing the nearest sailor backward.

"Lawks!" the other exclaimed as he went to help his colleague up. It was getting darker in the warehouse, and the already dim lights were flickering. As the two sailors righted themselves, a dark... something... swirled around them and everything went black.

At the gatehouse, the guard on duty reported that all lights in the compound failed about half past midnight and that he really hadn't fallen asleep on duty.

The admiralty report finished with a summary that questioned whether the two sailors had been drinking their rum ration whilst on duty.

A seemingly unrelated news item mentioned the disappearance that night of Admiral Thorne, who had failed to appear for a briefing the following morning.

Jason's family home was a grand affair, with all the usual accoutrements of a country home—a long winding drive, a large estate, a fishing lake (with herons), a stable block, numerous outbuildings, several wings and a complement of modest but adequate staff.

"Welcome to Pettigrew Hall," Jason announced as he helped Homily down from the carriage. "You are welcome to stay a few days. There are, after all, plenty of spare rooms." Jason smiled and waved his hands in the direction of the edifice that towered in front of them. "I'll have your bags sent for."

"Thank you. That's rather presumptuous of you, but I accept," said Homily. "I'm rather keen to see what happens next."

Jason grimaced and thought "So am I," and in a part of his mind, I had to agree. I was glad to be out of that vial and off that godforsaken island, but I was still a prisoner. The walls of my cell had just changed, that was all.

Jason led Homily upstairs to a bedroom, as a doctor was just exiting. "There's been no change I'm afraid, Mr Johnson, she eats, sleeps and so on but there is no-one home."

"Thank you, Doctor Preston," Jason answered.

And there, through the door lay a body, my body. It was a bittersweet reunion for me, so near and yet so far. Jason went over and kissed me on the forehead. He seemed to wait expectantly. Ever the optimist, it was clear that Jason hoped that just by bringing my ethereal self, trapped in his mind, and my body together, somehow we would miraculously and spontaneously unite. After a minute or so, Jason slumped down into the chair next to the bed.

Homily placed her hands gently on his shoulders. "Don't worry, we will find a way."

It seemed to be Homily's turn to be the optimist. Jason placed his hand on hers and smiled.

The next few days passed uneventfully. Jason spent the time in the library with Homily, both reading books and studying manuscripts that I had previously collected whilst researching Hopeless,

Maine. Sadly, I already knew they would find no answers there. Jason had also sent for a number of works by various experts in a variety of fields, ranging from psychology to witchcraft. They seemed to be making precious little progress.

Out of the blue, we had a visitor. One morning we were called downstairs by Jason's butler who had answered the door.

"It's a Mister Davies to see you, sir."

Jason looked at Homily, then back to his butler. "We don't know any Davies?"

"Oh, beggin' your pardon, sir, he said to say, Mr Owen Davies, recently of Hopeless, Maine."

Even though he was my favourite nephew, sometimes I despaired of Jason. How was he expected to win the heart of Homily standing there with his mouth open, looking completely gormless? Although to be fair, Homily was displaying a similar, stunned expression.

"I asked him to wait in the conservatory, sir," the butler added.

Homily, Jason, and of course myself (not that I had any say in the matter) made haste down the stairs, across the hall and into the conservatory. A young man awaited us, slightly bedraggled and unshaven, and possessed of piercing eyes and long black hair.

"Are you Jason?" he inquired somewhat brusquely.

"Yes," Jason replied. "I am Mister Jason Hercules Pettigrew Johnson." He accented the mister pointedly.

"I apologise for my plain speaking," Owen started, "but time is of the essence, and I've travelled a long way, a very long way, if you include my past week's sea journey."

"You've come from Hopeless, Maine? Is that even possible?" asked Jason incredulously.

"Well, clearly, since I am here," answered Owen. "I think I left the island around the same time you did. I left to find my fortune in the greater world, but I was given an errand to undertake, if I managed the leaving."

"An errand?" Homily asked.

"Yes, a warning and a missive," explained Owen. "You are in grave danger. And I believe you are looking for a solution to a problem." He looked at Jason intently then, although I received the distinct impression he was actually looking for me.

"I trust this boy," I said internally to Jason, for in truth, I did.

"Why should we be in danger?" asked Homily.

"Something, some... thing, followed you home," said Owen mysteriously.

"That's not very specific," pointed out Jason.

"That is all I know, all I was told. It's entirely possible the person who entrusted me with this errand was not able to see all the details."

That raised too many questions in Jason's mind, so he asked a more immediate question, "You mentioned a missive?"

"Yes." Owen reached into his coat and pulled out a small scroll tied with a rough piece of material and handed it to Jason.

"Thank you. Can you tell me anymore about this danger?" Jason asked.

"I'm sorry, I really wish I could, but I just know you should be careful and waste no time in acting upon the contents of the scroll." Owen apologised. "Now, I'm afraid I must take my leave. I am sorry, but it is not my path to help you further."

"You have been most kind to visit us," said Homily graciously.

"Yes, indeed, Owen," Jason added, "it is most appreciated. Is there anything we can do for you?"

Owen looked around the conservatory. "I was admiring your trees, your small trees."

"Ah, the bonsai? They were my mother's passion. A pastime that she picked up whilst travelling the Orient. Do you like them?"

"Yes, they are most curious. Something that is usually so big, but so small." Owen seemed to struggle to explain his attraction to the miniature trees.

"Please, take one, my compliments," offered Jason.

Owen walked around the shelves where the bonsai were displayed and seemed to consider carefully. .

"May I take this one?" He had stopped by a beautiful example of the art growing out of a rectangular Japanese pot.

"Yes, of course, an excellent choice. And please, have some refreshment before you go, I insist. I have thought of something else you can take with you."

Owen accepted the offer gratefully and had just finished sipping his perfectly English cup of tea when Jason returned a few minutes later clutching an envelope.

"Here is a letter of introduction for you. It may help open useful doors on your journey," Jason said as he handed the letter to Owen.

After Owen had thanked them and continued on his way, Jason and Homily sat down in the library and studied the strange scroll they had been gifted.

As they unfolded it, I was initially disappointed "It's just a recipe!" I exclaimed "What good is food to me!"

"It's not a recipe," Jason said, his eyes alighting on the initials A. N. in the corner.

"What?" said Homily.

"Sorry, I was talking to Auntie Ally. I forget you cannot hear her," Jason explained.

"It is a little disconcerting, but you know, I think you are right," Homily agreed.

"So, if it's not a recipe, what is it?" I asked Jason.

"I think it's a spell," continued Homily before he had a chance to respond, "with a set of ingredients and instructions. I think…"

"Yes?" queried Jason.

"Yes?" I echoed.

"I think it's what we've been searching for.

Did I mention Jason's family home was substantial? Toward the back was an old ballroom, not used for some years, but as a big open space it served a useful purpose now. It took a while to layout out the necessary items required by the incantation. All had to be in their proper place. My body was brought down and placed on a cot in the centre of the room, and candles were dotted around the room to provide illumination.

In addition to items and precise positions, the scroll also dictated the rite be performed in the evening after dark. So there was nothing to do but wait.

About six o clock, there was another unexpected visitor. It was Admiral Thorne.

"Good evening, Jason, Miss Homily. Sorry to disturb you, but there has been a development, and I must ask you to travel to London with me straight away."

"I'm sorry, Admiral, but that simply isn't possible. We are..." Jason tailed off.

"...in the middle of something," continued Homily. "So we couldn't possibly."

"But it's imperative, essential, crucial even," said the Admiral, sounding like a thesaurus.

"And we are expecting family," added Jason. "My aunt will be joining us later, so you see, we are completely unable to leave the house."

I found this amusing. Yes, hopefully I would be joining them later.

The Admiral looked as if he were going to argue, almost appearing to be searching for the right words, but all of a sudden his shoulders slumped, he lost his military bearing and said, "It doesn't matter, I will join you for dinner."

"Erm, as you wish," Jason responded, not used to dinner guests simply inviting themselves.

"Something is not right here," I warned Jason as he followed the Admiral into the library.

"Yes, I sense it," Jason whispered.

"Your aunt again?" questioned Homily.

"Yes, sorry. We need to keep an eye on the Admiral, I think."

Dinner was a strange affair. The Admiral sat at the head of the table and mostly stared off into space whilst eating in a very perfunctory manner. Jason and Homily exchanging glances, whilst even I could think of little to say. We needed the Admiral to go. We didn't want him to be present for the evening's affair.

The Admiral seemed to wake up at the end of the meal, after Jason said, "Sorry, Admiral, but we have to leave you. We have to prepare for our family visit. We have things to do."

"But a gentleman must allow for digestion. How about a game of billiards?" the Admiral suggested.

"Sorry, we have no game room here. It was not a family trait."

"Well, cards then. I'll wager some money on the outcome," the Admiral continued somewhat desperately.

"Sorry, I don't play, never learnt," Jason lied. Would the Admiral not just leave it be?

"Perhaps I can regale you with some of my stories of sea battles I've been part of, and you can, perhaps, tell me about all your adventures on Hopeless, Maine?" The Admiral now seemed determined to delay us.

Just what was going on?

"Apologies, Admiral, but we really must be getting on. Why not spend some time in my library, it has a wide range of books. There's even a small section on naval tactics, I believe." Jason was trying to be dismissive.

"No, I believe I will accompany you. Perhaps I can help," responded the Admiral firmly.

Jason shrugged.

"How can you let him join us?" I asked.

"What else can I do?" replied Jason under his breath.

It was almost time, and we made our way, Jason, Homily, myself and one unwanted Admiral, to the ballroom. It was weird that there were no questions about our actions from the Admiral. It was if he knew.

Jason took the precaution of calling for his butler and a footman to join them, a decision that shortly proved to be most fortuitous. We took our places and Jason removed the scroll from his pocket.

At the sight of this, the Admiral shouted, "STOP! Thou shalt not proceed," – this said in a most unnatural voice as he drew a small pistol and aimed it in the direction of Jason's head.

Jason turned toward the Admiral and took a step.

"Stop, or I will end you," said the Admiral resolutely.

Homily looked at Jason and they exchanged glances.

Suddenly Homily fainted, crashing to the floor. As the Admiral turned to see, Jason took one more swift step forward and brought his hand up inside the Admiral's, pushing his gun hand upwards, whilst Jason's other hand reached over and grabbed the gun quickly and smoothly out of the Admiral's hands.

"I'll take that," said Jason, as Homily picked herself up.

Jason considered Homily with a newfound respect, as indeed, did I.

"Amateur dramatics," was all she said in response to Jason's admiring stare.

Jason gestured to his butler. "Vernon, please take this gun and cover the Admiral for me. He's clearly not feeling himself. I suggest a leg shot if he misbehaves again."

"Very well, sir," Jason's long-suffering butler replied.

I didn't know the butler's background, but with his unquestioning obedience and loyalty, I would have employed him at the drop of a hat.

Back in our places, Jason once again turned to the scroll and started reading.

It was at that point that another unexpected event occurred. I honestly felt we had experienced quite enough surprises for one day, but clearly, I was suffering under a grave misapprehension. Amongst the ballroom's most noticeable features were the huge windows on both sides, currently covered by long drapes. These drapes were suddenly and dramatically thrust aside after a huge crashing of glass. Men appeared from both sides of the ballroom. I counted four in all, and they bore more than a passing resemblance to the plain clothes men that had accompanied the Admiral previously. But it was hard to see them as men for they moved differently, they shifted in shape, their faces were blank, and their eyes were completely black.

Jason was still reading the incantation, and I felt... something. I gasped. Could it be working?

There was no time to think though, as one of the men-who-were-not-men had grabbed Homily, one was grappling with the butler, one was being tackled by the footman and the other... headed toward Jason. A shot rang out, and the butler was standing over a body with the Admiral's revolver in his hand. A further shot, closer to hand. Jason had, for some fortuitous reason, kept his own pistol handy and had discharged it at point blank range into the approaching ghoulish figure. Even more remarkable, he carried on speaking and I felt a strange but definite tug on my spirit.

"Stop now," it was the Admiral, finding his voice again, "or your sweetheart will not live to see the dawn." He nodded toward Homily, held in the grip of a man-not-man.

Jason paused, and I felt the strange compelling force weaken. I looked toward Homily in horror. Somewhat bizarrely, Homily just smiled.

Before Jason wondered what that might mean, the Admiral spoke again. "Call off this absurd and dangerous ritual and I will let her go."

As you know, it is the prevailing opinion, mostly amongst ill-informed men, that women are inferior in some way, a weaker species. And whilst that may be physically true in the majority of circumstances, I would proclaim that we are as resourceful, as intelligent and as fortitudinous as our male counterparts. It is perhaps unwise for men to underestimate us.

Take Homily for example, a seemingly gentle soul, caring and kind, with a good heart. Passionate about what she believes in, like votes for women, for example – a cause about which she felt most strongly and indeed, to that end, she had joined the suffragettes for a time. And whilst part of the movement she had studied at the Garside School of Baritsu, learning a number of useful techniques to be used if an errant policeman should try to grab her inappropriately—techniques she had excelled in. There were many good aspects to Homily's character and fortunately an excellent memory was one of them.

She now put that memory to good use, jabbing the man-not-man in the shin with her heel and bending his thumbs back in a simultaneous swift movement. In mere seconds, she had him pinned to the floor to the astonishment of all present.

I do believe I was falling in love with Homily myself!

"Don't mind me Jason, do carry on," she exhorted matter-of-factly.

The butler had the Admiral back in his sights by now, and the footman, like many of Jason's staff, an ex-soldier, had the better of the last of the unearthly goons.

As Jason continued with the ritual, the power drawing me back to my body grew stronger, as the wind howled through the broken windows in an unnecessarily dramatic manner.

The Admiral was shaking now with his face convulsing and his eyes turning jet black.

"Mr Jason," the butler cried out, but Jason was otherwise occupied, sensing the changes happening inside his mind as my spirit was pulled inexorably toward my body in the centre of the room.

Jason's voice rose louder above the noise of the wind and became stronger too. A black fog surrounded the Admiral and appeared to be emanating from every pore of his body. Candles flickered and some faded to nothing. The room became dim, and through the windows a great wind came, carrying no end of leaves and dust, creating a great maelstrom of violent air all around the room.

Jason's voice reached a crescendo, and I found myself outside his body.

I could see the whole room, despite the physical darkness. It was a blaze of colour to me, there was a pure yellow aura around Homily, so beautiful, and a red flame around Jason, strong and magnificent. The butler had a solid blue, and the footman a similar blue but more fluid.

Everywhere was colour except around the men-not-men. All around them a grey fog swirled, and around the Admiral – there was a faint orange glow surrounded by monstrous, jet black clouds. And in that second, I recognised the nature of that evil, inky horror. Don't ask me how I knew, but I did know.

The malevolent blackness oozed out from the Admiral, stretching sinuously across the floor and walls, threatening to engulf the entire room with its corrupt fetid foulness. As it reached the butler, the good man clutched his throat and fell to the floor. It edged on, and the footman, too, succumbed to the hideous black horror. Then it was inching toward Jason and Homily, who by now had retreated to his side. There was little I could do but watch in my present form, caught between the two existences, without a body or a mind to host me. I knew that if Jason did not finish the spell now, I would be lost forever.

And still the loathsome black miasma slithered inexorably on. Now it was lapping at Homily's feet and ankles and nearly at Jason too...

But it was too late. Jason had uttered the very last word of the spell and I was drawn in from the ethereal to my body in the centre of that room.

At that moment, I saw everything, knew everything. I was more than just Lady Alison. My forced separation of body and spirit and my incarceration in the vial had added something, something powerful, and something uniformly good.

I realised my body was floating upright in the middle of the room some feet off the ground, and all remaining eyes were upon me. An incandescent white light flowed out of my body and streamed into the room.

I regarded the blackness with some pity now. I knew its nature, but more importantly, I knew its name, and I spoke it.

There was an enormous flash of the most brilliant light, beyond imaginable, and that was the last I remembered of that night.

Afterward Jason told me that everyone in the room was temporarily rendered insensible by the flash, and when they came to, there was no trace of the black evil or the men-who-were-not-men. To our great relief, both the butler and the footman recovered fully from their experiences, and even the Admiral, though greatly shaken, seemed none the worse for wear, save for a complete lapse in his memory. This was perhaps a kindness, all things considered.

I was found asleep on the cot, apparently smiling and "quite beautiful" in Jason's words. And it was true that I seemed to appear much younger after that fateful night, as well as perhaps feeling wiser and less inclined to adventure.

Whatever had happened to me, whatever I had become, I was still Lady Alison, and very much Auntie Ally to Jason, and now to

Homily. Although I was changed, different in some way, nothing like the experience I had that night has happened in the six months since. Who knows what destiny lies in my future? I do not. Although I can happily predict a family wedding before the end of the year. I am left wondering why something from that cursed island did not want me reunited with my body. Was it afraid of my new self, of what it might be capable of?

Which brings up a final, disturbing thought: Is my future inextricably linked to that of the island of Hopeless, Maine?

Thank you for listening to my story.

AN AFTERWORD
by Nimue Brown

I thought about doing a foreword, but the risk of spoilers would have been immense, so better to hide in the shadowy bit at the end and let you fall in here when you already know all the things.

Those of you who have read the graphic novels will no doubt have spotted most of the clever ways in which these tales tie into everything else. However, you may not know about The Aunties, so I need to fill you in on them. The Aunties—three named agents of change with distinct ideas about how to run everything—were the creation of Meredith Debonnaire, and she gave Keith her blessings to bring them into his story. You can find The Aunties on The Hopeless Vendetta website. Hopeless is in the process of becoming a community owned island with many people sharing in the intellectual property. This is appropriate because the fictional island is an anarchic state.

We know that something must have happened to Owen Davies between the end of *The Gathering* and the start of *Sinners*. Tom and I have never really known what that was. Owen doesn't talk to us about those experiences, except when he remembers real coffee and becomes awkwardly emotional. His appearance in this book has, however, given us a clue as to what happened...

Those of you who live in approximately the same reality as I do may remember a televisual dramatic entertainment serialisation called *Quantum Leap*. I have come to the conclusion that Owen's absence from the island may have had a similar flavour, as he spent a couple of years flung inexplicably from one adventure to another. Owen has a bit of a hero complex, and some part of reality appears to have decided to take him up on that and chuck him unceremoniously from one place to another for the purposes of fixing things. It has left poor Owen with a series of adventures so unlikely and preposterous in nature that he doesn't dare talk about it for fear of being laughed at.

We wait with interest to see if anyone else has caught sight of him during this outrageous period of his life.

Keith Errington, The Keith Of Mystery, sometimes Count Rostov and probably seven other people I haven't met yet, has brought a great deal to Hopeless, Maine. One of the things this book was unexpectedly responsible for is the figuring out of exactly how Hopeless relates to the rest of reality. But that, as they say (those annoying people who like to spoil your fun...) is a story for another day!

ABOUT HOPELESS

Life in Hopeless continues... You can follow the local news at www.hopelessvendetta.wordpress.com – this site has been many things, but at time of publishing it is a community project inviting contributions, and we mean to keep it that way.

For the next installment of the story, pick up The Gathering – the first part of the Hopeless, Maine graphic novel series, which begins just a few years after this tale ends. It's a child's eye view of the island and was written before New England Gothic. The graphic novel series moves forward from this point as its young characters grow, and you can see how the curses and predictions made in this story play out.

ACKNOWLEDGEMENTS

This book has been a long time in the making. When the first draft was written, we lived on other sides of the Atlantic and were not married to each other. It seems like a very long time ago. People who seemed helpful when we were first doing this – well, some of them we're very glad to still call friends, and some we are very glad not to have heard from in ages, and such is life. We look back fondly at the Below the Fold team (now folded) who gave us so much support. We really appreciate those of you who have stuck with the Hopeless, Maine project and been there from the start, and we also feel very glad to have met so many others of you by doing this and keeping it moving.

To everyone who has aided, abetted and otherwise encouraged, thank you. We hope you enjoy the peculiar tentacled offspring you have helped to birth!

Particular thanks to Meredith Debonnaire for editing, and to the growing family of people involved in exploring island life through The Hopeless Vendetta and other forms... there are too many people to name everyone, but particular mention must be made of Nick Rossert, Martin Pearson, Lou Pulford, Keith Healing, Laura Perry, Cliff Cumber, Paul Alborough, Charles Cutting.